Like a
RIVER
FLOWS

BOB JOHNSTON

ISBN 978-1-7772974-0-4 (Paper)
ISBN 978-1-7772974-1-1 (ePub)
ISBN 978-1-7772974-2-8 (Kindle)

Original artwork by Alida Cameron
Cover design and illustrations by Hutton Graphics
Interior design by FTF Book Production & Distribution
Printed in Canada by Friesens Printing

This is a work of fiction. Any resemblance to actual events or persons, living or dead, is entirely coincidental.

Dedication

In loving memory of my grandparents,
Bob and Jessie Johnston,

Who farmed in Downsview from 1926 to 1949,

Leaving me a rich legacy of happy childhood
rural memories.

Other Works by Bob Johnston

After the Honeymoon: A Family Counsellor's Guide to Marital Enrichment
(Welch Publishing, 1986)

From Toddler to Teen: A Family Counsellor's Guide to Effective Parenting
(Thorn Press, 1994)

A Time to Listen: The Ministry of Pastoral Counseling
(self-published, 1994)

weekly column for the *Peterborough Examiner*, 1975-1985

bi-weekly column for the *Saugeen Times*, 2014-present

PROLOGUE

Silver Street carefully winds its way down the two hundred feet of bluffs before dipping its toes into the slow-flowing Mississippi River. Charlie pauses and takes his time before slowly descending the deserted road. He is sweating from the oppressive late-night humidity of a Mississippi summer. His eyes are eager to absorb every detail of the vista opening before him.

It is near midnight and the town lies asleep behind him. Across the river he can clearly see the night lights of Vidalia in Louisiana. But it is the water which draws his attention.

The Mississippi wide, is sluggish and despondent, a murky mix of brown water and reflected moon glow. Despite the late hour, squat barges still work their quiet way downward. A long bridge span, part of Interstate Highway 145 connecting Mississippi to its Deep South sister state, dominates the scene, its string of shining lights arching across the entire flow like a row of diamonds in a queen's crown.

Charlie reaches water's edge and finds a park bench. Yesterday, he rode a crowded Greyhound bus from Jackson to Natchez, his eyes stinging from the presence of too many smokers. A white Canadian civil rights volunteer, he deliberately chose a seat toward the back of the coach, the section where the coloured folks were supposed to sit. Despite hostile stares and muttered threats from other white passengers, this time he had not been physically assaulted.

Tomorrow, another Greyhound will bring him to New Orleans and the flight home to Toronto. But tonight belongs solely to the river. He had long planned this side trip just to see the storied waterway, which helped create both Huckleberry Finn and Showboat. He could almost hear his father singing Ol' Man River to himself, like that deep-voiced black singer, Paul Robeson, would do. He smiled, remembering that unlike his idol, Doug never managed to hit the low notes.

A month earlier the FBI had pulled two bodies from that same water, both young black men murdered and dumped there by the Klan. Now the summer of 1964 was at an end, and a new job, this one thankfully danger-free and paying a real salary, awaits him back home.

Charlie stares almost hypnotically at the river, as it flows past his feet. Water and death. Yet the mighty Mississippi seems callously indifferent. But then so had the Humber River some ten years earlier. Memories begin to resurface like long-submerged debris, and he feels himself swept along, helplessly caught in a powerful current of nostalgia mixed with a heavy sense of loss.

CHAPTER ONE

The evening of October 15, 1954 unseasonably warm rains from the south swept across Lake Ontario, buffeting the unsuspecting city of Toronto with the remnants of Hurricane Hazel. Rising quickly, the Humber River had no difficulty escaping its crumbling banks. In the hours that followed, swirling dark debris-filled water spread destruction and death, a relentless rampage slicing through the west end of the city. A flood that would also alter the life-course of Charlie Thompson.

Four months earlier, the thirteen-year-old boy had stood on the river's muddy bank, taking scant notice of the wide stream flowing steadily past his feet. Instead, his attention was focused on the right hand of Roy Campanella.

The Brooklyn Dodgers catcher is crouched behind home plate, his thick brown fingers rapidly flashing a coded sign. "Campy" is signalling for a fastball, low and away from Willie Mays, the New York Giants batter. It's the first week of July and Major League Baseball is halfway through the 1954 season. The traditional rivalry between these two teams is intense.

On the pitcher's mound, my body turns toward third base, I begin a full windup, just like Carl Erskine. Arms stretching high above the head, weight shifting to the back foot, I pull my left knee toward my chest. Rotating my upper body toward the plate, right arm whipping past my ear, I hurl the baseball, aiming at Campy's big mitt.

Missing its intended target, the grey trunk of a willow tree on the far bank, his stone ricocheted instead off a half-submerged log and into a clump of bulrushes. Alarmed, a sleeping green-camouflaged leopard frog plopped into the murky water, abruptly drawing the boy's attention back to the river. Next time he would throw a better pitch.

* * *

The headwaters of the Humber are approximately 30 miles north of Toronto. The river's west branch is born within limestone along the Niagara Escarpment. Rainwater trickling down through cracks in the ancient rock mingles with cool subterranean springs before emerging to tumble down the Escarpment's rugged incline. The resulting myriad of creeks meander southward.

The east branch begins with a gentler birth. Running a hundred miles from east to west, the Oak Ridges Moraine is composed of a series of elongated hills. Molded by past glacial activity, its gravel beds and clay-sandy soil overlie a vast underground aquifer. The continual seepage of this water creates wide soggy wetlands from where cold clear trout streams emerge. Hundreds of these south-flowing brooks and rivulets wander unhurriedly through farm pastures, boggy swamps and hardwood. Just north of the city, the east and west branches finally merge into that flat shallow river which flows silently through Toronto before spilling into Lake Ontario.

* * *

Charlie Thompson slowly pulled himself to the top of the river's slippery eastern bank, his left hand clinging to an exposed twisted tree root for traction. Gaining level ground, he paused for an instant to catch his breath. Behind him, the slant of late-afternoon sun touched the water's breeze-rippled surface before scattering into a million dancing fireflies. On the far shore, the river's edge was hidden amid gently swaying bulrushes, bobbing green lily pads, long wild grass and Charlie's favourite willow tree target. Beyond that, a scattering of new homes and one half-built house squatted solidly on what had once been flat pasture land. Here, the Humber's west bank lacked elevation. Some years ago, when the river ice broke up, great jagged grey chunks were carelessly tossed up on its bordering fields like beached whales, to die a lingering death in the warm March sun.

Leaving the top of the embankment, Charlie turned and broke into his usual slow steady jog. He would sooner run than walk; that way, he got there faster. He liked the feeling of freedom, the wind in his face and most of all, a belief for those moments that he was a pretend athlete. In fact, Charlie was built for running. His long legs covered the terrain economically, his upper body carried neither muscle mass nor heavy bone structure to slow him down. What he didn't know was that, hidden under his slender frame, lay an unusually large set of lungs. To anyone who might notice, he ran with an efficient stride, arms and hands relaxed and loose, torso slightly inclined forward. Except, no one ever noticed.

* * *

Charlie steadily jogged toward home. He didn't need a watch to know it was time to eat. He was tall for a 13-year-old, and his thin body was impatiently awaiting the added muscle his reassuring mother had promised would soon appear. He wore a short-sleeved jersey with alternating red and white stripes, jeans with three-inch turned-up cuffs and black and white PF Flyers. His straight brown hair was trimmed above the ears and high on the neck and lay limply across his scalp with a neat part on the left side. Charlie's face was as thin as the rest of him, with a narrow nose and small blue eyes. Leftover from childhood, a few freckles were visible under his early summer tan.

Maintaining his pace, the boy soon crossed Jackson Park which bordered the river's east bank. Now that school was out, the sparse grass and weeds were brown and tired-looking, already worn down from daily pick-up baseball games played by the older neighbourhood boys. At the far end of the park next to a road, a row of swings, four teeter-totters and a wood-framed sandbox kept the squealing younger children busy. It was almost 5 o'clock and the park would soon grow quiet as youngsters reluctantly began the trek homeward. Charlie could hear the shouts of parents from nearby houses, each home voicing a different call. Mr. Hancock had the biggest yell with his distinctive "O, Billy, O Tommy," and two young ballplayers ran across left field toward the street, carrying their leather infielder gloves and ignoring the jeers of the bigger boys who urged them to at least finish their last at-bats before abandoning the game.

* * *

Westdale Road ran parallel to the river, every bend in its length mirroring the long gradual curves of the Humber. Beyond Westdale, the streets assumed the orderly grid pattern favoured by Toronto's city planners for 150 years. Avenues of stone or red brick and two story- homes, many with a third floor, street-facing gables and fronted with screened-in porches, were blended with newer compact stucco-clad bungalows. Most were sheltered from the heat under protective canopies of maple, walnut and elm trees. There were also a number of single-story wooden structures and shabby-looking duplexes, with dilapidated weathered siding and sagging verandahs that reflected the hard-luck histories of their occupants.

Despite his love of baseball, Charlie seldom joined the daily ball games. He preferred the river's solitude. Whether away from home or in his room, he was usually alone but seldom lonely. His vivid imagination offered him both escape and companionship. When he wasn't pretending to be a pitcher for his beloved Dodgers, he could assemble a phalanx of lead warriors from his collection of hand-painted British and German toy soldiers. He would carefully line Montgomery's Eighth Army in formation, each man clad in desert camouflage with their Dinky tanks, green jeeps, troop carriers and howitzers, creating endless scenes of combat. His bedroom floor became North Africa. The self- proclaimed Desert Rats would confront Rommel's elite Desert Corp. Bloody battles ensued until at last the British and Australians vanquished their enemy— and Charlie could put his soldiers away in closet barracks to rest before the next attack.

Doug had served in that actual struggle against Hitler. Yet despite a nagging curiosity, Charlie sensed that his father had no desire to talk about it; and he learned to content himself with imagining what war would be like. Inevitably, the bedroom battleground was at best a sanitized version of the real thing, and the former soldier content to leave it that way.

Arriving home on Lawson Avenue, Charlie was still a bit early for supper.

Charlie was content to lose himself in the tall stack of worn-looking well-read comic books cluttering a corner of his small room. He avidly followed the adventures of the Flash, Superman, the Green Hornet. These muscular heroes with fantastical powers relentlessly fought the forces of evil, eventually winning every battle, but never before the last page had been hastily turned. He was also drawn to stories of far-off Africa, his attention held by brightly-coloured images of jungle girls. Dressed in skins of wild animals, long bare legs prominently displayed, they bravely faced peril from stalking lions, massive, stampeding rogue elephants or huge pythons stealthily sliding down from overhanging tree branches.

Yet somehow, when it came to human threats—slave traders, fearsome native tribesmen, unshaven European adventurers looking for gold or diamonds—these jungle girls were clearly in need of a last-minute rescue. Whether bound in chains, tied to a stake or about to be fed to crocodiles, they never failed to cast about for a rescuing hero.

I could be an explorer except I don't like snakes, and I'm kind of scared of big jungle animals, they would scare me, and it would be awfully hot...

But those jungle girls! If I was stronger and older, I could be a hero. Especially if I got muscles like Tarzan. It might be fun swinging on a vine. And I do like Tarzan movies, Hope the new one comes to the Grant soon. I'll get Dad to take me, or go to the matinee. Wish I had a girlfriend, I'd take her. Pretty soon I'm going to ask one out...

Charlie's daydream was interrupted by his mother's call. "Wash your hands! Have you seen your sister?" Katie Thompson managed to keep a watchful vigil over the stove even as she tracked her children. A large stainless steel pot was already in danger of boiling over, bursts of steam and splashes of scalding liquid escaping from under its vibrating lid. A smaller pot on simmer held coin-shaped cut carrots. In a third, six peeled potatoes were gradually softening on medium heat until they reached a desired mushy consistency.

"No, she wasn't in the park. What's for dinner?" Charlie had moved away from splashing water over his hands at the kitchen sink and was hungrily eying the stove, already guessing tonight's dinner menu with a practised glance.

"We're having mince. Now go find Mary. She's likely in the backyard."

* * *

When Katie turned to face her son, her glasses were fogged with the escaping steam. She wore a royal blue sleeveless cotton dress, mid-calf in length, seamed nylons and sensible flat shoes. Her dark hair, short and perm-curled below the ears, was just beginning to grey above a wide forehead dampened with perspiration. Katie sometimes looked stern even when she wasn't, her long face and strong jaw conveying both concentration and determination in equal parts. Awaiting her husband's soon-arrival, she had just applied fresh bright red lipstick, its vividness contrasting with her pale complexion.

"If she's not there, go over to Rachel's house. See if they're inside."

Before Charlie could move, a sudden slap of the wooden screen door on their back porch announced Mary's entrance. At seven, she was tall and slender like her brother. Her summer-brown arms and thin legs poked out from a light brown cotton dress with gathered full skirt and puffed sleeves. Her long hair, blonde and worn in a ponytail, was bleached even lighter by the July sun. Her white socks were grass stained, her black leather shoes muddy from play. Unlike Charlie, Mary didn't wait to be told to wash her hands. Heading to the bathroom, she shouted over her shoulder in a rush of words:

"Mom, I was at Rachel's house. Mrs. Golson told me it was time for supper and asked if I wanted to stay but I didn't but I might next time. They said they were havin' goldfish. Rachel said that's what they sometimes eat on Fridays. Can you really eat goldfish? You'd have to eat an awful lot of 'em, if you didn't want to feel hungry." Before her puzzled mother could answer, Mary already had disappeared up the stairs.

Katie turned to a mystified Charlie. "I think she means 'gefilte fish. It's a kind of Jewish food. Never tried it myself. Anyway, it was kind of Mrs. Golson to ask her." Charlie simply shrugged, not knowing what else he could add to the conversation.

* * *

A few minutes later Doug Thompson's arrival completed the family's homecoming.

Although not much taller than his wife, Doug was heavily built, his thickly muscled arms and shoulders the legacy of 21 years as a stonemason wrestling heavy rocks and hods of bricks five- and-a-half days each week. Many sturdily built homes and offices scattered across Toronto stood as silent evidence of his skill. He was clad in a white undershirt and grey overalls, as earlier in the day he had discarded the sweaty red work-shirt now slung over his shoulder. Under his right arm Doug carried a battered black metal lunch pail, empty except for the Thermos bottle which kept his noon tea hot. Placing the pail on the kitchen counter, Doug opened his arms wide to receive Mary's enthusiastic embrace, her arms only half-encircling her father's waist. He then greeted his son with a meaty hand on the boy's thin shoulder. With a shy smile, Katie waited her turn. She was pleased to see him safely home, enjoying the attention he paid to their children, looking forward to the gentle kiss on her cheek that always came next. She deemed such displays of affection appropriate for little eyes to see.

By late afternoon, Katie was ready for the refreshing breeze her returning family brought with them from the outside world. After high school, she had gone to Shaw's Business School, then worked as an office secretary in a button factory on Spadina. But once she became pregnant with Charlie, Katie reluctantly left her job. Even now, at times, she missed being part of a successful business, of being recognized by her boss as an essential member of the staff, a nice perk to go along with her pay cheque. So it was with unexpressed ambivalence, Katie traded the role of income-earner for the greater responsibilities of a soon-to-be mother. Since then, her life was home-centered and intermittently tedious–children, meals, housework–but enlivened by occasional card parties with other couples and frequent visits with her parents in Downsview.

And, on occasion, movie night at the Grant or Colony or maybe one of the fancier downtown theatres like Shea's or Loews.

"'Tis good to have you home on time, Doug. You'll surely be ready for a good meal, and supper be ready for you." In moments like these, Katie could almost convince herself her life was one of fulfillment and meaning.

Still, she lived vicariously through the smattering of neighbourhood news and gossip she learned from the children and of the wider community from Doug's workplace stories of union politics and business dealings. She fed on these snippets of information like a hungry person grasping at breadcrumbs fallen from the table.

"You've had a hot one today, Doug." Katie smiled at her husband with a hint of concern in her voice.

"Yes, and it's to be even hotter all week." He shook his head ruefully. "I'll just be a minute." He clambered up the narrow oak staircase to their small second floor bathroom. Reaching for his tin of Snap, he scrubbed at his hands and forearms. The grey gritty paste had a pleasant fragrance, reaching his nostrils as he worked the cleanser onto his work-toughened skin. Bending over the wide basin of the porcelain sink, he ritualistically rinsed each hand and splashed warm water over his face, gratefully ridding himself of another day's worth of sweat, stone dust and cement powder.

With eyes still shut, Doug blindly grabbed for a towel within easy reach on a wooden rack. Wiping away the water, he glanced briefly into a small mirror above the sink and caught a glimpse of a tired 39-year-old man looking forward to spending time with family. While he worked long hours to provide for them, by this time of day there seemed little of him left to give.

* * *

The family sat for supper. Katie had added milk to the potatoes in order to mash them and placed a mound in the center of each plate. Man-sized portions for Doug and Charlie, smaller amounts for herself and Mary. She then vigorously stirred the contents of the largest pot before carrying it carefully to the table. Mince was an old Scottish dish, made by boiling ground beef until it turned grey. By not draining off the liquid, and adding chopped carrots and a cooked onion, the result was halfway between soup and stew. Using a soup ladle, she poured it over each serving of potatoes, the mince rippling to the edges of their china plates. With slices of white bread with butter, sugary tea for the adults and milk for the children, the first course was presented and ready to be consumed. Later, she would fill the bottom of a large square Pyrex dish with the rest of the mince, add a layer of leftover mashed potatoes, and pop it in the oven to create shepherd's pie—tomorrow's dinner.

"Good as ever, Katie." Doug knew his wife needed to hear that her efforts were appreciated, though he didn't always remember to tell her.

"Can I get dessert now?" Having gobbled down the mince in five short minutes, Charlie looked hopefully at his mother.

"Just hold your horses, young man. Let the others finish and the meal settle." With a dramatic sigh, Charlie accepted Katie's decree.

Come on Mary, Hurry up! Oh, why does she take such tiny bites? To bug me? Well, let her. I don't care.

That pie sure looks good.

Talk flowed easily. Mary chatted animatedly about her day: her friend Rachel, that strange menu of goldfish, and the Golson's newly erected backyard canvas tent. Every so often, Katie would gently redirect the conversation to father and son although neither felt any great need to compete with the bubbly monologue. Most days Doug was dog-tired from work and content to concentrate on his food. While he didn't always follow his daughter's narrative, he enjoyed the lilting singsong of her chatter. Charlie's conversations were usually inner ones, leading Katie to observe that his mind often seemed "far away."

Today, Charlie too was focused on his dinner. He knew from grade eight health class that the nutrition he needed for the muscles he craved were in the first course, and this particular first course was both tasty and lacking in limp overboiled vegetables. Still, it was but a prerequisite to dessert. And it would be no less nutritious for being eaten quickly.

Katie had spent two hours creating her pie, with fresh strawberries and homemade crust, and it was welcomed with anticipatory murmurs of pleasure by the rest of the family. Sticky red juice trickled from each slice as the overly sweetened dessert was cut into wedge-shaped portions and served, with one piece reserved for Doug's lunch next day.

* * *

O ye'll tak the high road and I'll tak the low road,
And I'll be in Scotland afore ye,
But me and my true love will never meet again,
On the bonnie, bonnie banks of Loch Lomond.

Later that evening as she washed the dishes, Katie sang quietly to herself songs that she had learned years ago at the knee of her Scottish grandmother. The children were asleep in their tiny second floor bedrooms. Doug was intently reading The Evening Telegram, the Toronto Daily Star too liberal for his taste. The day had unfolded peacefully, as it should; events in each of their lives had flowed smoothly. This sense of gratitude and satisfaction mostly outweighed whatever yearnings she might feel about her own place in the family. When a sticky dessert plate slipped from her hand, just for an instant her composure slipped as well.

She quickly placed the broken dish in the garbage can under the sink, and the mistake disappeared along with it. No one seemed to notice.

Soon the day would run its course, like a quietly flowing river and refreshing sleep would wash over the last two family members still awake. And the secret she had carried for many years remained securely buried in the back corners of her conscience for another day.

CHAPTER TWO

C harlie's transition into adolescence was moving at a slow un-
even pace. His child-body was beginning to stretch upward like
a spring weed, though still without widening, edging past his
mother's height earlier that year and giving Katie ample cause for teasing
mixed with pride. The finely textured hair on his body had finally begun
to thicken. Despite the absence of any formal preparation on his part,
Charlie was not surprised by what his body was doing.

* * *

It was early August a year ago and first thing. on a Sunday morning,
that the Thompson family's wood-panelled '49 Ford station wagon had
merged into a steady stream of traffic moving slowly north on Highway
27. A time when Charlies had both his sisters, a better time. They were
all on their way to Jackson's Point on Lake Simcoe, hoping to find respite
from the city's sticky humidity. Arriving before noon, Charlie's family
had quickly laid a well-worn red woollen picnic blanket over the hot
sand, staking claim to a few square feet of the crowded beach. Charlie had
gone ahead to the men's change house to put on his blue boxer-style swim
trunks. Old and wood-sided, with chipped and fading green paint, it was
noisy with male banter. He stripped quickly, piling discarded clothes and
shoes on the grey-painted pine bench behind him which ran the length
of the room. Hurriedly and self-consciously, he wiggled into his bathing
suit. Glancing around at the men and older boys, he noticed for the first

time what he too might soon become. He pondered this discovery as he carried his bundled belongings into the hard sunlight.

Those guys looked so big and strong. Some of the men had pot bellies, they were pulling up their trunks to hide the roll. What if I get like that? Wouldn't it be better than staying skinny? No, the best bodies are the ones with muscles. I wonder—did they just grow 'em, or did they have to do weightlifting and stuff? [Pause] It must just happen once you're a teenager. I'm sure it will for me. Except what if it doesn't?

* * *

Charlie found his family sitting cross-legged on their communal blanket. Eleven-year-old Sarah and their younger sister, Mary, had already emerged from the other change house, the one marked LADIES in bold black letters as if to deter any males from mistakenly (or otherwise) wandering in. Leaving their three children to watch over the brown wicker food hamper and red cooler, Doug and Katie quickly proceeded to their change rooms. Everyone was anxious to cool off in the lake's clear waters.

Waiting patiently for their parents to emerge, each child sat quietly on the blanket lost in thought. Sarah was scanning the crowd, hoping to see a familiar face from the neighbourhood; several of her friends had mentioned they might be coming this weekend. She was tall like her siblings, but with broad shoulders and long auburn hair courtesy of her mother's Scottish ancestry. Mary's gaze eagerly followed the other holidaying families as they moved to the edge of the water.

A few of the braver ones made a beeline across the sand, stepping nimbly so as not to burn their feet. Once in the lake, they paused only for a moment as the insistent push of the waves temporarily held them back. Then, launching themselves with strong kicks and a splash of bubbles, they quickly dove out of sight. Other more tentative bathers approached cautiously, dipping a toe to confirm its temperature. They paused on the shore, before proceeding to systematically splash water over legs and torsos to acclimatize their bodies. Both Sarah and Mary were impatient to join them. Charlie, as always, was more inclined to hang back and observe.

I wish we had the beach to ourselves—no noise, no crowds running around. But it's so hot, and the water's cool even if you have to share it.

So should I just run in? No, it's too cold. Better to get in slowly. I just know Mary's going to splash me if she gets in first.

The girls caught sight of their parents before Charlie did and bounded toward them. He noticed that below faded blue boxer-style bathing trunks, his father's hairy, muscular legs were winter-white, while the rest of him—face, arms and torso—was work-tanned like a walnut stain. He was relieved to see that Doug wasn't hiding any rolls. His mother, still slim and pretty at 35, had wrapped a beach towel around her, reluctant to display more than was necessary before going into the water.

Soon all five Thompsons had joined the crowds in the lake. After a two-hour road trip and a long humid week in the city, it was like the end of a pilgrimage. For the rest of his family, it was a moment to be enjoyed and celebrated. Still, for Charlie, it was always more ordeal than pleasure.

* * *

"Duck your head under. That's the first step." Doug was gently encouraging his boy to learn to swim. "Come on. The water's warm."

The object of his instructions stood uncomfortably, waist-deep and immobilized, as each small wave brushed cruelly against his belly button. Despite Doug's reassurances, the lake was too darn cold. Even raising himself on tip toes didn't keep the ripples from touching his exposed flesh.

"Do it, Charlie, we haven't got all day. I want to get swimming myself." Noticing a slight note of frustration in his father's tone. Charlie reluctantly leaned forward. Like a long-legged stork spearing an underwater frog in some swamp, he quickly poked his face into the water, coughed up an unexpected mouthful of wave water and just as rapidly returned to his former rigid stance.

"Dad, I don't want my ears to get plugged!"

"Charlie's a 'fraidy cat!" taunted Mary. She'd been watching the drama played out beside her and naturally seized this opportunity to demonstrate her own aquatic skills.

"Look Dad, I can do the crawl." She fearlessly dove into the water and proceeded to swim a few strokes, her arms moving rhythmically, thin legs wildly flailing. Intentionally or otherwise, just as he'd feared, Mary's performance managed to splash her brother with a shower of cold water.

"Dad, tell her to stop!"

Doug was about to gently chastise his daughter but she was already dog paddling her way back to shore. In reality, he was more than a little frustrated with his son who simply stood, arms wrapped for warmth around his frail underdeveloped body, dripping and shivering. With all the patience he could muster, Doug put his big hand on the boy's bony shoulder and suggested he head back to the sanctuary of their beach blanket. After eying him safely back to the sand, Doug pivoted toward the inviting lake and quickly disappeared under its rolling waves.

His powerful front crawl rapidly propelled him into deeper water, so much cooler and bracing on his skin. The exercise felt good after sitting in the station wagon for so long. His strong arms sliced the waves, first left then right. After every fourth stroke Doug rhythmically twisted his torso to the right to take a breath. He was soon far out into the lake, enjoying the sense of freedom and renewal it offered.

Meanwhile, Katie had laid out lunch. A large Thermos held still-cold lemonade. Ham, cheese, and egg salad sandwiches, all made with the family's favourite Brown's Bakery sliced white bread, were produced from the cooler. As older girl, Sarah was tasked with handing out the food. She began by passing around paper plates decorated with sticks of celery stuffed with bright orange Velveeta cheese. Dessert would come later: sticky Rice Crispy squares in a cookie tin which had once held British store-bought biscuits. On its patriotic lid was a colour picture of the young Queen, posed demurely on her throne in full regal dress.

"Who wants a sandwich? Mary, egg or ham?" Mary didn't answer and simply grabbed one of each. Katie suppressed a smile, while pretending to be indignant in the face of such bad manners.

"I know we're not at the kitchen table but there's no need to behave like little pigs," Katie gently chastised, echoing past admonitions from her own mother.

"Mom, pigs wouldn't eat ham sandwiches. It would be like eating their friends." Despite her hard-wired insistence on manners, Katie finally gave in and burst out laughing.

"At least the chicken didn't have to make any supreme sacrifice to give us these eggs," mused Doug.

"Then I'd rather be a chicken than a pig," Charlie added after a moment's reflection. "So I can call you 'chicken legs' and not get in trouble," crowed Sarah, at which point Katie returned to Scottish form and ended the teasing with a stern glance.

After cleanup, Doug and Katie moved the cooler so they could lie side by side on the blanket. In the background, the sounds of nearby swimmers and screeching children lulled them into a half-sleep. Sarah wandered along the shoreline looking for shells. Mary worked on an immense sandcastle, complete with towers and festooned with a grey-white seagull feather, with a new friend Debbie. They'd dug a moat around the perimeter and were busy filling it with lake water scooped up in Debbie's blue metal pail.

"Charlie, wanna help us?" asked Mary, hoping to assuage the tiny but still troubling bit of guilt she was carrying for splashing her brother when she knew he hated it. From the resounding silence, Mary concluded she was being ignored, and resumed filling the moat.

In fact, Charlie wasn't ignoring his little sister; he was simply absorbed with the hypnotic rhythm of the breeze-blown waves rippling across the water, gently touching the shore and just as gently slipping back to the deep. He was sitting by himself in the sand a few yards back from his family and well removed from the happy commotion of shore-side activities. He didn't trust the lake. Once the water became waist-deep he didn't like that he could no longer see the bottom. Even at its calmest, it was an immense flat-shaped sea monster, its massive chest steadily breathing in... pause... then out.

He thought back to a pleasantly warm Saturday afternoon. His father had borrowed a friend's rowboat to take him fishing. Hart Lake was much smaller than Lake Simcoe, but Charlie felt the same creeping sense of unease as the tiny craft moved slowly but steadily away from the reedy shoreline.

I like having my feet on solid ground. Why do we have to fish in a boat? It's starting to rock. If I grab on to the sides, maybe it won't flip over. Dad's so calm. I guess because he could easily swim to shore. He'd have to rescue me. That's scary too.

I just gotta hang on. Dad knows what he's doing.

Water was foreign territory—an alien land where he knew he did not belong. Peering over the edge of the boat, he watched his father row, the long wooden oars slipping in unison under the surface, the boat thrust forward by the concentrated strength of a mason's biceps and shoulders.

How deep is it out here? Do we have to go so far out? What if there's a really big wave and it knocks Dad out? I'd have to hang on to the boat until someone sees me.

What if no one does?

Charlie swore a vow to himself that afternoon: if he ever got a boat, he would only row back and forth in shallow water, never venturing more than six feet away from the safety of solid ground. No matter if there were no fish to catch, so long as he could see the lake bottom, with its reassuring presence of seaweeds, sunken logs and slippery rocks. Should the boat suddenly capsize or spring a serious leak, he could then walk calmly to shore.

* * *

As the late summer sun began a slow return home to its far horizon, the Thompsons reluctantly packed up. Each was beginning to feel the growing tingle of sun-reddened shoulders and back. By bedtime, Katie would be applying large gobs of Noxema, one by one, ending with herself. In a few days, their skin would blister, peel and be pulled off—a summer ritual about which no one ever gave a second thought.

CHAPTER THREE

"It's not music; it's noise!" Doug's body filled the doorway of his son's bedroom. "Why on earth do you like it?" His voice was more curious than condemning. In truth, he was pleased his normally reticent son was voicing a rare assertive opinion.

"It's new and different and I like the beat." Charlie was lying on top of his bed covers in the fading light of a summer evening. A small box-like Northern Electric radio stood on the brown three-drawer dresser beside his head. Its bakelite casing was grey with a gold-coloured decorative front. Each night, before sleep overtook him, Charlie would slowly and systematically rotate its red-knobbed tuner across the bandwidth in search of favourite stations. Two smaller white knobs controlled the off/on and volume.

Although Charlie was unaware of the greater cultural debate over this new music, Doug's question was fueled in part by what he'd been hearing at card games or at work: "This rock and roll stuff is Negro music. They can keep it." "This so-called music is of the Devil. Keep your kids away from it!"

* * *

It was the summer of 1954. Charlie's discovery of this controversial but exciting sound had happened by chance. For as long as he could remember, his family had listened to the polished-oak floor model Crosley which once had held a prominent spot in the living room until shoved aside by the recent arrival of an equally bulky RCA console television set. This second, smaller Northern Electric radio was a surprise Christmas gift from Grandma and Grandpa Ranwick—his own radio for his own room.

After years of listening to the Crosley, Charlie was familiar with most local stations: CBL-740 for Hockey Night in Canada or The Happy Gang, CKEY-580 for the Toronto Maple Leaf baseball game, CJBC-1010 for Mary's noontime Small Tykes Club with "Uncle Bing," and CFRB-860 for the 6:30 p.m. news, sponsored by Beehive Golden Corn Syrup. Nothing too radical or upsetting, only sometimes vaguely unsettling, reflecting the prevailing insular mood of daily life in Toronto. Regional or colonial wars and rebellions were far away; racial tensions were brewing, but mainly in the American Deep South; brutal Communist dictatorships were prevalent in Eastern Europe but even more remote. Through their radios and newspapers, Torontonians were aware of the world's troubles, but these remained at some safe peripheral distance.

* * *

For Charlie, the Northern Electric was a portal into a different world: specifically, American cities near and far—and the bold new music they carried across the miles into his bedroom. He could remember that first post-bedtime discovery in the quiet blanketed darkness of night, when he slowly rotated the tuner, its thin yellow needle impatiently slipping past the familiar call letters until he found not just nearby Buffalo, but Atlanta and New York, Albany and Cincinnati. Only after darkness had covered the city, did they speak; by sunrise they were gone. They called to him through crackling static on stormy nights when, just for an instant, flashes of jagged lightning bolts lit up his room. Even when they inexplicably faded, they were gone for only a few moments before returning stronger than before.

I wonder what it would be like to live in the US? They have Marlborough cigarettes and Pilsner beer. Except I don't smoke or drink beer. But I could go to Brooklyn to a Dodgers game. What must it be like to live in a city with millions of people?

Or what if I lived in a small town, maybe in Iowa or Michigan. But then I might get drafted and end up in Korea. Except I'd get to wear a uniform. The girls would notice me then for sure. Until I had to shoot someone. I'm not sure I could do that.

Better to stay where I am, and just enjoy the music.

Until the Northern Electric, Charlie had contentedly accepted the popular music of his parents' generation. He knew the lyrics to all their top hits and, when his mind wasn't otherwise occupied, he even liked to sing them. Drawn by one pop song's romantic melody, and blissfully ignoring its jarring grammar, he once found himself singing alongside the deep sultry voice of Rosemary Clooney as she confessed:

"Once I had a secret love

That lived within the heart of me."

Other popular female vocalists—Patti Page, Jo Stafford, Doris Day, Eartha Kitt—and the men—Eddie Fisher, Perry Como, Nat King Cole, Frankie Lane—sang of romance and falling in love, despite occasionally having their hearts cruelly broken. Charlie knew all the catchy melodies and folksy songs. "Cryin' In the Chapel." "The Happy Wanderer." They were soothing and sanitized, banal and formulaic.

But two weeks ago, Charlie's musical interests literally changed overnight. It was on a Saturday, when he could stay awake longer without fear of parental censure. His' nocturnal exploration of American radio frequencies had led him further down the AM band, and he stumbled across WJW, broadcasting out of Cleveland at 1210 on the dial. Half asleep by 10 o'clock, he was stirred into sudden alertness by a gravel-voiced disc jockey calling himself "the king of the moondoggers," Alan Freed. And he was playing music that woke Charlie up fast.

Freed called it "rock 'n' roll." Charlie had no idea that the more correct label "rhythm 'n' blues" was too closely associated, in the minds of uneasy sponsors, with "race music" and Negro culture. He only knew that he was hooked.

Following a commercial break extolling the good taste of Erin Breweries beer, Freed spun "Shake, Rattle and Roll," a current hit by Big Joe Turner. While the entranced Charlie was oblivious to its suggestive lyrics, he was instantly excited by the song's hypnotic backbeat and the raw and raspy voice of the singer. It became his music, a music that was nothing like what his parents listened to. He was completely unaware that Turner was coloured.

His next step was to acquire a phonograph. The thought of playing his songs whenever he chose was compelling. Which is how, a week earlier,

Charlie found himself in spirited discussion with his skeptical father over his need for a loan.

"Dad, I'm tired of Doris Day and Tony Bennett. They're okay for you and Mom. But it's not what kids wanna hear."

"Your songs are nothing but banging and noise. You can't even understand what they're saying. Besides, what makes you think we can afford a record player?"

"I could work with Grandpa on the farm in August and pay you back."

"So how much are we talking about?" Charlie thought a moment then tentatively suggested "maybe fifteen dollars?"

For Doug, money wasn't the real issue. It was his son's newfound preoccupation with rock 'n' roll. Drawing from his own memory bank, he felt more or less equipped to talk with Charlie about girls, alcohol, smoking and other adolescent temptations. He reasoned that some things never change from one generation to the next and assumed that when a situation required parental action, he would lay down rules and guidelines from his own experiences. With this new music, however, Doug had neither the experience nor any idea what the responsible paternal attitude should be. And as he realized he couldn't explain why he felt that way, he focused instead on the price tag. Even so, a part of him resolved to set aside these nagging concerns. He decided, instead, that he had now found the perfect present for the boy's birthday, two weeks away.

"OK, Charlie, let me think about it and talk the idea over with your mother." Though unaware of his father's decision, Charlie felt his hopes rise. Then it hit him. How many hours would he need to work? Would Grandpa be willing to pay him that much?

* * *

Planning the party was easy for Katie. She knew the boy's favourite treat would be a white cake, which she would make in the Scottish way: sweet vanilla icing roofing, a thick layer of cake, a thin jam-covered pastry on the bottom. Charlie's cousins lived far away, in Ottawa and Brockville, and he lacked close friends. So the only invited guests would be her parents, Tom and Jane Ranwick. Charlie's other grandparents,

Norman and Sadie Thompson, immigrants from Glasgow, had both died while their grandson was still a preschooler.

Katie felt a waft of nostalgia, a yearning for what might have been. She knew Doug still missed his parents and would love them to be a part of the family he and Katie had nurtured. It suddenly occurred to her that, as strange as that sounded in her head, Doug was an orphan. Does a grown man still need parenting? Of course he does. After all, she still relied on her mother and father for support, reassurance, guidance. For love. What a foolish question.

Katie snapped back to the party. To linger longer in the past would only reawaken other bitter regrets which were better off in cold storage, like the birthday cake she would hide in their pastel-green refrigerator.

She wished there could be other guests, boys Charlie's age and maybe a girl or two. She could guess the answer. She asked anyway, in case she was wrong.

"Charlie, would you like to invite anyone from your class? There's lots of room and we'll have plenty of food." The question hung in the air like a birthday balloon.

"No, it's okay. The family's good enough."

I'd be afraid to ask anyone. What if no one said yes? Or they come and they're bored to death? Maybe a girl, though, maybe Susan. No, I'm too chicken. Besides, I'd be embarrassed with everyone there watching us. No, the worst would be people saying they'd come but not showing up. Then I'd have my family feeling sorry for me and knowing I don't have any real friends at school.

Mary already has more friends that I do and she's only seven. And Sarah... no, I can't think about Sarah...

"Well, if you change your mind, let me know and I'll make a bigger cake. It's good to be with friends on your birthday, not just your dull old parents." This last part was accompanied with a smile and a wink, but also a soft reproach.

"I will, Mom." Neither mother nor son actually believed anyone else would be invited but were content to pretend it might.

Late on the Sunday afternoon of a rainy mid-July weekend, the family gathered together around the Thompson's solid-oak dining room table for Charlie's birthday dinner. An extra leaf had been inserted into its rounded top to accommodate everyone. Tom and Jane Ranwick looked forward to these times with their Toronto grandchildren. Tom, a ruddy-faced Scot, was a talker, constantly telling stories about his early years in the Highlands and gently teasing the children at every opportunity. English-born Jane was quieter, a patient listener to Tom's yarns which, after many years together, she could have recounted as well as he.

"Charlie, now that you are fourteen do you have your eye on a pretty girl?" Tom grinned mischievously at the blushing boy who promptly began to poke at his cake.

"I dunno," he offered shyly, hoping a minimal reply might be enough.

"When I was your age, twas the lassies chasin' me." He ignored Jane's quietly mocking laughter. "I had my pick of the prettiest of the lot. Ah but I remember Annie, the minister's daughter."

The unspoken message from her father—that Charlie *should* have a girl who caught his eye—roused Katie's protective maternal instincts and she moved quickly to shift the conversation. "Father, Charlie has plenty of time to find a girlfriend. He need not be in any hurry. How be I warm your tea?"

In these situations, Charlie didn't mind his mother speaking up for him. In fact, he counted on her to bail him out of awkward moments. The reality was that the birthday boy had never thought much about girls that way, except for the pretend ones in his comic books. By grade eight, though, his classmates were pairing off at Saturday matinees, which he'd hear about at recess. The more mature boys might brag about "feeling up" their dates, but it was mostly just talk. At least he hoped it was.

The birthday dinner ended early so that Tom could be home in time for the evening milking; some tasks couldn't be set aside even on a Sabbath. After they had left, Katie and Tom cleared the table, saving the remnants of the cake for tomorrow's dessert. Mary grudgingly helped with the dishes, so that the birthday boy might have a night off from chores.

"Don't forget, Mom, I don't have to do dishes on my birthday then. Charlie, you don't forget either. I hope we have ten pots and pans that night." She stuck out her tongue to amplify this last point while her brother pretended not to notice.

Charlie had been surprised and excited by his gifts. He'd already set up the boxy RCA Victor record player in his room, its red center-post and round turntable awaiting the first 78 vinyl disc.

His grandparents, in coordination with Doug and Katie, had given Charlie a birthday card with a five-dollar bill inside, more than enough to buy his first record. And before sleep overtook him that night, he had determined what that purchase would be.

* * *

Neal's Appliances on Bloor Street was only a short walk from the Thompson's home on Lawson Avenue, which ran north off it. Lawson was a quiet road. Bloor on a Monday morning was already humming with commercial activity. The grocers had set out boxes of peaches and plums, soft fruits now arriving daily from orchards along the Niagara Escarpment. Carrots, potatoes and lettuce from Holland Marsh were also on display. The butcher shop, owned by Italian immigrants who came to Canada after the War, was crowded with early shoppers buying cuts of beef, chicken and pork for the coming week's table. Skinned animals—Charlie guessed they were pigs or lambs—hung in the store window on iron hooks. He wondered as always why there was sawdust on the floor. It always seemed out of place and looked messy. What liquid was it meant to absorb?

This section of Toronto was just beginning to change its character. As well as the Italian newcomers, the War had pushed Ukrainian, Polish, German, Dutch, but mainly British, emigrants out of post-war chaos and the uncertain future of a broken Europe. Each group found comfort and kinship by clustering with those of their own who had come to Ontario earlier in the century.

The newcomers brought with them tiny pieces of their homelands: English fish and chips wrapped in newspaper and drenched with vinegar and salt, a small grocery shop featuring store- front European-style open displays of produce, a rare and hard-to-find Hungarian restaurant.

Nevertheless, the city easily absorbed her new citizens and remained for all intents and purposes "Toronto the Good." Just as, despite a large Roman Catholic population, it maintained its Protestant insistence on a commercially shut-down Sunday.

Mr. Neal, a short worried-looking man who habitually scurried around his store trying to keep his customers content, chose to change his name from the original Polish "Neligmann" because it was easier to pronounce. He also chose to cater to their musical tastes and had set aside a corner of his large store for records. These were primarily 78s and albums, although the new and smaller 45s were beginning to claim a share of the market. Bins were divided by category, with classical works and Broadway shows sharing shelf space with current hits popularized by the radio and movies.

It was the "Top Forty" bin that Charlie set his sights on, eagerly scanning titles that Mr. Neal himself had carefully arranged alphabetically by artist or band. For an instant he was distracted by an unexpected discovery, "Sh-Boom" by the Crew Cuts, currently the number one song on the charts, before resolutely returning it to its proper place. A moment later he found what he had come to buy. He had heard "Thirteen Women and Only One Man in Town" several times during the last few nights over his now-familiar American stations. The song described a post-nuclear apocalypse, but it wasn't the lyrics but the rock 'n' roll sound he sought.

That evening, Charlie played his record over and over again, each time careful to place the stylus on its groove without scratching the delicate vinyl surface. Then, out of curiosity, he flipped the disc to hear the B-side of the record.

The wailing tenor sax, steady pounding of the kettle drum, the driving cadence of the shouted lyrics unrelentingly drew the boy into its musical vortex. Excited and eager for more, he quickly closed his bedroom door before playing the flip side song again, this time at a much louder volume.

I like this side even better. What a great band. Bill Haley and the Comets. Great drum beat. Doris Day and Frank Sinatra sure don't sing like this. I don't know what all the fuss is about. It sounds great to me. One day I'm gonna dance in a high school gym with a girl and make smooth dance moves. Maybe swing her around and make her laugh. I wonder how you learn to dance like this? Some day...

Sure, Charlie, except you're too chicken to ever ask a girl out. How are you gonna feel if she says no? Better to not take a chance and never get hurt.

Or maybe someone will ask me to the Sadie Hawkins dance. That way I wouldn't get rejected.

But I still won't know how to dance or even how to hold her. Or when it's okay to kiss her goodnight.

Well, I still can like the music, even if I never go to a dance.

An hour later, at his own bedtime, Doug wearily climbed the stairs. As he passed Charlie's room, he noticed two things. For the first time, his son had shut the door. Previously, both his children had left their doors partly open, making it easy for him to look in before quietly closing them for the night. Even more unexpected was the sound seeping out from behind that door.

Nine, ten, eleven o'clock, twelve o'clock rock,
We're gonna rock around the clock tonight.

Doug shook his head and continued toward his own bed. As he dropped off to sleep, he muttered to his dozing wife: "Something is certainly going on with Charlie."

"I know," she replied drowsily and gently drew him into her arms. "I know," she said again, this time to no one except to the darkness which slowly encroached.

ed

l are

she

that
es to

NATIONAL WEATHER SERVICE:

A tropical storm developed rapidly in the west Gulf of Mexico on the 24th of June and by early on the 25th was of hurricane force. It moved inland south of Brownsville, Texas. Seventeen deaths were reported in Texas and an estimated 38 in Mexico. Dollar damage is not available.

record breaking teen

m
aga
H
Lyl
in
lin

National Hurricane Center 1954 Data archives, Miami, Fla.

CHAPTER FOUR

Charlie sat quietly on the Humber bank, chewing a tender stalk of timothy grass and watching the dark water roll by. A lonely, green maple leaf, reluctantly dislodged from some upstream tree, silently floated by, captive to the relentless current on its way to some unknown destination not of its own choosing.

It's fun to watch the river.

I can see the bottom, the slippery mossy rocks and the mud. It's not scary, not like the lake. I'll never see this bit of water again; it doesn't come around again like a merry-go-round. I wonder where it starts and where it goes. I know it ends up at the Atlantic but what happens after that?

Maybe we'll cover that in Canadian geography this year.

Ugh, I don't want to think about school! Not when it's still summertime.

* * *

Sarah had died last September. He had no idea how his family would react when the first anniversary of her death inevitably arrived. Sometimes when they were alone, he and Mary would talk about her. They instinctively knew not to include their parents, who never offered more than terse comments if her name came up, then awkwardly changed the subject. He never thought to question this.

For Doug, thinking on the death of his middle child created a powerful stinging sense of failure. Just before Sarah was born in June, 1942, Doug had rushed home, having been given special leave from army training in New Brunswick. After several restless hours in the waiting room, pacing the floor and making small talk with the other soon-to-be-dads, Private Thompson finally entered the recovery room to meet his daughter. Leaning in over Katie's bed, he gently kissed his newborn. As the baby's blue eyes gazed unblinkingly at her father, Doug mouthed a solemn vow to shelter this helpless little life from the dangers of a troubled world. Yet he had not been able to protect her, to keep her safe from a disease he couldn't see, that hovered invisibly beyond the sanctuary of home. At times, he tried to convince himself that Sarah's death was beyond anything he could have done. But logic was no match for the pervasive and lingering feelings of anger which Doug carried on his back each day like a stone mason's load of bricks.

It was the irony of the loss that created much of his bitterness. Nearly ten years ago, he was jammed into an overcrowded troopship, a converted passenger liner, with hundreds of other young men and shipped halfway around the world to defend his country and keep its women and children safe. Yet he couldn't keep his own precious daughter alive. If there was a God, he must be a cruel bastard, not worthy of belief or trust.

Katie too was burdened with unresolved struggles. Why had her prayers for Sarah's healing not been answered? Was God unable or, worse, unwilling to hear her pleas because of what she'd kept hidden all these years? But whenever guilt would rise like a circling black crow, Katie redirected her thoughts to happier memories. The bitter acid of self-condemnation still churned deep in her stomach, but at least the intensity was temporarily soothed. All she needed to do was remember those good days gone by.

Sarah had turned eleven and, even though it was a school night, they celebrated by going to see *Roman Holiday* at the Colony Theatre on Eglinton Avenue. Her daughter sat entranced as the princess in disguise fell in love with an American journalist. The very next day she was determined to cut off her shoulder-length auburn hair just as Audrey Hepburn did part way through the film. Katie recalled the amusing argument which followed:

"But she looked so beautiful with bangs," Sarah pleaded loudly.

"She looked like a boy" her mother countered. "When you're older, you can decide what to do with your hair. Not until then."

It took Sarah only an instant to reply. "But it's my own hair right now, isn't it?"

"Not as long as I have to look at it every day," Even as she said it, Katie knew that made no sense. The next day, Charlie overheard her admit to Tom that a short hairstyle would frame their daughter's face and probably look quite attractive. And maybe that was the problem, she continued; Sarah was growing up too fast, not according to the schedule she'd laid out for her the day she first held her in the delivery room.

In the end, mother and daughter agreed to reopen the discussion at Sarah's next birthday.

With a lump swelling in her throat, Katie was forced to remember that it would never come.

* * *

Perched on his riverbank, Charlie struggled to understand Sarah's death.

I don't understand why she had to die. I can still see her clattering down the stairs on school mornings—too much time in the bathroom and the rest of us banging on the door. I'd yell at her cause I had to get washed too. Now I wish I hadn't been so impatient. She'd grab a piece of toast and gulp her orange juice and leave most of her porridge. Then Mom would complain about her going to school hungry, she'd laugh and say "I left some for Goldilocks" And even Mom had to smile as she finished the bowl herself. Dammit! I miss her.

I still have Mary. Doesn't take away the hurt of losing Sarah, though.

* * *

It was near the end of August when Sarah got sick. The unrelenting heat of late summer held the city in a steamy embrace as temperatures climbed to over 100 degrees. When the weekend mercifully arrived, any residents with the means to leave did so quickly. Most drove north to Muskoka cottage country or up Number 27 for the beige-coloured sands of Wasaga and Balm Beaches. Left-behind Torontonians slept overnight on screened-in porches or spread tarpaulin ground-covers and blankets on backyard grass. Some took a short streetcar ride to the city beaches along the Lake Ontario shore with its notoriously cold water. Sunnyside extended open hours in its Olympic sized pool for those seeking a warmer swim. Families of picnickers crowded onto ferry boats for the short trip to Centre and Ward's Islands for the mere promise of a cooling onshore breeze.

Sarah lay listlessly in bed as the day drew to a close. It was a raging fever, not the weather, that caused beads of sweat to form across her forehead before sliding down to wet the white cotton pillow underneath. Katie patiently held a cold cloth against her older daughter's brow, her smiling face masking an inner dread. Charlie remembered how his mother spoke soothingly that night, as he lay awake listening anxiously in his room down the hall.

"You'll be feeling better in the morning," she offered by way of reassurance, as much to herself as to her child. Apart from seasonal colds and flu, illness in the Thompson home was an uncommon event. Katie was used to handling Sarah's cuts and scrapes, the inevitable result of raising an athletic energetic daughter. This was far scarier. Bandages, mustard plasters and ointments would be of no use. Still, she knew to keep calm and hold her emotions in check so as not to frighten the children.

By next morning, Sarah was no better; She complained of a stiff neck and overall achiness, while her temperature stubbornly hovered over 102 degrees. Katie kept a constant vigil at her bedside, urging cool drinks and bits of food. Finally, three nights later, with Doug at their side, the fever broke and Sarah drifted off to a deep sleep. Her parents, relieved but exhausted, soon followed, after one last brief conversation.

"Doug, do you really think the worst is over?" Katie needed reassurance despite the obvious improvement she could see for herself.

"So far so good. We'll take it one day at a time. In the meantime, let's get some rest. God knows it has been a rough week." He was by nature more cautious than his wife. Better not to set one's hopes too high lest trouble lay hidden like a mugger around the next corner. That was one big lesson he had learned in Italy; just when you thought the German paratroopers were beaten, back they came in a vicious counterattack. He could still see them, big men in dark green uniforms and muddy leather boots up to their knees. His buddies called them "green devils." They were the battle-hardened best from Rommel's North African campaign, tough soldiers that Hitler could now throw into the Italian fight. "We never experienced real warfare before Sicily," he muttered, "but we bloody well learned in a hell of a hurry."

Sure enough, their respite from worry was short-lived. Within four days, Sarah's symptoms had returned, this time much worse. Her fretful crying pierced the darkened quiet of midnight. Charlie remained in bed, hoping in vain that he was only dreaming. Even after almost a year, he could replay, reluctantly but accurately, the unbearable sounds of that night. First his mother's frantic cry:

"I'm coming, Sarah, I'm coming. What's wrong?" The sound of a bedroom door flung open, the light snapped on.

"Mummy, my head!" Charlie couldn't remember the last time his sister had called their mother that. The heavier footsteps of his father soon followed, down the hall then a moment later the stairs, his slippered feet flapping on each step. A narrow band of light now shone under Charlie's door. He instinctively grabbed his pillow and placed it over his face, successfully shutting out the brightness but not the fear.

Then Doug was climbing the oak staircase, two steps at a time. Katie joined him in a whispered conversation outside Sarah's closed door.

"Dr. Cranmore is on his way. It'll be alright, Katie, don't worry." As they re-entered Sarah's room, Charlie now heard Mary, who shared Sarah's bedroom, sobbing softly.

"Daddy, what's wrong with Sarah. Why is she crying?

"Don't be scared, Mary; Mom and I are right here and Dr. Cranmore is on his way. He'll tell us what is wrong and how to fix it."

Mary got out of bed and went over to her sister. "Sarah, the doctor's coming. He'll help you feel better." As his little girl voiced a reassurance that she surely could not feel, Doug turned away so she wouldn't see his tears.

Dr. Cranmore arrived within the hour, the tires of his old green Nash sedan crunching on the gravelled driveway, followed by the slam of a heavy car door. Still in his room, Charlie could picture the doctor. He was tall, taller than his father, with wire-rimmed glasses and always wore the same worn-looking grey suit with baggy unpressed pants. His dark wavy hair was matched by a small equally dark moustache that bounced up and down under his wide nose when he talked.

Charlie was surprised when Dr. Cranmore's examination was brief and ended with a hasty consultation downstairs at the grey arborite kitchen table. He could hear the rise and fall of their voices, his parents frightened and questioning, the doctor attempting in vain to reassure them. Overwhelmed by worries and questions too scary to indulge, he desperately switched on his radio and soon found a half-inning of a White Sox game and a few Top Forty songs. Eventually, as he hoped, the familiar sounds led him into a fitful sleep which mercifully lasted the remainder of that long summer night.

Still, morning arrived too early and Charlie stayed in bed, unwilling for the new day to unlock the events of a few short hours ago. His parents were back in the girls' room, their muffled voices blending with the sobs of both daughters. Suddenly the sounds grew louder and now came from the hallway, quickly followed by a sharp knock on his door. Then Katie was in the room, her face reddened from weeping although the tears had been hastily swept away.

"Come out and say goodbye to Sarah. She's going away for a while—to the hospital." Charlie was immediately struck with a stabbing fear that his mother's struggles to appear calm were out of concern for Mary and him. He looked over her shoulder and saw their father with Sarah in his arms. She seemed groggily half asleep and was still wearing her pajamas. Mary clung to Katie's hand. Doug's face was set, suppressing the painful jumble of fear and helplessness he felt inside.

Charlie looked at him expectantly. "Your mother and I will explain things to you and Mary. Right now we need to take Sarah where she'll get better," Doug answered, as he and Sarah moved quickly toward the porch.

"Bye, Sarah, see you soon." Charlie's weak farewell was strained with worry.

"I'll visit if you have to stay overnight—but I hope you don't," called out Mary, who hastily added that she would make a get-well card that very day. Then father and daughter were in the car, leaving in their wake a slew of unacknowledged emotions and questions.

Katie, Charlie and Mary had no appetite as they picked away at their corn flakes and toast. As they tried to swallow, Katie began to explain, picking each word carefully and stringing them like beads into sentences she prayed would ease not only her children's minds but hers as well. She stared at the far wall as she spoke.

"Dr. Cranmore says Sarah is very sick. He thinks she has polio, but we won't know for sure until they do some tests at the hospital."

"Is that bad?" Mary looked at her mother, her voice conveying a mix of anxiety and confusion.

"It can be, but not always." When she turned toward her children, her eyes were desperate, her mouth tight-lipped. She was determined to say no more.

Charlie was thinking of Andy, a classmate last year. "But Mom, polio can make you not walk." Andy had been away from their classroom for over half the school year. When he came back, it was with crutches and iron braces on his legs.

"We are not going to even think about that." For just an instant Katie flashed a look of anger at her son, impossible to contain in her exhausted fear-stricken state. "Now listen carefully, both of you. Your Grandma will be coming to stay for a few days. As soon as she gets here, I'm going to the hospital. Sarah will be at St. Joseph's and Daddy is there now with her."

* * *

In 1953, Canada experienced its worst outbreak of infantile paralysis since the Depression years. By the end of that twelve-month period, about 8,800 cases of polio were reported across the nation, almost twice the number of the previous year. In Ontario alone, over 2,200 residents, most of them young children, were stricken with the insidious virus. The year before, only 700 incidences had been tracked. Although he had often listened to news reports, Charlie's knowledge of the disease was not statistical. For him the word "polio" meant yellow QUARANTINED signs on neighbours' front doors and mothers not allowing their children to swim in the city' pools. "Polio" meant Andy and the memory of him watching sadly and silently from behind the baseball cage as the rest of them played ball at recess, his pale white legs kept straight by the metal braces and leather straps imprisoning his skinny limbs. Now "polio" also meant Sarah, stolen first from his home, then from his family, then out of his life forever.

* * *

Charlie pulled himself back to the present. *She's gone and there's nothing I can do about it. She was here and then she was gone. I hope she's in heaven, wherever that is. Death is so final. And it takes good people, not just bad ones, and they never come back.*

Maybe I'll see her in heaven. I wonder, would she still be eleven or older?

The lonely green leaf, which earlier caught Charlie's eye, had disappeared long ago, pulled silently around the next bend by the river's unrelenting force. Stiffly, he rose to his feet, and mechanically slapped at the seat of his pants, shaking off a puff of dust and sand but unable to rid himself as easily of those last memories of Sarah. The dirt was soon gone but depressing uninvited thoughts stalked him all the way home. Even at his customary jogging pace, they ran as fast as he did.

CHAPTER FIVE

"Those bloody downtown politicians are only interested in getting their bloody hands on our bloody tax dollars." Tom Ranwick was on a typical rant. Once he calmed himself down, he would hastily assure his slyly grinning grandson that "bloody" was not a swear word "back where I come from." When Tom got wound up about politics, his ruddy Scottish face turned even redder as he railed against complainers who were always trying to bring about unwelcome and unnecessary change in his community. This time, "outsiders" and "newcomers" were moving into the area and making demands. Tom and his farming neighbours were certainly not going to stop spreading manure on their fields just because a strong breeze would blow the smell downwind toward the newly built subdivision. Just as predictably, his wife's' halfhearted and embarrassed efforts to settle down her husband were brushed aside like pesky ants on a picnic table.

Jane Ranwick had long ago learned that it was impossible to head off Tom's longwinded monologues once he got rolling. Her only hope was to redirect his thoughts toward some less controversial topic. Once in a while, she even succeeded! Most of the time, however, she could only imagine speaking boldly to her husband:

"Tom, you would get a better reception from your audience if you would just turn down the volume and take a breath." Assuming he even heard her gentle admonition, she knew exactly what he'd say: "Janey, m'dear, you need to hear me out. This is an important matter, not just for me but for you and your grandchildren.' Somehow, the young ones always became "hers," as if Jane were responsible for whatever catastrophe would befall them for failing to heed his warnings. But Jane was vexed with local politics for a different reason.

As a volunteer with Downsview Presbyterian Church, Jane regularly brought donated groceries to local families facing some financial crisis. During her visits, Jane was frequently made aware of other pressing needs in these homes: parents who could not afford dental care or medicine for their children; aged frail grandparents lacking the money to live in private nursing homes but dreading the large, impersonal government institutions. In some cases, both parents had to work in order to make ends meet but couldn't find anyone to care for their young children. In others, the family couldn't afford hospital insurance and feared serious illness.

Whenever Jane tried to present these concerns to the local politicians, she was soon reminded that they governed through financial prudence not by expanding welfare programs. So alongside the other church volunteers, she resolved to carry on, even as she hoped for more compassionate community services some future day.

The Ranwick farm was in the Township of North York, twenty-five productive acres of clay soil just west of Keele Street. In 1953, the Township, along with eleven other suburban municipalities, had reluctantly joined the City through an arrangement engineered and mandated by the Province. Naturally, Tom had kept a watchful eye on the proceedings. This new creation was called "Metro Toronto" to distinguish it from the smaller, identically named city, the only partner eager to consummate the union. It was a kind of arranged marriage, an experimental two-level model of municipal government. As Metro would now control property taxes, the merger was strongly opposed by 'the Ranwicks and most of their neighbours. The fact that North York was allowed to retain its name, local school board and emergency services, plus the promise of new Metro-wide planning for roads and parks, were of little reassurance to them.

"My taxes are bad enough already," Tom would readily complain to any listening ear patient enough to hear him out. "What do I need to pay for garbage collection for? I've been burnin' my garbage for 30 years and what I can't burn I bury. Then we're gettin' sidewalks. We've not needed them all these years—why now? Not on my road. Let the subdivisions have 'em— and pay for 'em. And don't get me started on the sewers." (Of course, he then promptly got started on the sewers.) "We've always had septic tanks and they work just fine. Can you imagine what that'll cost?"

Charlie would live to see Metro endure for the next 45 years, despite his grandfather's objections, until the final amalgamation process was completed with the creation of a fully integrated municipality to be called, once again, the City of Toronto. By that time, the farm was no more than a distant reflection in his storehouse of memories.

The Ranwicks always knew they would eventually have to sell— sooner or later. Journeying together through their eighth decade of life, each was finding the challenge of maintaining their rambling old brick home and running a working farm increasingly onerous. But each also carried their share of the burden without disclosing the depth of that physical struggle with the other. No point in causing worry! Then, shortly after Sarah's tragic death a year ago, Tom had received his own dose of bad news. Dr. Prentice, the cardiologist, bluntly told the old farmer that he had to give up heavy work. The decision to sell would now be made sooner, not later.

* * *

After 44 years of marriage Jane read her husband's face like an open book. When he returned from the doctor's office that day, what she read was bad news.

"Tom, what did Dr. Prentice say?"

"Nothing good," He spoke while his back was turned to hang up the cap and old worn leather jacket he habitually wore to town. Jane waited, knowing that he would share in his own time, not hers.

After pouring a glass of water from the refrigerator, Tom lowered himself slowly into his rocking chair with a deep sigh and stared for a long moment at the bright red-patterned wallpaper which suddenly seemed too festive for the occasion.

"It's my heart, all right. He tells me that I shouldn't be doin' any more heavy work. Of course, most of what I do is heavy work. No one yet has invented a light bale of hay or a pig barn which cleans its own manure."

Jane rose from her rocker and went to him. Open displays of affection were uncommon in their marriage, but she instinctively moved to stand behind Tom and encircle his neck in a loving hug.

"Tom, we're not getting any younger, and I don't want to lose you before I have to. Maybe it's time to think about making some changes." He said nothing in reply but sipped a mouthful of the cold liquid, staring at the glass as if he had discovered the taste of water for a first time.

As he carefully lowered it to the pine floor, his rough farmer's hands found Jane's bare arms. Well aware of the ever-present arthritis rampaging within her slender fingers, he held her hands in a gentle embrace. No matter what the morrow might bring, together they were alright.

The morrow brought the Reverend MacDougall. After a sleepless night, Jane had called their minister. As always, she was more worried about Tom than herself. Ever the stoic, the old farmer had grown silent and gloom-burdened in the hours after their decision to sell the land where they had laboured together so many years. In past times of family crisis—like Sarah's death—they had sought and found comfort from their faith.

The Reverend Donald MacDougall was a fellow Scotsman and had pastored Downsview Presbyterian Church for the past four years. Despite his diminutive stature, he was a commanding presence in his pulpit. His sermons brought Biblical stories to life, well-flavoured with eloquence and delivered in a distinctive Glaswegian brogue. Through vivid word pictures, he easily transported his congregation all the way to ancient Israel.

The minister balanced Jane's finest china teacup on his knee, the experience of many pastoral visits evident in his practised manner. He seemed lost in the overstuffed horsehair parlour chair; and his white clerical collar was too big for the small neck it encircled, leaving a circular, noticeable gap of empty space. Raised in Glasgow's grimy council flats during the War, the Reverend MacDougall had climbed his way out of poverty using the tools of a brilliant mind and steely determination. After graduation from seminary and ordination in 1951, and having then been invited by Tom and the rest of the local church council to lead worship services in Downsview, he packed up his few bachelor possessions and migrated to Canada.

Once the obligatory small talk was dispensed with—the wet weather, the price of hogs—conversation turned to the reason he had been summoned. Jane described the painful decision and her concern over the effect it was having on her husband. Both had fought successfully to save the farm from creditors during the Depression, only to lose it to age. Tom reluctantly acknowledged his sadness that there was no one to carry on their legacy. His son-in-law was a stone mason, not a farmer, and Charlie and Mary were obviously far too young.

The Reverend listened with empathy. Most of his parishioners were farmers and the land was their workplace; they defined themselves by its bounty. He then brought out his small Bible and quickly brushed through its pages to find Ecclesiastes, chapter three. Setting aside his big Sunday voice, he began to read, softly and quietly, 'the words already familiar to his two listeners:

To every thing there is a season and a time to every purpose under heaven.

"Tom and Jane, you well know the seasons of farm life. You have lived, not by calendar months like city folk, but season to season. Winter is when your land rests and restores itself; spring is for planting and seeing your animals produce their litters; summer is for growth, and autumn a time of harvest and marketing of livestock. It's the same with us humans."

Tom spoke with a wry smile. "So you think we're ready for a season of rest, like winter?"

"There is a season for everything. It is God's plan." The minister smiled reassuringly and continued to read.

A time to be born, and a time to die,
A time to plant and a time to pluck up that which is planted;
A time to kill and a time to heal,
A time to break down and a time to build up.

Jane chuckled: "I sure do remember when we finally tore down the old outhouse and put in plumbing for an indoor toilet."

"And think of all the times we had to decide whether to put down a sick animal or call the vet to try and heal it ourselves—never an easy choice." Tom shook his head, remembering how the cost of a veterinarian's visit had to be balanced against what was needed to achieve profitable milk or beef production.

A time to weep and a time to laugh,

A time to mourn and a time to dance.

"You never were much for dancing, Tom, but we've had lots of laughs in this house." Jane nudged him playfully.

"Yes, and weeping as well. I still can't get over losin' our bonnie wee girl to polio." Both were silent for a moment, lost in the painful memory. The minister continued:

A time to cast away stones and a time to gather stones together;

A time to embrace and a time to refrain from embracing.

Tom looked down at his calloused hands. "I can't recall how many rocks I had to get off our back fields, usin' that old stone boat so's we could get on the land after spring thaw."

"And how many times they were right back next spring." Jane smiled at the memory.

Still, neither was ready to put into words what they felt about that coming day when death would rob them of life's embrace. Better to stick to the stones!

A time to get and a time to lose;

A time to keep and a time to cast away.

"And that, I suppose, is the point I'm trying to make, friends." The minister gently put down his Bible. "When you think about it, no one really owns this land, although you obviously have title. It was here before you came all those years ago and it will be here long after we're gone. For a time, you were handed this land, this farm, to tend and make productive, just like the farmers here before you. Soon, you will pass it on to someone else. Then it's their turn to be a good steward."

Tom pondered that idea for a moment. He did feel he'd been a good steward. "That makes good sense. I remember you saying that God put Adam and Eve in charge of the Garden, not to ruin it but to look after it. God did the same thing with us."

"And we've done our best to look after it properly—the land and the animals." As always, Jane drew comfort from this, though she suspected Tom wasn't yet convinced.

"You know, Reverend, I can see what your're gettin' at but there's still one thing weighin' heavy on my mind. Look around Downsview these days. You won't find farmers buyin' the land, it's developers. Like the old Mathews place. Torn down, house and barns. And Fowler's. A hundred acres of good soil, now sittin' under a foot of gravel and asphalt for new roads. Now it's us!" As usual, Tom was getting worked up, his face reddening like a warning light.

But the Reverend knew how to defuse his anger. "You're right, Tom. It doesn't seem right to pave over some of the Province's best agricultural land. After all, city folks need to be fed, same as everyone else. And someday, when everything's covered in concrete, they might be sorry. But there's another side to consider."

"This city is growing fast—war vets getting married and having kids, immigrants leaving the old country, just like we once did. They need places to live, good country air to breathe.

Maybe your land will still be productive, except now for growing children, not corn." He paused to let his words sink in. Tom's chuckle was evidence it had. They would sell the farm next year.

* * *

Eleven months later, Charlie still knew nothing about the pending loss of his beloved summer home away from home. He was completely focused on maneuvering the front wheel of his red C.C.M. bike around deep potholes in the summer-softened asphalt on Keele Street, as he pedaled north on a Monday morning where a week's worth of farm work awaited. The road he travelled was a familiar route, usually taken by car as part of a family visit. Getting there by bicycle, especially on his old one-speed, was definitely a bigger challenge, especially as the August sun was already moistening his back with trickles of sweat under his white cotton t-shirt.

Tom had taken Charlie up on his offer to help, for that last month before high school beckoned. Even though he already had his treasured record player, Charlie liked the idea of extra pocket money. A month of hard outdoor work would also deepen his tan and maybe help him grow some arm muscles. And it made him feel grown-up and responsible. In the past, he had helped a bit with chores, but now it was an actual paying job.

The Presbyterian work ethic, first defined by Calvin and Knox centuries ago in Europe, played a dominant role in the Ranwick side of the family. Hard work would be rewarded by prosperity, and prosperity was a confirmation of God's blessing. Although he certainly could not articulate this doctrine, Tom lived it every day as he farmed his land, pulling crops of wheat and oats out of the ground and raising pigs and cattle to market-maturity.

"Those potatoes aren't goin' to pop out of the ground themselves," he warned himself whenever a temptation to take the day off whispered in his ear. He would often remind Charlie about the Bible passage in Proverbs which scoffs at the "laggard" who lies in bed with some fanciful excuse that a lion might be in the streets.

Charlie thought about his grandfather's favourite phrases as he steadily pedaled toward the farm. Hard work, especially the physical kind, was something to be proud of and soon he too would be getting his hands dirty. The prospect appealed to him.

All this pumping is gonna build up my leg muscles. I'm breathing hard on these hills, but I'm not tired. I'll still have lots of energy left over for the hay and straw. I'm skinny but I got endurance, I guess. Only two miles to go. Damn, it's hot! I'll be able to run a marathon someday if I keep this up.

* * *

Keele Street began its long journey northward at the edge of Toronto's High Park. This Toronto landmark featured 400 acres of forested hardwood which, over the years, had been zealously protected from development. It included a miniature zoo, crooked dirt paths which meandered up and down the rolling hills and weedy Grenadier Pond (so named in memory of a long-ago British soldier who, the story went, had fallen through the ice and drowned in its boggy waters.)

The road angled through the heart of the Junction where early in the morning, sleepy men and women left for work in factory, trade or shop. It continued past the rancid-smelling stockyards where cattle and pigs, imprisoned by whitewashed wooden fences, bawled and squealed their farewells to an indifferent world, past Canada Packers where many of those same creatures were reborn as bacon or lunch meats, through York Township with its British population, and finally into North York with its farms and open spaces.

Tired and sweating, Charlie reached his destination by mid-morning. He pedaled at last up the long dusty dirt laneway, where he immediately was hugged by his grandmother, relieved to have him safely off the roads.

He was soon devouring a grilled-cheese sandwich and a bowl of Campbell's tomato soup with soda crackers crushed on top, followed by three oatmeal squares and a tall glass of cold milk, refrigerated fresh that morning after being supplied by Bossie, the family's fat little Jersey cow.

"You want to eat up, boy, if you expect to lift those bales." "Grandma, your food sure is good. But I can't eat no more."

"You mean you can't eat any more." Grandma was a stickler for this sort of thing. "Whatever I mean, I mean I'm full, but thank you." The boy always remembered his manners if not his grammar.

"But I've got to fatten you up. I want to see some muscle on those bones."

So do I. Nothing yet. He looked at his forearms and flexed the left one, hoping it might suddenly bulge out like Popeye's. *Maybe a can of spinach. Wonder if Grandma has some of that in her pantry?*

As long as Charlie could remember, this North York farm was his favourite place to be, especially in the long, school-free, hot days of summer. There, in the countryside, he could escape his neighbourhood, full of people he barely knew and always wanting to start a conversation. On the farm there was plenty of time to be alone, to discover some quiet corner in the rambling three-storied house where he could read. Painfully well aware of his lack of social skills, he preferred to poke around the old barns where the penned animals would not expect conversation and were content with an occasional overripe apple or armful of sweet-smelling hay.

Time with his grandparents was different from city life. Jane, a tiny dynamo of energy in her younger years, was now inclined, at age 76, to spend time in her wooden Boston rocker, a heavy, multi-hued, woollen afghan protecting her back from its hard wooden spindles. After temporarily abating her grandson's hunger, she was back to knitting, the arthritic fingers expertly engaging in a productive repetitive ritual of motion. It would not be long before the ball of brightly-coloured wool on her lap was transformed into a warm sweater or sturdy pair of socks. As she worked on her current creation, she talked about her childhood in England and the family still there.

"Are you sending this stuff to them soon?" he asked, eying a large cardboard packing box in a corner near the kitchen door.

"Almost, I'm wanting to add some apples now that the McIntosh crop is ready." Since war's end, she regularly sent food to the old country, mostly supplies from her own modestly stocked pantry. Tinned ham, white sugar, flour, thick wedges of cheddar cheese and packs of powdered eggs: all were dutifully mailed and gratefully welcomed by her extended family who lived in Luftwaffe-bombed Coventry. Along with the rest of the Island's inhabitants, they persevered patiently and stoically, although nine years after Hitler's defeat, they still lived with food rationing.

"But they had good news in their last letter," she continued with a wide smile of relief. "The government has finally ended ration books. Now the little ones can eat a proper meal." Proper meals were the height of his nutrition-conscious grandmother's value system. In contrast, thought Charlie, everyone finally having their own chocolate bar was a better reason to celebrate. Despite Popeye's example, he had a hard time imagining these English children fighting over soggy green lumps of spinach suddenly appearing on their plates. But he could easily picture their brown-stained lips as each square of a Neilson's bar quickly disappeared into an eager mouth.

"Do you miss your family?" Charlie knew she hadn't been back since coming to Canada as a young bride a few years before the Great War.

"I have you and your family right here." Her non-answer was a typical response whenever a potentially emotional discussion was imminent. Charlie knew from his mother that Jane, safely in Canada, had passed many long and sleepless nights during the German air attacks on British cities, finding comfort only when, in 1944, R.A.F. spitfires had finally driven them off for good. But even that respite was short-lived, when Hitler's V2 rockets began to fall from the sky.

"Do you think you might go back to visit some day?"

"I might have, when I was younger but there was the Great War, then the Depression, then another war. Besides, there wasn't money for travel. Now I'm too old to think that way." For an instant, she looked away as if remembering a time when she didn't think that way.

She felt a twinge of sadness and quickly buried it. Jane had learned long ago to put a wall between her thoughts and her emotions. It started on a damp spring day in 1910, as she sailed from Southampton, eyes fixed resolutely on the western horizon, her grieving parents on the long concrete dock waving a tearful farewell. The new bride clung desperately to Tom's arm as she forced her thoughts forward. She did the same when the news came that her younger brother had died in the mud of Verdun. There was no place for self-pity. Weeping would not bring him back from France.

The Depression years which followed required a similar fortitude. She and Tom struggled together to keep their farm out of the clutches of the bank. She laboured alongside him in the barn and in the field when they could not afford a hired man. She dutifully raised Katie to be responsible and hard-working. There was no time to regret her inability to have other children— some problem with fertility, the doctor said.

Jane wondered when and how to tell her grandson this most recent bad news. The decision to sell the farm was weighing down her spirits like a lumpy, fifty-pound sack of potatoes. She would need to lay it down soon.

"Maybe they could come here to see us," Charlie offered helpfully, breaking into his grandmother's wistful thoughts. He knew she had a younger sister, and several nieces and nephews with their own families now. Before she could reply, he heard his grandfather taking off his boots in the summer kitchen, an unheated storage room that adjoined the rest of the house.

Entering the room, Tom pulled a blue sweat-stained cap off his head, revealing his farmer's tan, the sun-exposed dark brown of his face which vividly contrasted with the hat-protected whitened top half of his forehead. Behind him stood a tall round-faced older teenager, shirtless and muscular, his body already molded into a man's physique. Gary Bellover lived with his large family down the road on Wilson Avenue and worked with Tom when an extra pair of hands was needed during summer months.

"Day's half done. Where's that help I was promised?" His grandfather's smile belied any attempt at a scolding.

"It was Grandma's fault!" Charlie returned the smile and pointed to the dirty dishes still cluttering the round oak kitchen table. "I had to be polite and finish, right?" He winked at his grandmother before dutifully carrying them to the sink and thanking her for lunch.

He felt satisfied, fueled by good food, ready to face the challenging rigours of farm labour, but still unsure whether he could keep up with the older men.

The three workers were soon out the door, heading for a recently combined ten acres of wheat. While the grain was already stored in the barn, bales of straw lay scattered across the field like huge loaves of bread. Over the past two years, Charlie's task was to slowly drive Tom's tractor, pulling a straw wagon back and forth across the stubbled land, while Gary lifted and tossed the bales one by one onto the wagon. Grandpa, keeping pace, stacked the bales into orderly rows, ten-high. Charlie was always amazed how he managed to keep his balance on the bouncing wagon. This year though things would be different.

"Charlie, how be you handle a real man's job? Think you can wrestle these bales all by yourself?" Tom sat on the edge of the empty wagon, causing it to tilt to one side. He slowly wiped his face with a blue cotton handkerchief, which also managed to hide an involuntary grimace caused by a sharp pain which had just begun to rhythmically bang out a warning drum beat inside his chest.

"Sure, Grandpa," he replied, hiding a slight tinge of disappointment beneath his assent. Although several years away from a driver's licence, Charlies had developed a strong sense of pride and responsibility by running the bright red fume-belching Case tractor. This time around it would be his grandfather driving the machine, Gary on the wagon building the stack and the rookie lifting bales up off the ground. Far less important, or so it seemed.

Like all children, Charlie viewed his grandparents as immortal; they would always be there, just like the farm. And it was this willful blindness that caused him to miss the otherwise obvious fact that his beloved grandfather was getting old.

* * *

The job of clearing the field, hauling each swaying load back to the barn and returning for more, kept them busy most of the day. The only interruption was Jane's timely arrival with cold lemonade and ham sandwiches, which they consumed by a stone fence in the welcoming shade of a wild apple tree. Charlie was pleased and proud that he could keep pace with the moving tractor, grabbing each 30-pound bale by the two brown strands of encircling twine and tossing it onto the bouncing wagon for Gary to stack. The best part of the job, though, were the rides back to the barn. The two teens sprawled on their backs atop the swaying load, eyes closed against the sun's brightness, as they rested and talked.

To be more precise, Gary talked and Charlie listened. The older boy considered himself an expert on women and liked to brag about what he called his "romantic life." He also liked the thought of passing on his wisdom to this obviously uninformed younger boy.

"I got my licence this spring. Dad lets me take the Chevy as long as I'm home by eleven.

"Most weekends, I take Sandra to the drive-in. She lets me French kiss her and touch her breasts... over her sweater," he added somewhat sadly. "Wait 'til you get to Brock. You won't believe all the good-looking broads there." Gary went on to describe in vivid detail a long list of girls who had caught his eye over the past year.

"Yeah, but I bet they aren't interested in grade nine guys." Though he tried to sound disappointed, Charlies was in fact wary about dating. In his mind, even if he managed to secure a date there would be those long and awkward silences once his rehearsed opening words quickly ran out.

"Hey, you gotta start somewhere, just like I did. Grade nine girls will give even you a look-over if you dress sharp. I always made sure I looked cool, from the very first day."

"My mom's going to take me shopping later this month. What do the girls like guys to wear?"

"Well, for sure you aren't allowed to wear jeans." Gary went on to describe the importance of drapes which were fashionable tapered cuff-less dress pants, polo shirts and black pointed shoes. But his own favourite item of clothing was inspired by a movie he had recently seen.

"Have you seen *The Wild Ones*?" Did you see Brando in that leather jacket? I got a beauty to wear this fall but it cost me most of what I've made so far working for your grandfather."

However, wearing the right clothes was the least of Charlie's worries about September. The whole notion of leaving the relative security of King Edward Elementary for a much-larger Brock scared him most. While he had lacked close friends there, at least he knew the names of his classmates. The schoolwork was manageable, even if his grades were only average. He could navigate the corridors with the comfortable familiarity of nine years' experience. The large dirt field offered quiet corners at recess where he could watch soccer or softball games. Running the three blocks home for lunch provided a temporary sanctuary, hiding him away from social demands expected by the school community. And being in grade eight conferred on him at least some status among the younger pupils. He might be ignored but neither was he bullied.

Brock Collegiate would be something else entirely, an unfamiliar world of unknown demands and expectations, coupled with an ever-present risk of failure, both socially and academically. And he sure wouldn't be able to run home for lunch.

If only summer lasted longer. Maybe I could drop out and work full-time on the farm. Except I don't know how to do most of the things Grandpa does. Besides, Mom and Dad would have a fit. He quickly and silently berated himself for wasting time on such unrealistic thinking. He'd be better off listening to Gary about how to survive. Grade nine was going to happen whether he liked it or not.

The now empty wagon bounced into a second field, this one newly shorn of its crop. Tom had rented a noisy green combine and driver, which had already cut the stalks and was spewing the valuable stream of grain into Tom's truck. Once the grain was safely housed in the barn's granary, the leftover rows of straw could be scooped up by the baler, a second rented machine which transformed the loose straw into tightly bound bales and tossed them one by one out its back end.

Charlie could never figure how a dumb machine could wrap each bale in two lengths of twine, tightly tied together with a perfect knot. It had taken him years to learn how to tie a lasso knot, and his Sunday church-going necktie still proved a challenge.

Charlie preferred baling hay to bringing in straw, but it had already been harvested by early July. It was the sweet smell of the hay, essentially long grass, that he most enjoyed. Newly cut, it lay in raked rows along the length of the field, drying under the sun before being baled.

Charlie would tell himself that heaving a fifty- or sixty-pound bundle into the wagon would build his muscles even more quickly than the lighter straw he was now hauling.

Back at the barn, a belt-driven elevator carried the straw, a bale at a time, on its 45-degree lift to the loft. Charlie preferred to unload the wagon, dropping each bale onto the clanking mechanism. Inside the barn, at the other end of the straw's upward journey and under the elevator, Gary would hurriedly grab each bale as it tumbled off the lift, then compactly stack them into neat rows in the few available seconds before the next arrived. Falling behind in this task meant an unrelenting stream of tumbling bales would soon pile up in a tangled mess.

Whenever he changed places with Gary to give him a fresh air break, endless small bits of chaff would blow off the bales into his eyes. There was no breeze to cool the oppressive heat fueled by a galvanized tin roof overhead. Worst of all, if he wasn't vigilant, Charlie would lose his sense of timing and suddenly feel the full weight of a bale unexpectedly crashing on his head. Brief though these experiences were, he was miserable.

Yet, somehow, by day's end, once he'd washed off the barn dust and chaff in a well-earned shower, Charlie had already forgotten about the heat and noise; he remembered only the fields of straw that had been cut, sun-dried and stored in the barn. His grandparents' animals would be warmly bedded and adequately fed through another long winter.

* * *

With the looming challenge of high school creeping ever closer like a threatening high tide, Charlie clung to his remaining August days on the farm with renewed appreciation. He liked the predictable and satisfying routines of rural life. In the fading daylight of late evening—cow milked, pigs fed, pens and stalls cleaned and layered with fresh straw—the boy would climb the old pine stairs leading to his small back bedroom. There he would gratefully turn down the patterned quilt and quickly disappear into a deep chore-induced sleep.

Only one embarrassing incident spoiled the otherwise rich memories that Charlie was gathering about the farm. Almost two years ago, the Boyd Gang escaped from the Don Jail, a forbidding-looking old stone prison in East Toronto. The four desperate men had each been recently convicted of a series of bank robberies. Two of them were also accused of fatally shooting a police detective and wounding his partner. According to the Telegram, they were possibly hiding out in North York.

By unlucky coincidence, Charlie happened to be visiting the farm the September weekend when the escapees were still on the run. A neighbour had been invited to dinner, and the topic turned to the Gang. Tom was sure they'd fled to the States by then, Charlie equally sure they had a local hideaway. As luck would have it, Tom asked him to go into the hay barn and throw down a bale for Bossie. It was dusk and the building was already deep in shadow.

"I'm too tired."

"Come on, lad! It'll take you five minutes." "I'll do it in the morning, first thing."

"Charlie, it needs to be done now." Tom was surprised and annoyed by the boy's resistance to what had always been a routine request.

"But what if the Boyd Gang is hiding in there?" Embarrassment reddening his face, Charlie voiced his fear aloud. Grandfather and Angus the neighbour simultaneously looked at one another and burst out laughing, Angus poking Tom in the ribs with his elbow.

"I didn't know you had a granddaughter visiting this weekend!"

"Look, Charlie, the Boyd Gang won't be found anywhere around these parts. It's foolish to be afraid. Just go and do your work—now!" The grandfather's exasperated tone ended further debate.

Charlie quietly turned away so the men wouldn't see that tears were welling up in his eyes. Leaving the house, he reluctantly walked the familiar fifty steps to the barn, cautiously opened the door, and stepped inside. Once his eyes grew accustomed to the dark, he clambered up a homemade, rickety wooden ladder to the loft. He hastily grabbed a bale and tossed it down, then another. While a cold fear surrounded him as he worked, he was more afraid of appearing cowardly in front of his grandfather than the Gang.

I won't look anywhere except right in front of me. There is no reason to be afraid. (But I am.) There is no one else here. (But there might be). That creaking noise is only the sound of the tin cooling on the roof because the sun has set. (I hope.) I'm not a baby. (I'm scared but I'm not gonna show it.) And even if someone was here, they would want to stay hidden, not hurt me. (Besides, I'm almost done.)

Yeah, but one of them's a killer. I should've grabbed a pitchfork. Just get it over with, toss the hay and stop worrying!

After ten seemingly eternal minutes the task was finally done, and Charlie was once again back to twilight and safety. By then, Tom and Angus were relaxing on the side porch. With amused smiles, they watched him approach. Tom called out reassuringly:

"What did I tell you, lad? Nothing to worry about."

"See any robbers while you was in there?" Angus chimed in, laughing.

Ignoring them, Charlie proceeded to deliver his armload of hay to sleepy-eyed Bossie waiting patiently in her stall. Then he slipped quietly into the house where Jane sat dozing beside the radio. He silently climbed the carpeted stairs and into the shelter of bed. Alone with thoughts and feelings that had nowhere to go, he felt them inside his body like a lump of raw dough. In the rough-and-ready world of rural manhood, he had clearly failed some test, despite keeping that failure hidden from the men. Fear as always had won out, seeping through his mask of courage. Embarrassment lingered long after the fears had melted away. He was still afraid of the dark—at age 12.

Four days later, police arrested the Boyd Gang. They had in fact been hiding in a North York barn. Neither Tom nor Charlie wished to revisit that awkward subject; and the news of their 'recapture was never mentioned again.

Whenever Charlie wasn't needed by his grandfather, he roamed the inviting pastures and woodlots which bordered the farm. His only companion was Lindy, his grandparents' black and white border collie. During their shared adventures, the little dog busied herself by relentlessly and silently stalking groundhogs as they peered out of their hidden burrows. Charlie was most content when travelling at a relaxed running pace along the edge of ripening fields of oats and wheat, through knee-high lush second-crop hay, past orderly rows of cattle corn already taller than he was. On days when neighbouring farmers weren't on their tractors, the land was still and soundless, save the occasional raucous cawing of black crows in the trees, sounding a loud alarm over his unwanted human presence.

* * *

On a still-hot Sunday morning, a few days before holidays' end, Charlie finished his shredded wheat and toast and quietly slipped out the summer kitchen's back door. He whistled for Lindy, then broke into his usual steady run down the dirt road which neatly bisected the farm fields. Long legs carried his slight frame effortlessly. His spirits lifted by the exertion, he was breathing rapidly when he finally arrived at the back of the 100 acre property. He happily rested in the corner of a fallow field, his back against a cedar fence post. Cocooned in rural solitude, the boy let a sense of peace wash over him. Charlie had long ago determined the deep waters of a lake or pond to be alien territory, full of unknown murky danger. On the very few occasions when he had ventured into the granite rock-strewn maple and spruce forests of the Canadian Shield, he experienced a similar unease.

Last summer while visiting a family friend's cottage perched on crown land at the edge of Raven Lake, Charlie trekked but a few hundred yards into the woods before anxiety overwhelmed him.

I can hardly see where I'm going. What happened to the path? Too many dark shadows and scary noises. How do I get back?

Farm landscape was different. Each field was neatly bordered by wire or cedar rail fencing, within them a comforting sense of order and tranquility. He looked out at the gentle vista before him, the browns and greens of plowed soil and evolving crops—no dangers hidden or lurking.

Refreshed by his respite and inspired by the pastoral panorama spread before him, Charlie eagerly resumed the run. Lindy kept pace at his side, her long wet tongue hanging from one side of her open mouth. She was getting old, as evidenced by the greying of her snout, but still able to keep up with him.

His destination was Black Creek, a gentle stream which wandered erratically through the western end of North York before finding its way to the Humber. Across the mile and a quarter which separated Sheppard and Finch concession roads, it was sheltered by a thick overhanging forest, which kept its clear waters cool. Unlike the Raven Lake experience, this terrain was familiar and so posed no threat. He could watch crayfish, which looked like miniature lobsters, lurking in the shallow depths. Fat green frogs with yellow eyes watched him as he watched them, as they perched on rocks to enjoy the few rays of sunlight which made it through the leafy canopy. Hiding in deeper pools were small catfish and, occasionally, a lonely brook trout.

Charlie had a favourite spot beside the creek, in the crook of a willow tree which overhung the flowing water. With a now-tired Lindy dozing at his feet, her fur splashed with mud and festooned with burrs, he would let his mind drain itself of all the questions and concerns he habitually carried around: high school, Sarah's death, life itself. That newly emptied space in his head could now be filled with imagination.

I'm a woodsman trekking through the quiet forest a hundred and fifty years ago. I know every tree and plant by name; I can track deer, bears and even humans by skillfully following trails too invisible for the ordinary eye. I run effortlessly along narrow paths trampled out in earlier times. Both white men and Indians respect my wisdom and bravery.

The village folk often invite me to stay in town, to settle down and marry some pretty young girl. I always politely decline and, supplies in hand, return to the bush as they watch in admiration.

"He's a different sort," the blacksmith would mutter mostly to himself, though the other men gathered in his shop nodded in agreement. The unmarried girls would watch me as well: walking steadily toward the beckoning tree-line, a heavy sack of flour slung over one broad shoulder, my rifle on the other one. It is well known that I am more at home in the woods than within the restrictions of town life. Still, each secretly hopes she could be the one to change all that.

Such scenarios played out regularly in Charlie's mind, providing him with a great deal of escapist pleasure. But to the rest of the world, he was a slender boy in his early teen years gazing contentedly at an endlessly rolling stream.

Inevitably, he would become aware of the passing of time and, calling to patient Lindy, would head more purposefully back to the farm where his grandmother's roast beef was already browning in her huge cast-iron oven.

August, with its suddenly cold nights and daylight which was gone before the dinner dishes were washed, would soon yield to September and autumn. Charlie found he could no longer avoid the jolting reality of his move to high school and the first anniversary of Sarah's death. Both bore down on him like some massive CNR train engine—its shrill whistle echoing across the pastoral landscape, its jagged trail of black smoke scarring the bright blue sky—with him firmly and hopelessly stuck between those two shiny rails.

It was in the midst of these troubling days that the boy would return to his farm memories, forged in that last summer of boyhood innocence, remembering them with a gut-deep yearning that was almost audible.

HURRICANE CAROL HITS NEW ENGLAND HARD

NATIONAL WEATHER SERVICE:
By the morning of the 31st of August Carol was just south of Long Island and moving rapidly north-northeast-ward. It crashed into the New England States, diminishing rapidly as it swept into Canada. The storm left 60 dead and over $460 million damage to prop-erty in the North Atlantic States.

National Hurricane Center Data Archives, Miami, Fla.

CHAPTER SIX

A loud first ring burst from the Thompson's shiny black telephone mounted on the kitchen wall by their back door. The jarring sound, unexpected so early on a Saturday morning, caused Charlie to lift his head from the current issue of *Jungle Comics*. Once someone picked up the receiver, he would be able to overhear the conversation. He rightly assumed nobody would be calling him. His parents were lingering over breakfast. Mary had left to play with Rachel.

He'd already gobbled down three blueberry pancakes in his eagerness to continue the adventures of "Rulah the Jungle Goddess."

Over the past few weeks, when not on the farm, Charlie had found himself irresistibly drawn to these half-dressed heroines. *Batman* and *Captain Marvel* were gradually being replaced by *Wonder Woman* and *Nyoka Of The Jungle*. In his always-active imagination, Charlie now fantasized himself among them.

I've got broad shoulders, like John Wayne. My skin is tanned, even under the cover of banyan trees. In fact, I live way up there, where it's densely branched, like Swiss Family Robinson. I hear a sudden scream from below, and there's a beautiful woman being attacked by a huge lion. I know how to use my knife with deadly force, so the battle is short-lived and he soon lies bloodied and sprawled in the dirt. The woman rises on long unsteady legs to thank me.

Shyly, I turn away and disappear silently away into the dark forest. She stares in puzzlement as I am gone as mysteriously as I had appeared.

It was the man of the house who first reached the receiver. "Yes, this is Doug." Then a long silence as his father listened. Charlie pictured his father patiently nodding his head, while using a foot to pull one of the arborite kitchen chair closer in case the conversation dragged on. But it didn't.

"I think you should probably discuss this with my wife." Another silence, followed by the voice of his mother sounding curious and a bit tentative.

"Who is it, Doug? She mouthed before taking the receiver from his outstretched arm. "Your minister. He wants to know if he could come over." Doug's voice was flat, revealing no indication, at least to Charlie, of how he felt about the matter.

"Pastor Hanson, so thoughtful of you to call." She sounded more relaxed and chatty than Doug, or was she just being polite; Charlie couldn't tell. Then she was quiet again.

While he had not officiated the funeral service because of Doug's objections, Pastor Hanson had visited the family in the week following 'to offer support and prayer.' Now, a year later, as the anniversary of Sarah's death approached, he was checking in.

Pastor Frank Hanson was tall and stocky with a crew cut that made him look more like a teenager than a grown man at the head of a large congregation. As he listened, Charlie remembered the pastor's large blue eyes. They glowed with an intensity which grew even brighter whenever he talked about Jesus.

"I'll speak with my husband and then let you know. Thank you again for calling." After carefully returning the receiver to its hook, and with Charlie now perched on the top step to watch, Katie slowly turned to face her husband. Doug's jaw was set. Katie opened her lips slightly but said nothing. A rare tension between his parents was beginning to percolate.

* * *

The family's initial encounter with Faith Tabernacle had occurred last August, shortly after Sarah was hospitalized. Agnes Goodwan, a widow who lived a few houses away from the Thompsons, had stopped by the house with a large batch of her thick Irish beef stew, still bubbling and simmering in its crock—her expression of concern and support for a neighbour in crisis. Charlie recalled their front porch conversation, after Mrs. Goodwan had been updated on Sarah's worsening medical condition.

"We've been on our knees at the church for that little girl of yours."
Charlie found it hard to picture Mrs. Goodwan—old, heavy-set and arthritic—getting down on her knees for any reason, even to talk with God.
"You know," she continued earnestly, "Doctors and nurses do good work
but there is nothing like the power of prayer. Like Jesus said: 'You don't
receive because you don't ask." The visitor paused to gauge the reception
her words were having.

"Well, we're certainly open to receiving help from wherever it
comes," Katie replied diplomatically.

"Then perhaps you and Mr. Thompson would be interested in
attending our prayer-and- praise service this Wednesday evening. Or you
could come Sunday morning for our regular worship service. We meet at
eleven."

Charlie's grandparents on his father's side had been Presbyterian,
and he knew that his mother's parents were long-time faithful members
of Downsview Presbyterian Church. As far as his own family was concerned, though, church-going was more of an Easter and Christmas tradition, part of familiar customs reserved for special holidays. Otherwise,
Sundays were for rest and visiting, not pews and prayers.

While Charlie had always been indifferent to his family's non-
attendance, his mother occasionally expressed an interest in reclaiming
her Presbyterian heritage. She had ensured all three children were baptized
as infants at Downsview. She loved the historic red brick church, with its
heavy carved oak pews and richly coloured stained glass windows. But
any further religious involvement by the Thompsons was strongly and
quickly vetoed by Doug. Charlie had never heard his father explain this
antipathy toward religion; so he was understandably surprised when,
that Sunday a year ago, Katie directed both children to dress up and be
ready to leave at 10:30 for Faith Tabernacle It didn't surprise him that his
father had not joined them on the sidewalk as they nervously waited for
Mrs. Goodwan's little grey Austin to pick them up.

"Doug, we're leaving now," Katie had advised her husband a few
moments before. Earlier that day, Charlie had expected his mother to at
least invite Doug to join them. Or asked if it were okay with him that
they were off to church instead of their usual Sunday morning routines:
sleeping in, reading the newspaper with its large coloured comic section,
listening to or watching the radio or television.

Instead, there was no discussion at all. "Say hello to Mrs. Goodwan for me. See you at lunchtime," Doug said without lifting his eyes from the sports section of the Telegram.

Doug always checked yesterday's scores before reading the accompanying articles. Both Doug and Charlie loved baseball and faithfully followed the fortunes of the Dodgers. On the strength of the powerful bats of Duke Snider and Roy Campanella, Brooklyn was continuing to lead the National League pennant race. Carl Erskine, on his way to a 20-game-win season, had admirably filled the pitching gap created when the Dodger's ace, Don Newcombe, was called up to serve in Korea. In the American League, the Yankees were already on the verge of clinching the pennant.

Despite the best efforts of Burleigh Grimes, their frustrated manager, Toronto's local ball team, the Maple Leafs, continued to have a mediocre season. Doug and Charlie had been intrigued to learn that Grimes, in his playing days, was the last major league hurler who could legally throw a spitball, a pitcher's trick banned in the 1930s.

Doug found himself thinking about Don Newcombe and the Korean War. While some of his World War Two buddies had volunteered for Korea, he was glad he was too old for that. He had seen more than enough of war and had no desire to play a part in this new chapter, perhaps this time written with his own spilled blood. His thoughts drifting back to 1943 Italy, he was quickly reminded why he was not with his family that morning.

* * *

Doug hadn't begun the war with that bitterness. October 2, 1941 had been a cold, cloudy day with a swirling north wind blowing piles of brown and yellow fallen maple leaves back and forth, up and down the street as if uncertain which direction to go. Newmarket was a town of 4,000 just north of Toronto. As he stood in line to enlist, Doug scanned a bronze plaque honouring Quakers who, in the early nineteenth century, had founded a village beside the Holland River. Considering the irony of signing up for war in a place settled by devout pacifists, he allowed himself an inward chuckle.

Doug was no pacifist, but neither was he eager for war. Always the pragmatist, he reasoned that serving his country was a duty he was expected to fulfill. With family roots in Scotland, it was an easy decision to enlist with the 48th Highlanders of Canada. As he learned more about the history of his regiment, he felt that he was following in the footsteps of generations of Scots, who fought against the English at Culloden and later soldiered in India, Canada and other far-flung corners of the Empire. Sometimes patriots, more often mercenaries for hire. After many months of arduous and sometimes boring training in Quebec and the Maritimes, 25-year-old Private Douglas Thompson, rifleman, began preparations to embark with his regiment for England, a prelude to the invasion of Europe.

In September 1942, Doug was granted special leave to be with Katie when she gave birth to Sarah, a sister for 2-year-old Charlie. Mother and children would move to the farm with Katie's parents soon after Doug sailed for Britain in the spring of 1943. Katie was grateful for their offer of support; the thought of coping on her own with the heavy demands of a newborn while chasing after a rambunctious toddler seemed over- whelming. She was similarly burdened with worry for Doug's safety. But in front of her parents and, especially during Doug's brief visit home, she maintained a mask of confidence and faith, as if it were Hallowe'en. In August, a month before Doug came home on leave, headlines in the Telegram finally forced Katie to voice her fears. She had brought Charlie for a brief visit with his grandparents.

"Oh my God, Dad, have you seen this?" Tom quickly looked up from his book, startled at his daughter's urgent tone. "What is it, Katie?"

"Canadian troops have attacked the French coast... Hundreds of our men are dead or captured. The paper calls them '—a brave raiding party to test German defenses.' But at what cost?" She looked stricken. Tom, rarely one to show tenderness, immediately clambered to his feet and enveloped her in his arms, as if he could keep her safe, hidden and protected from both those large black headlines and the war itself.

"There, there, I know 'tis a bad time for us all, but especially for you, with these young'uns."

"Dad, I didn't want him to go. He didn't have to enlist. He could have earned an exemption from service with his age and already having a child. I don't understand. Yes, he's soon training safe in England, he's not on some bloody beach, but next year..." Her voice trailed off in a sigh.

"Did Doug know you felt this strongly about his joining up?"

She paused before answering. Her father must never know the whole story but this much she could admit: "I should have said No! But he was determined to go and I was not going to send him off with our last moments together ruined by a quarrel."

Jane had been drawn by the upset and joined them in the front room. Tom took over the paper. "It says about 5,000 Canadians raided a place called Dieppe, in France." He further perused the story behind the headline. "My God, the Germans killed 900 and another 1,500 are wounded or captured. They don't actually say it was a disaster, but it must have been. The rest retreated. 'Twas all over in half a day." Grabbing the armrests of the old rocking chair, he shakily sat down, having frightened himself along with Jane.

Mother, father and daughter sat mute for a few moments as the room filled with end-of-day darkness. Upstairs in the old farmhouse, as if she shared her family's pain, Charlie began to cry.

* * *

On July 10th, 1943, as part of the British 8th Army, the First Canadian Infantry Division stormed Sicilian beaches at Pachino. Doug was finally at war. Now, some 11 years later, he could still recall the equal parts of confusion and fear that were his constant companions those first days. He struggled with the possibility of having to kill another human being. He was afraid of being wounded and returning home, no longer a whole man. Yet underneath also lay a sense of duty and honour. Although the connection seemed remote, he knew—and had been told enough times by his commanders—that he was in the mud of this foreign land to protect his family. His bitterness over the irony of this wouldn't emerge until later.

War games in the English countryside had provided some excitement and relief from the tedium of drills and cross-country marches. One incident in particular always made Doug chuckle. The games commonly pitted British against Canadian, mockingly referred to as "colonials." During one exercise, an English tank commander had boastfully proclaimed his Churchill tank was unstoppable, especially by a bunch of "colonials" who thought they could defend their dug-in positions with only small arms and a jeep-mounted Bren gun. The stubborn Canadian corporal boasted back that his Bren gun would whump their tank.

As the tank rolled slowly toward the Canadian trenches, the corporal suddenly grabbed a roll of barbed wire and threw it under the Churchill's treads. As the wire entangled itself, the tank screeched in frustration and ground to a halt, its driving mechanism hopelessly emmeshed. The Canadians were declared the winners. The English grumbled.

But July 10 was no laughing matter. It was early morning when he saw his first combat. Their practice landings in Scotland had been wet and arduous, but manageable and certainly not frightening, even for a man who preferred to be on solid ground.

Sicily was the real thing. That ugly reality hit home even before they reached the designated invasion point near Pachino. Speeding toward shore, crouched low in their Landing Craft Infantry boats, the 48th Highlanders were spotted by German, low-flying Messerschmitts. As the planes dove, the boats hastily and prematurely unloaded their human cargo, then desperately tried to scatter. The troops waded ashore through warm waist-deep sea water, rifles carried high above their heads, tracer bullets from the Messerschmitts pinging all around. Doug saw two men from his platoon slip silently beneath the surf, bloody stains on the water the only testimony that they had been alive mere seconds ago.

Once ashore, Doug's platoon regrouped within their battalion. It was at that point they realized the boats had sped away with their personal gear. Now they would have to fight without extra socks, eating utensils, shaving items, parts of uniforms, saved-up rations and, worst of all, precious letters from home. Hardship and deprivation, relentlessly close companions for the next traumatic months, had made their unwanted introductions.

Apart from this setback, the 48th initially met with little resistance. Italian troops were surrendering so fast there was nowhere to store the POWs. Once disarmed, some were simply turned loose, stripped of their uniforms and ordered to head home. Others were herded into large outdoor compounds ringed by barbed wire. Doug had no idea how this bedraggled crowd of tired thin dust-covered prisoners could all be fed and cared for.

Canadian spitfires from RCAF 417 squadron had finally driven off the Luftwaffe, affording the First Division a chance to rest. They had had to wait until the weather cleared, then came roaring in from the coast and, diving from 20,000 feet out of the high clouds, swooped down on the unsuspecting Messerschmitts. By then running low on fuel and ammunition, the German fighters quickly vanished.

But while the Allied army celebrated, they had yet to meet a far bigger challenge. German soldiers lay just ahead. And unlike their Italian allies, they would not gratefully surrender.

* * *

Faith Tabernacle was not much to look at from the outside. It was a newer yellow brick building, much smaller than any church Charlie had been in. If it weren't for the large metallic cross reaching skyward from the roof peak, a row of small, square windows on each side of the building and a wooden lawn sign advertising the 11 a.m. service, it could have been easily mistaken for an overly large elongated bungalow, sitting at the edge of a quiet block of single- family homes.

Early arrivals had already filled the small asphalt-covered parking lot next to the church, so Mrs. Goodwan carefully parked her car on the street, her short, thick neck twisting to locate the curb. Even before reaching the building, Charlie could hear the sound of congregational singing flowing through its open windows.

"Are we late, Mrs. Goodwan?" Katie asked worriedly.

"Not at all. This is pre-service gospel time. We choose our favourite hymns and sing them together. It gets our hearts ready for worship." She led the Thompsons up three concrete steps and into the sanctuary. Pastor Hanson looked quite youthful in his shiny blue suit with his even younger slim blonde wife standing at his side, her flared brown skirt almost scraping the ground. They stood just inside the door, so that they could greet the arrivals. He quickly extended his long arm in Katie's direction. She tentatively grasped his hand in return. But it was the pastor's wife who surprised her when she impulsively stepped forward, capturing Katie with a hug.

"Pastor Frank and I were so sorry to learn of your daughter's illness. I'm sure Agnes told you we have been praying for Sarah every Sunday. How is she doing?"

It may have been the genuine expression of concern or perhaps the accompanying embrace, but Charlie noticed his mother beginning to tear up, something he had never seen her do in a room full of strangers.

Katie had been prepared to enter the building anonymously and slip into a back pew.

Instead, before having time to put on her usual public face, she had been caught off guard. The omnipresent burden of sadness, fear and most of all guilt she carried was supposed to be hers alone, not for the world to witness.

"Sarah is not doing very well, but we're still hoping for a turn-around." Her voice weak and shaky, Katie could say no more.

Mrs. Hanson quickly guided her into the church's little office at the right of the entrance and closed the door. At the same time, Mrs. Goodwan directed Charlie and Mary to some wooden chairs near the back of the church. There were no pews, the fifty or so assembled worshippers arrayed across several rows of sturdy-looking matching seats. When Katie joined them moments later, she was once again composed. With a reassuring smile, Mrs. Hanson quietly settled herself next to them.

Charlie looked around with interest. He had already noted the absence of stained glass and pipe organ. But it was only when the service began that he realized this worship service was unlike anything he'd ever encountered in the Presbyterian church.

"This is the day that the Lord has made. Let us rejoice and be glad in it!" Now positioned behind the pulpit, Pastor Hanson abruptly began the service, his booming voice filling the small room. "Can you say Amen to that?" He looked expectedly over his little flock, who immediately returned a ragged but loud "Amen!" Then, all by himself, he began to sing a hymn Charlie had never heard, but which grabbed his attention with its lively beat. The congregation quickly jumped to their feet and enthusiastically joined in:

Oh, worship the King, all glorious above,

Oh, gratefully sing His pow'r and His love.

Mrs. Hanson passed two bright red hymn books to the Thompsons although no one else seemed to need one. The singing seemed to go on forever, at least to Charlie, but gradually the tempo grew slower. They now sang of being cleansed by the blood of Jesus, while the pastor raised his arms skyward, as if to pull God down into their midst. Most of the congregation was similarly positioned, swaying back and forth, eyes closed the singing interwoven with ecstatic shouts of "Hallelujah!" and "Praise the Lord!" Mary anxiously reached for her mother's arm, but Katie was completely transfixed. Charlie stood stiffly at attention, the hymn book clutched but long-forgotten in his sweaty right hand.

Pastor Hanson continued to subtly dial down the intensity of worship by quieting his voice until his "Amens" were mere whispers. He quickly and discretely pulled out a white handkerchief to wipe away the perspiration trickling down his forehead and stinging both eyes. He discarded his suit jacket, flung it casually over a chair, loosened his bright green tie, and began to preach. His voice no longer fettered by the lasso around his neck, words began to stream freely from his mouth.

Forty-five minutes later he was still sermonizing, long after Charlie and Mary had tuned him out, like clicking the OFF button on the family's radio. Mary was drawing pictures of horses on the back page of her mother's church bulletin, having already filled her own. Charlie was lost in thought, reflecting on this first encounter with a Pentecostal church.

The building seems bare and shabby. There is no stained glass and no organ with its big cluster of golden pipes. The minister doesn't even wear a robe like the Presbyterian guy at my grandparents' church.

Still, there's something going on here.

Maybe this "something" was bound up in the raised arms or fervent prayers, or perhaps it was the frequent "Praise the Lord" or "Preach it, brother" coming from the congregation, which seemed to motivate Pastor Hanson to talk louder, more excitedly—and longer. Or maybe the fact that when they weren't shouting, they were scribbling notes in their Bibles, capturing the best of the preacher's wisdom for future enlightenment. While Charlie might not understand what was going on, for this pastor's raucous flock it was real and meaningful. But one further surprise lay ahead.

Pastor Hanson finally concluded his sermon, and with no advance announcement to his congregation, he suddenly began to pray, while in the background, the pianist played a hymn so quietly it was like a soft cushion for his words.

"With every head bowed and every eye closed, we call upon you, O Jesus." Charlie and even Mary dutifully shut their eyes, imagining some divine entity staring down with watchful scrutiny over the now-silent gathering.

"O God, some of your sons and daughters assembled here this morning greatly need a touch from You. Our God is a healing God. We pray against disease; we pray against sickness; we pray against the enemy of our souls, that one who seeks to rob us of our health, to rip away our hope for the future."

The minister continued, his voice now more gentle and concerned. "While we remain in prayer with heads bowed, I want those of you with sickness in your home to raise your hands in faith, believing the Holy Spirit for that answer to prayer, yes, even for that miracle when the doctors may have told you there is no hope. But our God is still the Great Physician." Charlie opened one eye to peek at his mother. He saw her cautiously raise one arm slightly higher above her head. She was crying silent tears.

The congregation was now shouting words which Charlie couldn't understand, words that sounded like moaning and stuttering. The noise level alone was anxiety-provoking but it was the intensity and raw emotion in those primal sounds which almost frightened him. Were they shouting to get God's attention? Did that actually work?

The pastor quickly re-asserted command of his flock. "Now I invite all those who in faith raised their hand to walk down this aisle and come to this altar so we can pray for you and with you. Don't let the enemy keep you away. God is here and God is waiting." He then began to sing all by himself again and Charlie quickly recognized it as a Christmas carol, even though it was nowhere near December:

O, come let us adore him
O, come let us adore him
O, come let us adore him, Christ, the Lord.

The congregation joined in, standing as one, with hands reaching skyward and eyes still closed, as if they really could picture Jesus in their midst. At that point, Charlie discovered that his mother was gone. He looked around and caught a glimpse of the back of her dark hair and burgundy sweater as she knelt at the front, the pastor and his wife on either side. More people came forward to kneel and be prayed for; and behind them came others who stood behind each one, men with men and women with women, to lay hands on their shoulders in a show of support. Pastor Hanson rose, and moved back and forth in front of them, dabbing each forehead with liquid from a small vial that seemed to contain cooking oil. The pianist then led those still standing patiently in their rows in singing a lively song about "power in the blood."

What is she doing up there? I hope she doesn't embarrass herself, or us. Is this music ever loud. I like the tune, though. I hope I don't have to clap my hands or shout. Would they make me? It's never this noisy in Grandpa's church. I wonder what they'd think about all this. I would love to see Rev. MacDougall try to do this with his long robes and serious face.

Gradually, the "commotion" (as Charlie later described it) began to subside, like air slowly leaking from a birthday balloon. First, the children and teenagers who had been scattered among the mostly adult congregation streamed down the center aisle like puppies let off the leash. The older members were less eager to leave, the men lingering to shake hands while the women exchanged carefully positioned hugs and cheek-brushing kisses.

As Charlie watched, a human bottleneck formed by the door as everyone paused to speak with the pastor and extend some positive comment on his sermon or praise the music.

Katie soon followed, her white silk handkerchief quickly wiping away any evidence of distress, but not before her son had noticed with an unspoken concern. She gathered both children in a reassuring embrace, as a hen might shelter her chicks under each wing, and they moved toward the exit and outside world. Pastor Hanson thanked Katie for coming, smiled broadly at Mary, and suddenly extended his right hand toward Charlie. Caught off guard and unfamiliar with this end-of-service ritual, he tried to return the handshake, but only managed to grasp the pastor's fingers in an awkward embrace. Nonetheless, his arm was pumped up and down for a few painful and embarrassing seconds before his hand was finally liberated.

As they made their way down the front steps, Pastor Hanson called out, "We have a Friday night program for teenagers, Charlie. You'd like it. How about maybe coming along next Friday?"

"Sure, I'll think about it," he responded with a polite non-answer. Inwardly, he knew there was no need for that.

How does he know I will like it? He doesn't even know me. That's kind of pushy. No way am I getting involved with people I never met. Even if he does seem nice.

Might be some girls there, though, maybe even some good-looking ones my age.

"How about you, Mary?" Clearly, Pastor Hanson was anything but passive when it came to helping unchurched folks get to know Jesus. "We have a midweek club for children that meets here every Wednesday—lots of fun and some good snacks too."

Mary stopped in her tracks and gazed up at her mother. "Can I? It sounds like fun." She was pleased he remembered her name.

Katie looked uncertain, silently wishing the pastor hadn't put her on the spot in front of her daughter. Little did she know that "fun and snacks" would not be the only items on the agenda. In this group over the following months, Mary was not only strongly encouraged toward a life or death decision to accept Jesus as her saviour but to carry the burden of sharing him with her little friend, Rachel, who also "needed to be saved."

Their ride was patiently waiting on the sidewalk after the service. As the group moved toward the grey Austin, Mrs. Goodwan looked satisfied, having achieved her goal of introducing the Thompson family to Faith Tabernacle and to her Lord, Himself.

NEW ENGLAND READY FOR DATE WITH EDNA

BOSTON (AP) Hurricane Edna packed winds of 125 mph as it approached Southern New England. New Englanders have been charting the course of Hurricane Edna since earlier this week...

The New London Evening Day, September 11

CHAPTER SEVEN

Katie wondered if she had missed an opportunity to leave her guilt behind at that altar, along with some of her tears.

There was little doubt that she had felt a sense of hope for Sarah's recovery. There really was a power in prayer, just like the pastor shouted when they gathered in front of the congregation. She had felt a surprising sense of peace as hands were laid on her shoulders and voices cried out to God on her behalf. And not just peace. A comforting warmth had enveloped her, which was not just sanctuary-heat on a sunny day. As well as tears, she also left much of her fear.

No, it was not hope versus doubt over Sarah's recovery that she struggled with during the drive home. It was guilt and, as always, it weighed heavily. Before the service, God had been a distant presence, a heavenly father who apparently made the world, sent Jesus who had twelve disciples, loved children and healed sick people, all before dying on a Roman cross. She could also recite the Ten Commandments, remembered from long ago Sunday School lessons.

Now, God was different. More correctly, Katie's perception of him had altered. Suddenly, he was close and wanting to be involved in her life. She had always accepted his love in an abstract way. Now, not only that love but his righteousness and condemnation of sin (she found herself using church language) grew very real, and very personal.

Pastor Hanson had insisted, during his long sermon, that God, being holy, could not have a relationship—"fellowship" was his term—with sin. Those with unconfessed sin in their lives would never have spiritual union with God. So in order to be "born-again," sin would need to be removed through confession and seeking God's forgiveness through Christ.

What Katie had done years before was surely a sin. Most definitely, it was an unconfessed one. Consequently, she had cut herself off from God. How could he hear her prayers? And did that mean her altar experience was no more than an emotional few moments without lasting substance? By the time Mrs. Goodwan's Austin had reached Lawson Avenue, Katie's hope for God's intervention in Sarah's illness was dissipating as quickly as the smoky exhaust from the little grey car.

And then Sarah died. Exhausted by her long and desperate struggle to breathe with lungs that no longer worked, she was diagnosed with pneumonia which soon brought that struggle to a close. Her grieving parents by her mechanical iron lung prison, Sarah's spirit was finally liberated from her frail body like a butterfly escaping its cocoon.

CHAPTER EIGHT

On the Tuesday after Labour Day, and following his usual breakfast of shredded wheat, freshly squeezed orange juice and raisin toast with peanut butter, Charlie began the slow walk down Lawson Avenue toward Brock Collegiate. He had lingered over his cereal as long as he could. Staring at the elongated biscuit in his bowl, its woven strands of wheat half-submerged in a pool of milk, Charlie sought in vain to find some reason not to take that morning walk. He felt like a condemned prisoner awaiting a one-way trip to the electric chair.

Katie was understandably anxious that Charlie not be late, today of all days. "You'd better get a move on," she urged, adding supportively at the sight of his worried face, "I know the first day of high school can be hard, especially when..." She stopped short of voicing her unspoken belief that his shyness was surely compounding the problem.

"Maybe I should have flunked grade eight," he muttered ruefully.

"It wouldn't be any easier a year from now. Besides, would you really want to spend a second year with Mrs. Kerk?" That remark drew a fleeting smile from her boy and sent him toward the front door.

Mary was right behind her older brother but quickly headed in the opposite direction toward King Edward. For her, the return to school sparked excitement and anticipation. Entering grade four meant she would be in Mr. Rowar's class, her first male teacher. A conscientious student, she looked forward to the challenge of her studies, especially since they would be learning about the British monarchy, with its long list of kings and queens. She was equally eager to renew friendship with

Rachel, now a classmate, who had been away part of the summer at her family's Georgian Bay cottage. Along the way, she spotted another friend, Frances Pickard, who had just returned from the Salvation Army camp that she attended every year.

At the school yard, most of the grade eight boys were involved in a pick-up baseball game, while young ones watched from behind the old torn wire mesh screen. Junior graders always hoped for an invitation but stoically accepted they would remain spectators (unless one team needed an extra body in the outfield.) To occupy their time, some of them listlessly tossed a softball back and forth, hoping a player might notice a good catching glove or strong pitching arm. As a strategy, it seldom worked.

Other children from the lower grades created their own fun. Some were playing "frozen tag": each "caught" victim standing frozen in position, stiff as a statue until freed by another player. Others formed two opposing lines, each team linked by hands joined together. Once in place, the cry went up in a raucous chorus from one side:

"Red Rover, Red Rover, let Jimmy come over!"

On cue, Jimmy burst from his team's side of the field and charged aggressively into the opposing line, determined to break the chain. Instead, the opposing team held firm and Jimmy simply bounced off, landing on his behind in the dust. Rules then required him to join the enemy line, strengthening their ranks. Eventually, one side would run out of players— but not before the game would have to be adjourned until recess.

Mary wasn't fond of Red Rover, so she turned to the choir of grade four girls skipping Double Dutch:

Miss Mary Mack, Mack, Mack, all dressed in black, black, black,
With silver buttons, buttons, buttons
Down her back, back, back.

The sixth graders had their own ritualistic skipping songs:

Down in the valley
Where the green grass grows, Sat little Annie
As sweet as a rose.

And if the playground teacher was busy elsewhere, a few grade eight boys would break into their own ribald version:

Down in the valley
Where the green grass grows,
Sat Betty Grable without any clothes.

Mary was happily at home here. After five years, she knew almost all the students except the newest little ones. Spotting Frances and Rachel skipping Double Dutch, she quickly lined up for a turn but instead was handed the ends of two long braided ropes, one for each hand. With a practised rhythm, she twirled each rope so that they swung in huge circles, the left hand moving clockwise while the right, in perfect unison, circled in an opposite rotation. Frances and Mary matched each other's motions. *Miss Mary Mack, Mack, Mack—*

Mary finally tired herself out, handed off her lines to Rachel and, without missing a beat, jumped right in. She felt as if she were flying, her feet scarcely touching the ground. Such fun!

Promptly at 8:55 a.m., the bell rang and everyone instantly stopped in place as if joined in a game of frozen tag. Silence descended like a blanket, as the teachers on yard duty scanned the playground in search for any moving offenders. Ten seconds later, a second bell clanged and the children moved in a slow surging wave toward their separate door—the younger grades to the heavy, green-painted wooden door on the left, older grades to a similar one on the right. The stone arch above each separate entrance was engraved BOYS and GIRLS—a relic of more regimented and gender segregated times.

With Rachel and Frances at her side, Mary moved quickly down the long hall to room twelve. She hoped they would be able to sit together when desks were assigned. They had a lot of catching up to do. She looked forward to them working together on a science project or a skit for the Christmas pageant. Frances already knew about Jesus and his birthday from summer camp, but Mary felt sure God would open a door for her to tell Rachel about him. The only condition she imposed on God was that He not require her to eat any of those goldfish at the Golson's dinner table.

* * *

Brock Collegiate was located on Bloor St., a few blocks east of the Thompson's neighbourhood. The solid-looking three-story fading-yellow-brick structure had been built in 1911 and by 1954, now welcomed second and even third generations from some local families. The school offered a Senior Matriculation Diploma (also known as grade thirteen), a Junior one (grade twelve) as well as four-year programs in Industrial Arts or Commercial for those seeking a job right after high school.

Shortly before the nine o'clock bell rang, Charlie nervously climbed the few concrete steps, took a deep breath and entered the front door.

I can't turn around now. How does my hair look? Shit, so many people. Maybe I can spot Gary. Where am I supposed to go?

I wish I was smaller—there's nowhere to hide!

Inside, the grade nine students were directed by an unsmiling older woman, perhaps a secretary, to a spacious auditorium. Her sullen face suggested she would rather still be on summer holidays, her vacation abruptly and unfairly cut short by the appearance of these hordes of noisy teenagers. In the auditorium and flanked by two Union Jacks, a large picture of the young fresh-faced Queen seemed to solemnly survey the gathered youngsters. Under the portrait and occupying center-stage on the raised platform stood the principal. Mr. McGiver was quite at home on these occasions, having been at Brock for eight years and well-experienced at handling a crowd of adolescents. Most of them, the chatty noisy ones, had brought their opening day excitement and anticipation, while the insecure, quieter minority conveyed a sense of confusion and apprehension.

Charlie, of course, was in the latter group.

Mr. McGiver was a short, rotund man, with broad shoulders made even wider by his grey tweed sports jacket with its padded shoulders. Gary Bellover had told Charlie over the summer that he'd driven a Sherman tank in Holland during the war and was someone you didn't want to mess with. And Gary spoke from experience, having been summoned to Mr. McGiver's office more than once for various infractions of school rules. Still, he added, it was the vice-principal, not Mr. McGiver, who had given him the strap on two of those occasions.

After some brief welcoming comments, Mr. McGiver called out the names of those students assigned to 9A as home room. Thirty or so pupils clambered up from their hard wooden seats, made their way to the back of the auditorium and disappeared through the heavy wooden doors. The class of 9B, then 9C followed.

Charlie was called as a member of 9D. He followed the group, now much more subdued, down a long hall, its pale-green walls decorated with photos of past graduating classes, former principals and winning sports teams. As the last to enter Room 109, Charlie's heart sank; almost every seat had been taken. Never before had he sat near the front, and he had no intention of doing so now. He scanned the rows of faces impassively staring back at him. One desk remained, in the middle of the room. The young female teacher smiled and pointed toward it. He quickly sat down and, ignoring other students around him, resolutely fixed his gaze on the blackboard upon which was written "Miss Manton."

I made it. I'm okay, so long as she doesn't ask me a question. Just to be safe, I'm not even going to look around. Keep my eyes straight ahead. Wish I could shrink out of sight. I feel like I'm surrounded.

"This is where you will begin each day. After I take attendance, I will endeavour to teach you something about Canadian history." She smiled assuredly. Miss Manton was tall. Charlie had noticed her height when he first entered the classroom, and found that her blue eyes briefly met his on the same level. Although she was slender, the padded shoulders of her dark brown dress gave the impression of added weight.

As Miss Manton went through her checklist, Charlie's attention wandered and he finally risked checking out his classmates. A few he recognized from grade eight. The rest were strangers. The boys ranged from muscular well-groomed almost-men to short slender still-children. The girls too ranged in development although they all seemed to have chosen pleated skirts, short-sleeved blouses, white socks and saddle shoes.

The students of 9D had been assigned the early lunch period which, on this first day, came next. Freed from the tension of the morning's initiation, they quickly replaced the enforced formality of the classroom with loud spontaneous chatter. The next several moments were spent searching for their assigned lockers. Green metal doors banged open, then quickly shut as they stored books and notepaper, grabbed bagged lunches, clicked padlocks and headed for the cafeteria. Some groupings were resurrected from last year, others were forming new friendships.

Charlie purposely lagged behind, not confident enough to insert himself into one of these cliques. By the time he reached the cafeteria, all of the tables were occupied not only by his grade nine classmates but, more alarmingly, territorial upper-level pupils who had clearly staked out their territory.

I can't go in there—too many people, too much noise. Nowhere to sit.

Gotta walk in and get it over with. It'll be the same situation tomorrow. Where else is there to eat?

Charlie noticed Gary Bellover among the older students. This was the answer! He could sit beside his farm workmate. But Gary's only reaction to his hovering presence was a look of awkward embarrassment, while his table mates glared menacingly. Their postures made it clear: Charlie was to look elsewhere. There was no place for him at a table claimed by twelfth graders. Gary turned away, choosing to abandon his summer friend in favour of his buddies.

The late-comer then did what he instinctively had always done, quickly withdrawing in preference of quiet and isolation.

He ended up outside in an asphalt parking lot behind the school. Beyond the double rows of teachers' cars was the football field ringed by an oval red cinder track. Past that, and outside of school property to the north, was an empty field, once the site of some old factory torn down years ago. Climbing a rusty wire fence, he entered an open space with a few scrawny lilac and hawthorn bushes scattered amid the overgrown weeds and long timothy grass. In that place of refuge, Charlie slowly unwrapped a peanut butter sandwich from its waxed paper, then a second one with cheese slices and, without any enthusiasm, began to eat.

Definitely better than the cafeteria, at least while the weather is good. Yeah, but I'm still a chicken shit coward.

* * *

On the Friday of that otherwise awkward first week of high school, Charlie finally found a positive experience; or to be more precise, a positive experience found him. It happened during an outdoor Physical Education class. The boys of 9D were clustered on the cinder track in their school-coloured red and gold shorts and white tee shirts, listening to Mr. Tavener's instructions.

Standing at the far edge of the circled students, Charlie failed to hear the complete instructions. All he was able to discern was that they were supposed to run—and keep going.

At the sound of the teacher's whistle, the pack set off at a trot counterclockwise around the track. Even before reaching the first turn, several of the fitter students had created a gap between themselves and the rest. To his surprise, Charlie was among the lead runners, as if psychologically pulled along by their collective energy.

As they headed into the final turn of the oval track, an innate sense of male competitiveness took over and a frantic race to the finish began—except for Charlie, who seemed unaware there was even a finish line. Ever obedient in the presence of authority, he simply kept running, determined not to stop until Mr. Tavener blew his whistle.

Last year, Danny Blake had captained the grade eight cross-country team which won the North York championship. Now, a year later, and a muscular twenty pounds heavier, he found himself aggressively matching Charlie stride for stride as both sprinted down the homestretch.

Still under the assumption he was following orders, Charlie kept right on running past the teacher and began a second circuit of the track. After initially slowing for a few seconds, Danny perceived a direct challenge and sped after his opponent.

Mr. Tavener and the rest of the class stood frozen in place, watching what had apparently turned into a grudge match. Blake's friends began to cheer him on, their crackling adolescent voices resonating across the grassy football field.

Charlie knew only to keep running until directed to stop.

Halfway around the track, Danny's stamina began to wilt. His legs grew heavy and hot, his breathing laboured, his arms flailing as if to pull him forward. His weight gain had become a liability. He dropped behind his adversary.

Charlie felt only lightness. There were no extra pounds for him to carry. Many miles of jogging across country fields and wooded trails had made him strong in a way he never expected. On he ran, alone and effortlessly, toward the assembled group.

"Ok, you can stop now." Mr. Tavener stepped out in front and held up his arms like a traffic cop. "What's your name, son?"

"Charlie Thompson, sir." He wondered if he was in trouble for not stopping earlier. "Come to my office after school today. I want to talk with you."

"Yes, sir." Now he was certain he had transgressed. But what?

By this point Danny Blake had pulled up beside Charlie and paused long enough to glare at him, sweat rolling down his flushed cheeks. Fortunately, his target was too busy studying Mr. Tavener's face to notice.

Promptly at 3:30 p.m., Charlie arrived in the Phys. Ed. office and was waved in and toward a chair by the teacher.

"That was quite the race you and Blake were having. What was going on between you two?"

Charlie began to unravel the misunderstood communication which had inadvertently led to the contest. Mr. Tavener quickly brushed aside his explanation.

"What I'm really interested in is getting you on my cross-country team. Are you interested?"

Despite his shaky entry into the overwhelming world of high school, Charlie had found a measure of unexpected success and acceptance. He was on a team! In that moment he almost felt like he belonged.

"Yes, sir" was all the surprised runner could reply. His grin said much more.

CHAPTER NINE

The dreaded first anniversary of Sarah's death took place two weeks after Charlie entered high school.

Despite Doug and Katie's desperate efforts to reassure the children (and themselves) that she would recover, Sarah died in the hospital, her frail body imprisoned in an "iron lung" during the last difficult days.

Charlie would always carry that image in his mind: Sarah's head protruding from one end of what resembled an elongated tin can, long auburn hair framing a thin pale face. A black rubber collar encircled her neck to maintain air pressure inside the tube—fifteen pounds per square inch, the nurse had explained. A small wooden device above Sarah's head held open the pages of a book so that she might find some small measure of distraction through reading.

Though of course, this well-meaning gesture only worked if someone else was there to turn the pages.

Mary voiced the anxiety which Charlie inwardly shared. "Mommy, why is Sarah in that machine?"

Katie gently explained that their sister's diaphragm was paralyzed. "She can't breathe well enough on her own right now. The iron lung is helping do the breathing for her until she gets stronger."

The shiny cylinder with its protruding hoses and wires would remain Sarah's home for her remaining days.

All these months later, Charlie could still hear the rhythmic whoosh of the life-giving air as it was pushed into Sarah's prison. Only during the few seconds when the air flow was reversed could she gasp out a few words, the sound pushed out with the stale air.

How can she stay in that thing? She can barely move. Is that why she looks so white and skinny? She must be scared, like I am.

The doctors will help her. Remember that guy at school last year? He got out. Even if she gets leg braces like him, at least she'll be home.

I love her. I hope she knows that. Yeah, she does. I don't have to tell her.

But doctors and iron lungs could only delay, not avoid, the inevitable. Pneumonia found a home in those damaged lungs and launched an attack against an already weakened system. Sarah died on September 17, as her body was finally freed from its prison for one final embrace by her distraught parents.

Sarah's funeral took place in her grandparents" Presbyterian church. When Katie initially raised the possibility of Pastor Hanson conducting the service at Faith Tabernacle, Doug reacted with a surprising fury. His outburst, uncharacteristic of a man indifferent to matters of religion, had frightened Katie and the children, and she immediately abandoned the idea. It was only later, after the funeral, that an apologetic Doug had shared the reason for his bitterness.

"Your church and that Mrs. Goodwan said Sarah would be healed. They misled us. You should never have believed their nonsense."

He turned away but not before Katie could see the angry tears.

"Pastor Hanson did phone and offer his condolences and assured me Sarah is in a better place. Can't you find any comfort in that?" By now, she was choking back her own tears.

"Our daughter's better place is here with her family." And with that, the discussion quickly ended. Katie understood but had no answer for Doug's bitterness.

It wouldn't be until Charlie had grown into manhood and become a father himself that he finally understood his father's inner turmoil. Doug was a strong loving man who took seriously his role as protector. Sarah's illness and death had robbed him of that certainty, and left him feeling powerless and guilty.

Generations of Thomson men, neither competent nor comfortable with diapers or stoves, had nevertheless put food on the table by wresting a living from the land, the factory machine, a pile of lumber, or granite stones which, under their chisels, became decorative gargoyles. When

Doug talked like this, Katie would often counter with a resentment-covered smile that she too put food on the table and it was high time he appreciated that reality!

Of course, these days protecting one's family no longer meant fighting off wolf packs, hostile highland bandits or marauding soldiers. Now it was a matter of laying down rules to keep children away from bad influences or being hit by a car on some busy street, and watching closely when they swam at the lake. Thus, no matter what his mind told him about Sarah's death being unavoidable, Doug's heart told him differently. He had failed to keep her safe.

However, Doug's guilt had deeper roots. He had been part way through basic training in New Brunswick when he opened Katie's telegram announcing her pregnancy. Later, in her ninth month, he was granted leave to be at her side, and arrived home on the CPR train in time for a few days' visit with his family before rushing with Katie to Toronto Western Hospital when her water broke. Ensconced with other similarly nervous soon-to-be fathers, he stood watch and paced until a labour and delivery nurse shared the good news that Sarah had arrived safely.

In those first moments with his daughter, a love affair began. For the week that Katie remained in hospital he visited daily, one time bringing Charlie so the toddler could be lifted up and have a peek. His nose pressed against the nursery room glass, the little big brother met his cozily-blanketed baby sister. Once home, Doug was an attentive, protective father, walking the floor at 3 a.m. those first nights, Sarah snuggled against his shoulder until she finally gave in to sleep.

But all too quickly, Doug was back on the train to Quebec City then Fredericton, leaving his forlorn-looking family gathered on the porch.

Doug always regretted and at times resented those three and a half years of service which robbed him of time with his young family. He also bore feelings of guilt for leaving Katie to raise the two children on her own.

In Europe, during those endless months away from home, Doug constantly reminded himself that at least Katie had moved in with her parents on the farm. He knew the Ranwicks were eager to help out and to spend time together with their only grandchildren. While this somewhat eased Doug's conscience and worry, he longed for the day when he could resume his rightful place as head of the family.

The war had separated them. Now, death had stolen his precious girl away from him once again.

Charlie had his own struggles accepting Sarah's death. In the days following her funeral, he found solace on the Humber riverbank. Watching the muddy stream roll endlessly by, he could engage in a lonely inner dialogue.

"The pastor had said that God loves us"

"Right"

"He said that God is in control and has the power to even make miracles."

"True"

"He believes that God hears our prayers—and answers them."

"I remember that."

"So if he is that loving and that powerful and hears our prayers, why did he let Sarah die?"

A year later, Charlie walked along the edge of the slow-moving water. His presence frightened two crows who had been feasting on the remains of a small fish, likely a yellow perch, which had somehow ended up on shore. As he looked, he immediately realized what had happened. The perch had strayed into a shallow pool of water, perhaps in pursuit of bugs floating on the surface. As the pool shrunk in the hot weather, it became separated from the river, cutting off any hope it could return to its home.

Day by day, as it gradually and relentlessly transformed into a stagnant puddle, it was unable offering neither shelter nor life-giving oxygen to its trapped captive. Death was inevitable.

Charlie was struck by the random nature of life: for a now-rotting yellow perch, for his dead sister, and ultimately for himself. Meanwhile, the river silently continued its unending flow, indifferent to the loss of one of its own.

NATIONAL WEATHER SERVICE:
Tropical storm Gilda formed in the Central Caribbean Sea on September 24. It moved westward, reaching a peak of 70 mph winds before hitting Belize on the 27th. Gilda caused heavy rains and flooding, leading to 29 deaths and extensive flooding. No damage figures are available.

Consejo Belize weather/storms

CHAPTER TEN

The girl was walking rapidly along the flat west bank of the Humber River. Her bare feet hopped acrobatically from one smooth rock to another in a concentrated effort to avoid the oozing brown mud which lay between the stream and the tangle of wild grass and ferns beyond the shoreline.

Charlie was sitting unseen across the river on its much higher east bank, his feet dangling over the steep embankment. He watched intently as she drew closer. He first took notice of those prancing legs, then the dark hair which gently bounced across her narrow shoulders with each calculated jump. He reckoned her height as almost matching his own. As she moved closer, he noticed she had tied her white short-sleeved blouse around her rib cage, leaving her flat stomach bare. Red shorts exposed her long tanned thighs.

The girl was now directly across from him, still focused on her river-dance, arms outstretched sideways for balance, each hand clutching a sandal. She was close enough for Charlie see she had large brown eyes, clear dark skin and red lips. Two minutes later, she had disappeared around a sharp bend in the riverbank, the tall bulrushes and milkweed blocking her passage from his lingering gaze.

Questions immediately began to compete for attention in his brain. He systematically processed his inventory of girls from Brock but couldn't recall ever having seen her.

Who was that? Where is she going? How can I see her again? How do I find out her name?

Yeah, and what good would it do you?

Charlie was also aware of new responses elsewhere in his adolescent body. They caused his stomach to flutter, his heart to pound, a sweaty dampness escaping from under his arms.

As he turned to go home, though reluctant to leave this now-sacred site, Charlie glanced one last time at the Humber, suddenly puzzled that the river seemed to be flowing faster than when he had arrived a mere hour ago.

Charlie's experience with girls was virtually non-existent, apart from the obvious exception of his family. His earliest encounters were, of course, through comic books. Those who roamed through the African jungles had lean muscled frames barely covered by lion skins, Others were more demurely dressed, like Lois Lane or Dale Evans, loyal sidekicks of Superman or Roy Rogers. But most of all, it was Wonder Woman who captivated him. Through hundreds of comic pages, loyally and vicariously, Charlie fought alongside this powerful Amazon warrior against villainous crime bosses, their henchmen and especially treacherous Nazi spies.

I wish I could be Wonder Woman's sidekick, like Lois and Dale. She never has a partner.

Everything she does, she does all alone.

Except she doesn't need men to help her; that's the whole point of the story.

When he first started reading comics, these female characters might just as well have been male. As long as they were the centerpieces of some storyline, gender didn't matter one whit. Now it was different. Charlie never fully realized that he was not alone in his infatuation with Wonder Woman. In those days, only Superman and Batman were more popular with readers. She even ranked ahead of super soldier Captain America, Captain Marvel with his magical incantation—SHAZAM!—and Plastic Man, who always managed to elongate his body when danger threatened. As for other heroines—Sheena, Batgirl, Black Canary—everyone one of them finished a distant second, despite their undeniable beauty and allure.

What was so special about Wonder Woman? For girls, of course—and if he'd had any female friends, he would have known this—she was a strong female role model in a fantasy world otherwise filled with masculine superheroes. Her iron bracelets could deflect bullets; her golden lasso, when encircling an enemy, compelled him to tell the truth. She possessed superhuman strength, could defeat almost any man and, like Superman, even stop runaway locomotives. Yet all this power was disguised in her modest quiet alter-ego, Diane Prince.

For boys (and men), though, there was another attraction. Long, flowing black hair crowned with a golden tiara, tiny waist, tight star-spangled short shorts: Wonder Woman was undeniably gorgeous, a babe even in the midst of battle.

Charlie was content for Wonder Woman to remain an unattainable fantasy, to be possessed only through comics and imagination. Not unlike the pretty, dark-haired teenager who floated across his vision at the river. Except in this case, he wasn't quite so content.

* * *

Fortunately for Charlie, cross-country practices had not yet started. After school, over the next few days, he kept a daily vigil by the riverbank, in the hopes of seeing her again. This change in routine did not escape the notice of his parents. Katie was used to him arriving home by four o'clock, ready for a snack of three slices of raisin bread thickly spread with peanut butter and washed down with a glass of ice-cold milk. Now, home had become a way station, as he dumped his books on the old Windsor chair in the corner of the front hall and took right off.

"Charlie, aren't you hungry?"

"Just wrap it up, please, I'll eat it for supper." And then he was gone, screen door flapping in his wake.

Doug had different concerns. One evening after dinner, he asked "Where are you after school? Has cross-country started already?" The answer offered no reassurance.

"Just hangin' around the river."

Doug knew his son wasn't one to get involved with troublemakers like the Christie Pits gangs. Nor was it likely he was smoking or drinking. Wanting to probe further but unable to express the unease he was feeling, all he was left with was "Well, stay out of trouble when you are around the river."

Trouble was an unlikely companion. No one else was ever around. Over the gurgling sound of the slow-moving current, Charlie could hear the shouts of boys playing baseball and the hum of rush hour traffic heading for home along Westdale Road. He passed the time by throwing a stick upstream as far as he could, then pretending it was a Japanese aircraft carrier. As it floated by, he lobbed pebbles in the hopes of scoring a direct hit before it could successfully sail around the bend to safety. Victory for the Marines at Iwo Jima depended on his accuracy.

I'm piloting a fighter plane, like John Wayne in The Flying Leathernecks. I finally see my target, a carrier cruising in the South Pacific and filled with troops to reinforce the exhausted Japanese garrison. They're desperately trying to hold out against us. Aim— Steady— all guns fire! Ha, I got his flight deck! The admiral's a dead man!!

Once his arm grew tired or his mind bored, he sat quietly watching the frogs watching him. He considered, then rehearsed, what he might say should the dark-haired girl reappear. As he did so, a mixture of fear and excitement bubbled up inside. He both hoped she would show up and feared she might.

Gotta make sure I'm smiling, or maybe whistling. Hi, I'm Charlie.

Then she'll tell me her name. Glad to meet you, Nancy. Unless she doesn't say anything. What then?

I'll just keep on walking along the river with her, like I'm heading toward the bridge. I'll just be silent and walk with her.

But wouldn't that scare her? Maybe I should go the other way instead and let her wonder who this stranger is. That way, she'd regret not stopping to talk. Then next time give her another chance—if we ever would meet again.

* * *

Charlie's lonely vigil by the river left him with too much time to reflect upon yet another source of sadness. Tom and Jane had concluded that late September would be the best time for their auction. It had been a year since they first decided to sell, a decision made slightly less painful by their meeting with Rev. MacDougall. But that pain was sharply reactivated when it came time to tell Charlie and Mary. Doug and Katie, of course, had been made aware of the news the evening of the minister's visit. Katie especially was not surprised, since she had long been concerned over her father's health and onerous workload. While she would never admit this to them, she was, in fact, somewhat relieved.

When to tell the children? Why spoil Charlie's last summer at the farm? Then more delay.

Finally, it was decided to let him get settled into grade nine. With Mary, the timing was not as critical, as she had never forged the same emotional connection. Being far more outgoing and less in need of sanctuary, Mary's interest lay in her neighbourhood and especially in particular her new best friend, Rachel.

Two days after Charlie's fateful sighting of the dark-haired girl, his parents drew him aside after dinner. Mary had been dispatched to her bedroom to do homework.

"Charlie, we've got some news about your grandparents," Tom began, sitting rigidly in his armchair, his mouth working to find the right words. "Grandpa and Grandma have decided to sell the farm. It's become too much for them to manage."

Charlie instantly looked away, avoiding his parents' concerned scrutiny. Inwardly, a rush of shock and loss poured up from his stomach like bitter vomit. Outwardly, he maintained the mask he always wore when painful emotions threatened to reveal themselves. Which is why he replied from his head, not from his aching heart

"When will the deal go through?" By focusing on the facts, he could sidestep the heavy sense of loss and panic that was beginning to weigh on him.

"Very soon," Katie mechanically replied, "But right now, we need to know how you're feeling about this. It's okay to be sad or angry." Though she knew from experience that emotions could not be pulled from her son like some imbedded sliver, she had to try, for her own as well as his sake.

"I guess it's okay. Where will they move to? Charlie stayed rooted to his emotionally safe ground.

"They've been looking at a nice apartment on Eglinton near Dufferin. You and Mary can come with us on the weekend to see it." With that, Katie reluctantly accepted her son's need to avoid the pain.

Tom took over. "Charlie, Grandpa has had some heart troubles this past year and the doctor told him that he has to avoid heavy lifting."

"I get it, I don't want Grandpa to get sick. Can I go now? I've got homework."

He walked out of the room through a heavy silence. Tom and Katie could only exchange helpless shrugs.

Why didn't they tell me sooner? Could I quit school and help Grandpa out? I already loaded bales. Maybe Gary could get hired full-time after he finishes grade twelve, or is that too far away? Shit!

We're going to lose the farm. What about my summers there? What about Lindy? Can they have dogs at the apartment? Or maybe she can come here to live. Except she would never be happy stuck in the city—like me.

In the sanctuary of his bedroom, Charlie finally allowed tears of frustration to escape.

* * *

Potential buyers began to arrive well before the advertised start time of 9 a.m.

Experienced auction-goers knew to give the most desired items a close inspection before bidding began, taking the opportunity to scrutinize vases and jugs for cracks, books for first editions and furniture for too much wear and tear.

It was a diverse crowd: the few remaining local farmers had come for the machinery and the tools. Antique dealers, pickers and collectors searched for pioneer-era chairs and tables, Victorian chinaware, silverware, whatever might increase their inventory. Another group was made up of more practical people wanting to find housewares, obviously used but still serviceable. They clustered around displays of bedding, towels, pots and pans, lawnmowers, records, dressers, end tables, lamps and clothing. Then there were the merely curious, neighbours drifting over from the new Cedarwoods subdivision across the field behind the barn. They came to investigate what all this commotion was about on a quiet Saturday morning. Unlike the other groups who knew their way around a farm auction, these folk were novices. They found themselves instantly transported like time travellers from a 1954 North York suburb—asphalt-paved streets with concrete sidewalks, compact brick bungalows with neatly trimmed, tiny patches of green grass—to farm life straight from bygone rustic Ontario. Two worlds separated by an empty and neglected corn field: one pointed ahead to modernity and progress, the other mourning a soon-to-be-lost way of life.

Charlie sat glumly at the edge of a noisy crowd, his back against the old chestnut tree near Jane's vegetable garden. She was not there, nor was Tom. A week earlier, they had completed their reluctant move to York Township and town life. Downsizing meant leaving behind most of what they owned, to be picked over by this assembled assortment of prospective buyers.

Naturally, Doug and Katie had been given their choice of whatever items of furniture or personal effects were not destined for the new apartment. Though their small home could not accommodate much, they took a few paintings, several photo albums, three hand-sewn quilt blankets and some garden tools. Today, recognizing the inherent sadness and pain of this day, they were spending it with her parents. Alone with his memories, Charlie quietly witnessed the dismantling of almost three decades of his grandparents' lives, a helpless bystander unable to reverse the inevitable tide of change.

As for the animals, earlier that September most of the livestock had gone to the auction barns at Maple, the rest to the Toronto Stockyards for slaughter. Then there was Lindy. "I guess we could take her home with us," Doug offered hesitantly, "though there's not much room for an animal that's been free to roam all her life."

"Charlie would take her for walks every day before and after school," countered Katie, well aware of the bond between the old border collie and her son. A sacrifice of added responsibility and expense was a small price to pay to keep him from further loss. Surprisingly, it was Charlie who made the sacrifice. "Dad's right, Mom. Lindy would never be happy in the city. We should see if Gary and his family would take her. That way she can stay in the neighbourhood where her surroundings are familiar."

* * *

Before the auction crowd gathered, Charlie had whistled for Lindy. It was time for another hike. Arrangements had been made by phone with the Bellovers to take Lindy. Gary was fond of Lindy, and they had gotten to know each other over the course of summers. It would work out. Besides, Charlie reassured himself, he could always visit.

Of course, no one had been able to consult the old dog about this decision. When she and Charlie reached the Bellover property after a ten-minute run through ripening fields of oats and corn, the plan began to fall apart—for both of them. Charlie tried his best to make it work. He bent down to offer a loving pat on her head, then buried his face in her fur in a desperate effort to hide his tears. As he hastily turned to leave, Lindy strained wildly at her leash, poor Gary holding on tightly against her frantic pull.

Suddenly, without warning, Lindy understood and stopped tugging at her restraint. She quietly sank to the ground, her grey snout resting on her front paws and watched mournfully as Charlie disappeared from sight. As for Charlie, he knew there would be no further visits. One goodbye was hard enough; a second one would be unbearable.

* * *

Bert Carruthers had gone to auction school in Iowa and knew a thing or two about how to efficiently dispose of farm chattels. Promptly at 9 a.m. he clambered up on the hay wagon, his grizzled old helper holding up a box of nails and, already red-faced and sweating, began his singsong delivery to a suddenly silent crowd:

"Who'll gimmee five-five-five? I'll say five-afive-afive.afive. Gimmee two-uhtwo-uhtwo. Who's got two for a big box of nails?"

Interested buyers, mostly farmers, quickly raised their right hands to offer bids on the displayed items. The rest of the crowd quickly grew bored and wandered around the yard where more interesting treasures might be found.

Within that first hour, the wagon was cleared of its mix of power sanders and drills, hammers, glass bottles of screws, old pioneer scythes and sickles, buck saws, leather and brass horse harnesses, whippletrees, coils of thick hemp rope and dangerous looking pitchforks.

Charlie recognized many of the tools, each of which had been carefully cared for by his grandfather. He recalled wistfully how Tom always insisted that each tool be cleaned off and returned to its proper place in the shed once the boy had finished using it: "A place for everything and everything in its place."

When Carruthers moved on to household effects piled on long tables on the back lawn beside the house. The women now pushed in closer. Jane's everyday china dishes, most of her pots and pans, her kitchen utensils, all went quickly. The crowd then followed the auctioneer to piles of bedding, oak dressers, the round pedestal table with six extension leaves where Ranwicks and Thompsons had sat for many Sunday roast beef dinners. Competition heated up when Carruthers reached a well-maintained made-in-Quebec set of eight Windsor chairs and a 100-year-old Mennonite pine corner cupboard elegantly towering seven feet.

By noon, the action stopped briefly for lunch supplied by the Presbyterian ladies as a fundraiser. Plates of sandwiches—thick slices of white oven-baked bread containing huge slabs of turkey, chicken, ham or cheese—awaited the hungry customers. In the cool of early autumn, hot coffee and tea washed down the food. Further down were dozens of homemade pies: apple, strawberry, lemon meringue and cherry, dribbles of fruit and juice spilling out from their pastry covering to entice even the most rigorous weight watcher. The ladies moved quickly and efficiently, and it was clear they had worked together as a team on many similar occasions.

Once the initial rush had subsided, they allowed themselves a break before cleanup. Gathering around a picnic table, they discarded aprons, wiped sweaty foreheads and consumed whatever was left over.

Despite the hour, Charlie had no appetite. He watched potential buyers as they aggressively pawed through his grandmother's personal items—sturdy shoes, old imitation jewelry, photo albums, treasured vinyl LP recordings of her favourite Gilbert and Sullivan—all reluctantly abandoned by the downsizing family. It seemed callous and intrusive. This change, all the changes, were too abrupt.

His worst moment came right after the auction resumed: a suitcase filled with Grandma's woollen stockings, her extra cumbersome-looking girdle with hooks and straps hanging down, and Grandpa's long underwear. Items which had been stored away in a closet for winter wear and the family had forgotten to take.

Sensing a growing post-meal sleepiness permeating his crowd, Carruthers decided a bit of humour was called for. He held the girdle up for inspection, then clumsily tried to step into it. Next he waved Tom's long underwear in a grand circle around his head, as a ripple of laughter spread across the onlookers. Helplessly witnessing this crude violation of his grandparents'privacy, Charlie turned away in disgust.

* * *

By two o'clock the auction was over. What had taken the Ranwicks decades to accumulate was crammed into dozens of trucks and car trunks en route to destinations near and far and gone forever. The crowd left, followed by Carruthers, the tired-looking assistant and the auctioneer's wife-bookkeeper who kept track of the purchases and carried the cash in her large leather pouch.

The troubled boy was alone with his thoughts and memories. He impulsively decided to take one last walk through the barn now empty of livestock. He stopped by the vacant stall where Bossie had provided the Ranwick household with her rich Jersey milk and cream. As he continued, he could almost hear the hungry squeals of the pigs at feeding time; now there was only the frantic buzz of hundreds of flies. He clambered up the rickety ladder to the hayloft one last time. With the bales now sold and no longer filling the barn like a safety net, the heavy pine beams loomed high above the floor, far too high for him to scamper across as he had done in happier times.

Back outside, he noted how the front lawn which Tom had kept neatly trimmed was trampled and marked with tire treads, discarded paper plates and cigarette butts. Parts of the garden had seemingly been overrun by kids having fun while their parents were preoccupied by the auction's bargains. The chicken wire fencing which had kept the rabbits at bay was pushed over, and some of Jane's roses which she had lovingly tended for so many years were now flattened.

His tour complete, Charlie returned to his old red bike, pedaled down the long dusty laneway and headed home without a backward glance. The now-vacant farm was left to mourn in silence.

CHAPTER ELEVEN

As September plodded toward October, Charlie's life woes continued to rotate between isolation at school and discouragement at the river. His self-induced ostracism was compounded by the mysterious girl who had seemingly disappeared for good. Train after school for cross-country or keep his daily 4 p.m. vigil by the water? When Charlie inevitably succumbed to the hunger in his aching heart, he knew he must face Mr. Tavener.

"Come in!" Charlie half hoped he wouldn't answer.

"Sir, can I talk with you for a minute?" He wondered if his voice sounded as strangled as it felt.

"Yes, of course, sit down, Charlie. What's going on?" Mr. Tavener smiled warmly across his cluttered desk.

Charlie gulped. "I can't stay with the team, sir."

"What! Is it your grades? Need more time to study?"

"No, my grades are okay." He left the conversation hanging, hoping there would be no need for further interrogation. No such luck!

"Then what's the problem? Are you sick? Do you need a few more days before practice starts?"

This was not going at all well. In desperation, without forethought, Charlie lied: "My mother needs me at home. She's the one who isn't well." He was invested in his lie he could almost see her on her death bed, too weak to ask him for the bottle of red pills and cool drink of water that would assuage her raging fever.

He rearranged his face into what he hoped resembled an expression of worried concern coupled with a caregiver's burnout weariness.

"I need to be there to help her. She's really sick." Repeating the lie might make it more believable. Inwardly, he felt sick spinning these lies.

"I'm sorry to hear that, Charlie. I'm sorry to lose you. I think you have real potential to make it in distance competition. I hope your mom will be better by spring for track season. We want you back for sure."

Charlie felt an odd mixture of relief and guilt. "Thanks, Coach, for understanding. I'm sure she will be fine by then." And that was certainly no lie. She would definitely be fine by then, if not already. He figured it was best to end on a truth and got up to leave.

"One more thing, Charlie." Mr. Tavener stood up and came alongside his student. "What can I do? How be I phone Mrs. Thompson to wish her well from all of us at Brock?"

"Uh no, but thanks anyway. I'll let her know." Charlie's reply burst out of his mouth so quickly he feared it would be heard as the lie it most certainly was. Fortunately, the coach seemed not to notice. He gave Charlie a firm handshake, followed by an encouraging heavy pat-pat-pat on the boy's bony back.

* * *

Through the balance of September Charlie managed to keep pace with his classwork but without much enthusiasm. Since that first day of school, he had made a mistake common to most shy students—failing to raise his hand during discussion time. By the second week almost everyone else had spoken up: offering answers, expressing opinions, and making their presence known to teacher and peers alike. By now, the ritual was little more than a relaxed routine for most of his classmates. Hands raised skyward, some waving frantically to be noticed, others reluctant, but making an effort. The teacher pointing and calling the chosen one: boys by surname only, girls by Miss then surname. The chosen pupil standing beside his or her desk and delivering an appropriate response. The next waggling hand called upon to continue the discussion. Over and over.

In some classrooms, students who did not participate were left alone unless it was clear they weren't paying attention, when they were generally brought back to reality with a sarcastic comment or unexpected question on the topic under discussion. Occasionally, a frustrated teacher would substitute the tossed question with a tossed piece of chalk, or even banishment to the vice-principal's office.

But there were other teachers who were not content with non-involvement from their attentive but passive students. It was inevitable that this fate would eventually befall Charlie. It happened in history class toward the end of September. The day's lesson plan centered on the 1498 voyage of Jacque Cartier to the New World. After several others had put forth their ideas about the purpose of this epic journey, Miss Manton slowly surveyed the classroom until her dark blue eyes rested on Charlie. Earlier that month he had managed to get his coveted back-of-the-class spot when she offered the students one final opportunity to choose their own seating. Uncharacteristically, amid the ensuing scramble, Charlie assertively pushed his way to the last desk in the row beside the window. Others were more concerned with finding a seat beside a friend or next to an attractive member of the opposite sex. One notorious sleeper cleverly claimed a desk behind Hugh Blackstone, the mountainous captain of the Junior football team, where he could quietly nod off, his sleeping frame well hidden behind Hugh's bulk.

"Thompson, why do you think Cartier was so motivated to reach the New World?"

Charlie had quickly and instinctively lowered his eyes once he saw her looking his way. But it was too late. Now, hearing his name called, he was startled into frozen fear. Forgetting to stand, he offered the only answer that came to mind:

"He might have been looking for fish."

But no one heard his mumbled response. "Please stand before you answer," she continued.

She thinks I'm rude.

"Cartier might have been looking for fish—Miss."

By this time the entire class, curious at the sound of a voice they'd never heard, had collectively swiveled their heads in his direction. This was followed by a wave of giggles and snickering, beginning with Peter Senton and swiftly spreading across the room like ripples in a pond. Miss Manton, with one stern glance at her charges, quickly reversed the flow of laughter, until only Peter realized he was the only one still chuckling. An instant later he too lapsed into awkward silence.

"Class, Charlie's answer was not what I was looking for, but I think he has made a valid point. Let us not be so quick to judge next time."

After the bell had rung and the room was emptying, Miss Manton asked Charlie to stay behind for a moment. He feared he might be in trouble though he couldn't figure why. She gestured for him to sit close to her massive walnut desk which, at that moment, was cluttered with their handed-in class assignments. She lowered herself gracefully into the wooden swivel teacher's chair and smiled at him. The ensuing conversation surprised him.

"Charlie, I know from your written work that you have a good understanding of what we're studying but you never say anything during class discussion. Other students would benefit from your ideas."

"I've always been quiet in school."

"There is nothing wrong with being quiet. I am thinking, though, of next year when you'll have to give oral presentations in English class. If you don't get comfortable answering questions now, how will you manage a ten-minute talk in front of everyone? "

"Maybe I could just catch flu on those days." He was only half-joking.

"That's no answer," she replied with mock disapproval to let him know she understood the fear underlying the joke. "What if I offered to help you during lunch hour? I've worked before with other—shy students." Miss Manton paused, uncertain about using the term, but quickly decided to label what they both knew was the problem.

"What would you do?" he asked, both scared and hopeful.

"It's more like what would you do."

Charlie smiled at the friendly word-jousting. "OK, what would I be doing?"

They spent the next half-hour devising a strategy, neither noticing they'd forgotten to eat. It was a simple plan, inaugurated the very next day. Miss Manton presented an Agree-Disagree question to the class. Instead of verbal replies, all students were asked to stand to her right or left depending on their answer. After some jostling and the inevitable wisecracks from some of the boys, a long line stretched across the room. Those who strongly agreed or disagreed were at either end of the line while those uncertain clustered around the middle. And this was how Charlie found himself participating in a classroom "discussion" without having to utter a word.

The following week, Miss Manton began each class by again raising a question for debate, this time requiring each student to reply with a simple Yes or No. But while Charlie had awkwardly managed to join other silent classmates strung out along the continuum, he blanched at the thought of having to utter that single word. He felt a growing anxiety in his stomach as his classmates, one by one, up and down each row, said "Yes" or "No." When it was finally his turn.

Miss Manton smiled encouragingly and, to his surprise, he managed to pull a "Yes" from his reluctant mouth.

Two weeks later, shy Charlie was still mostly quiet but occasionally took part in a discussion; and the determined teacher was understandably pleased with her achievement. But what Charlie had not anticipated was falling in love with her! In his head, he knew it wasn't actually love, but how else to make sense of what was happening. He had once heard his mother laughingly use the term "crush" to describe an attraction she'd felt long ago toward some boy in grade ten. It was the closest he could come to understanding his own emotional turmoil.

His crush on Miss Manton probably began when he first entered Room 109. He had noticed her tall stature and slender body even before he thought about finding a seat and being inconspicuous. The whole month of September, whenever the lesson became boring, he focused his attention on the woman presenting it. He had noticed her sensible brown leather flat shoes, but grew suddenly more attentive the day she showed up in high heels, the rhythmic sound of their click-clicking on the hardwood floors preceding her entry into the room.

Miss Manton's skirts were appropriately and modestly mid-calf but still revealed slim ankles and shapely, toned legs. On warmer days, her bare arms looked tanned and smooth. But it was during that after-class meeting that he was, for the first time, close enough to admire her wide blue eyes and full cherry-coloured lips, and even detect a gentle waft of perfume. And despite the brevity of that meeting, he was overwhelmed by the combination of her physical closeness, her femininity, and her interest in him.

Charlie kept his feelings a secret. He neither acted upon them by seeking more time with her, nor did he disclose them to anyone. At night, when he reflected on the situation, he recognized a connection among Wonder Woman, the dark-haired girl by the river, and the beautiful Miss Manton: all were all part of the same evolution of a vague and growing awareness of his own sexuality.

* * *

"Why do you talk about Jesus so much?" asked Rachel, as she and Mary played crokinole on the Golson's screened-in back porch with its sagging tin roof. Rain tinkled off the metal, creating a irregular drumbeat of sound. The inclement September weather had forced the two friends inside on this Saturday afternoon.

Mary lined up her tan wooden disc, aiming for Rachel's black one partially hidden behind a rubber bumper. "Jesus is my friend. He can be yours too." Her shot missed its target and was swiftly removed from the board.

Rachel was certainly not opposed to having another friend, but she was confused about Jesus becoming one of them. "Isn't he dead? Anyway, I'm Jewish."

"He did die but got raised again. His disciples saw him. Now he's in heaven with God." "What's 'raised' mean?"

"It means that he came out of the cave where they put his body." "But how could his body walk?"

"Simple. God brought him back to life."

Rachel's face revealed a blend of skepticism and curiosity. "How can anybody come back to life? My zaydie died when he was ninety-four and he's still dead. Can he come back too?" She flicked her disc and expertly knocked one of Mary's pieces out of the fifteen circle and right off the board.

"Rachel, what about when you die? We all are going to die someday. We just don't know when. Do you know what happens when you die without knowing Jesus?"

Rachel looked up from the crokinole board, her face puzzled but intrigued. "What do you mean?"

"I never knew Jesus before I went to Faith Tabernacle and the pastor told me."

"What did he say?"

"That everyone has a choice in life; they can become a Christian and go to heaven, or not be a Christian and not go to heaven." She carefully avoided the word Hell. "I accepted him at our kids' group a while ago. I'm getting baptized in water soon," smiling proudly at the thought.

Though she was curious to know what Mary meant by accepting him, she had a more important question. "Did your sister know Jesus before she died?" She shot another piece squarely in the twenty hole. "I win."

Mary was stricken by Rachel's casual question. Crokinole no longer mattered.

"I'd better be getting home. The rain's stopped and I gotta help Mom." She left in a rush, leaving her friend clutching the winning piece in her hand and wondering about this Christianity business. Was being Jewish good enough for God? And if it weren't, what did that mean for Sarah?

In bed that night, Mary talked with God about her failure to convert Rachel.

"Jesus, I don't want Rachel to go to Hell when she dies. I will feel like I didn't try hard enough. Then I'll guilty of not doing what Pastor Hanson asked me to do. Can't you make her see what I'm talking about? And God, what about Sarah? She never got a chance to meet Jesus like I did. But that wasn't her fault. We only went to church on special days. I knew Jesus was born at Christmas and died at Easter, then got raised from the dead. But we never heard anything about him wanting to be our friend. Is she safe in heaven with both of you?"

Mary listened closely as if God were on the other end of a telephone line—except he didn't answer. She struggled to stay awake so she wouldn't miss his voice, but within a few moments had drifted off to a troubled sleep.

CHAPTER TWELVE

Maria's parents, Donato and Rosa Lupozzi, tried to keep a tight rein on their only daughter. At fifteen, she was a woman in body, not yet in wisdom. Back home in Calabria she would have been more sheltered. There was the convent school for girls, with stern Sunday admonitions about chastity and modesty from the village priest. There were the omnipresent watchful eyes of both grandmothers, Maria's *noninas,* as well as their vigilant neighbours up and down the cobblestone village streets. No opportunity for anyone going astray without being caught. And she would have been assigned many household chores—washing clothes in the old wringer machine, plucking fat green worms off the tomato vines, daily trips for bread and flour—activities which would have kept her too busy for boyfriends. Here, in her new home, she occasionally babysat for neighbours' children and did the supper dishes. From her parents' perspective, that still left too many hours of freedom.

The Lupozzis found Canada to be a far different place than their homeland. They had been lured to this new world by the expectation of a better life for their children. Jobs were plentiful, especially for anyone unafraid of hard manual labour. Donato and many of his countrymen brought with them skills in construction, assets much in demand to assist with Toronto's suburban growth. Other newcomers, both men and women, worked long shifts in factories or optimistically began their own little businesses.

* * *

Maria's father had little formal education beyond being able to read and write. Yet he was strong and eager to work. The family's arrival in Toronto had coincided with the beginning of construction of the Yonge Street subway, Canada's first. On September 8, 1949, the dig began.

The plan called for a combination of beneath-ground tunnelling—burrowing slowly through solid rock—and using a cost-saving open-cut, basically digging an above-ground trench.

Donato was hired on as a labourer, but soon given greater responsibilities. Over the next four years, he and hundreds of other workers removed thousands of cubic yards of dirt, hauled millions of bags of cement, lifted into place endless lengths of reinforced steel and got out of the way when the dynamiters moved into action to blast rock. Finally, on March 30, 1954, he proudly joined the crowds at Davisville Station to celebrate the job's completion. Of course, all the dignitaries were there, including Ontario's Premier, Leslie Frost, and the mayor, Allan Lamport. Donato, though, only had eyes for his family. He was proud of his contribution to the building of this transportation marvel and knew they were proud of him.

This new land truly offered opportunity, peace and prosperity, an inviting alternative to the shattered post-Mussolini economy of Southern Italy and the endless legacy of European conflict. Yet life here was not without challenge. In the brutal cold of a Canadian February, the Lupozzis wistfully yearned for home. On those frigid days, they fondly remembered their homeland's mild winters and allowed themselves a rare moment of regret. In summer, they missed the rows of olive groves and oranges fresh-picked from the tree. But all these changes were manageable; it was the social customs which created the bigger clash of cultural expectations.

Back home, especially in rural Italy, life for children was far more home-centered even through their teenage years. In Canada (and despite her attending a Catholic school,) Maria and her friends expected—and sometimes demanded—the same level of freedom enjoyed by their Canadian-born peers. At times, Donato and Rosa felt helpless, trying to balance the old world of traditional restrictions and unquestioning obedience to their authority with this new world of family discussion and negotiation. And at the very center of this tension was the issue of dating.

In Canada, dating no longer required a chaperone, a potentially dangerous oversight in their eyes. They set curfews for their daughter and she obeyed, albeit at times with a grumble of complaint. They ensured that her social life revolved around two or three close female friends, none of whom was as yet formally "going out" with a boy.

Unlike many Italian newcomers, the Lupozzis did not settle in the College Street area of Toronto and had built their own house further away from the core of the city, despite Donato's longer commute on the Bloor streetcar. They had found an inexpensive lot on the edge of the city, near the Humber River, with room for a garden to grow tomatoes and onions and eventually cultivate grape vines so that they could one day make homemade wine.

Donato and Rosa planned carefully for the building of their new home. From their network of fellow Italians, men were recruited to help dig the hole, lay cement blocks for the foundation and pour the concrete basement floor. Working mostly on weekends, Donato nailed the joists that would eventually underlie the first floor. Once these were in place and covered with plywood and tarpaper, the family had a temporary home.

Living in the basement literally put a roof over their heads while work slowly proceeded on the first and second floors. Casement windows allowed some sunlight and fresh air to penetrate the family's below-ground accommodation, which occasionally, in moments of petulance, Maria scornfully referred to it as a dungeon hole. Though Donato was stung by these thoughtless comments, he said nothing. Maria was too young to remember the war years which devastated the land of her birth. He was thankful just to be living in Canada, even in a "dungeon hole."

The Italian dictator, Mussolini, had rashly declared war against Britain in June, 1940. His ill-conceived goal was the expansion of his nation's African empire. Soon after that, Donato was conscripted into the Italian army. With hardly any time to harvest his wheat and fruit, he found himself aboard an overcrowded and stifling hot troop ship steaming across the Mediterranean to the shores of Libya and on to Abyssinia, the fabled Horn of Africa. In a long fume-belching truck convoy he was then transported across three days of dusty roads north into Eritrea, at that time part of Italian East Africa. January, 1941, found him dug in on top of a 400-foot-high plateau, defending the town of Keren against an impending British and Colonial Indian assault.

It wasn't just the oppressive heat and throat-drying thirst that Donato would always remember. In the recurring nightmare which relentlessly followed him to Canada, he would hear the thunder of the British guns sending wave after wave of artillery shells crashing into the sandy ground all around his hastily dug trench. Once again, he would watch with fear gripping his guts as Indian and Sikh infantry scrambled relentlessly up the steep slope, coming closer and closer to his position. He would see the glint of the fixed bayonets in the sun and the death-screams of those stuck on the other end. He'd wake up just as they were about to get him.

The Italians had fought bravely, determined to hold the town which was a vital railway and road link to Asmara, the capital city. British Hawker Hurricanes continually strafed the defenders, quickly followed by Wellesley bombers to complete the devastation. By the end of March, the battle was over, leaving 300 of his compatriots dead on the killing fields.

Donato had been among those war-weary soldiers who were eventually evacuated back to Italy, only to find themselves reluctant allies of the Germans who had occupied and defended his country. So when the American and British Eighth Armies, supported by the First Canadian Division, invaded Italy, Donato and his fellow soldiers were once again thrust into battle.

* * *

Now the family had laboured to make their new home livable. Insulation lined the walls to ward off cold drafts and dampness, sheets of plywood were nailed to the studs and then painted a warm light yellow. Two tiny bedrooms, a small kitchen and bathroom were created, plumbing and wiring added, and a barely sufficient coal furnace installed. On weekends, Donato and his friends began work on erecting the main floor structure. Because the home was situated just outside the city boundaries, building code enforcement was less rigid.

When Maria wasn't in school, socializing with friends or babysitting little Roberto down the road, she would walk to the Humber for a few moments of solitude unavailable anytime else. She loved the calming song of the river as it splashed over green mossy rocks and swirled around half-submerged fallen tree trunks.

It was during those contemplative times that her thoughts ventured into questions about future hopes and goals.

Maria knew she wanted marriage and motherhood. That was expected. But she also wanted education and a career, perhaps nursing or teaching. How she would manage these conflicting achievements was unclear, but not yet a pressing concern for a girl still in grade nine.

As was her custom, Maria stopped her casual exploration of the shoreline just before the sweeping bend which carried the Humber further south. She had never ventured beyond the curve, for to do so would place her out of sight of the house and beyond the watchful scrutiny of her mother. Rosa was in the habit of emerging from their basement home every so often to check on her daughter's whereabouts. Maria resolved that one day soon she would discover what lay beyond that bend. Meanwhile the river seemed to murmur happily, rejoicing in its own freedom.

CHAPTER THIRTEEN

The weather during the first half of October was mostly wet and cool, complicating Charlie's daily pilgrimage to the river. His parents wondered why anyone would bother going for an after-school walk in the rain but didn't press the matter. Dumping off his books at home, he would trudge through the mud, its sticky clay clinging to his rubber boots. Eventually, the sheer weight of the dirt forced him to stop long enough to scrape it off with a pointed stick. His father's old green raincoat shielded him from the worst of the steady drizzle, but he still returned home most days damp and chilled. On Saturday, he had gone earlier in the day because, for a change, he had more on his mind than the dark-haired girl. There was a World Series game scheduled for later that afternoon.

"Charlie, you'll catch your death. Take off those wet things at once and get yourself some hot chocolate." Katie shook her head at the sight of her bedraggled son coming in the back door, water dripping from his nose.

"I'm okay, it's really not that bad." Even Charlie didn't believe his own words but offered them up in a vain hope to reassure his mother he was still sane.

Doug glanced up from his newspaper. "You really enjoy wandering around in this weather, don't you?" he asked, even though he knew he'd be rewarded with the vaguest of answers.

"Yeah, I like watching the river now that it's running faster with all the recent rain."

Charlie was glad to follow his mother's direction, and took a large cup of hot chocolate to his bedroom where he quickly changed into dry pants and shirt. As quickly as he could, he returned downstairs where the ball game was just getting underway. Watching the World Series had become a father-son ritual these past few days.

The large TV set was already glowing, its blue-grey screen casting a flickering light over the curtained dimness of the mid- afternoon. Doug had tuned in to channel 4, the NBC affiliate from Buffalo carrying the game. The 20-foot spindly aluminum antenna mounted on the Thompson roof ensured clear reception.

The New York Giants had already jumped in to an early 7-0 lead over the Indians. They had won the first three games of the series against a team with the best won-lost record that year. Urged on by a raucous hometown crowd of 78,000, the Cleveland Indians mounted a brief comeback, but still fell short, 7-4. Doug and Charlie talked animatedly about the over-the-shoulder catch Willie Mays performed in center field during the first game in the Polo Grounds. With his back turned completely toward home plate, Number 24 had tracked down and caught a long fly ball hit by Vic Wertz. In Doug's opinion, that had surely demoralized the Indians.

Father and son liked these relaxing times together. Sitting side by side, they found conversation flowed easier than in their rare face-to-face dialogues which too often left them squirming in awkward silence. Baseball gave them common ground.

Earlier that year, they had made a point of attending several games at Maple Leaf Stadium where the AAA Leafs were leading the league. It was the closest to major league action Toronto would experience for several more decades. Under the inspired and innovative ownership of Jack Kent Cooke, the Leafs regularly drew 20,000 loyal fans. Even before Jackie Robinson, he had brought in several top players from the Negro League who had been denied access to the majors.

When the Leafs played away games, Charlie and his father would listen on the radio. CKEY's Joe Crysdale and Hal Kelly provided exciting play-by-play coverage of all the action. It wasn't until years later that Charlie learned they were not actually situated in far-away stadiums such as Havana, but were in fact broadcasting from a Toronto studio, reproducing the game with details relayed from the site by telegraph.

NATIONAL WEATHER SERVICE:
A "very weak" easterly wave west of the Bahamas was watched during the night by the Miami weather bureau – Easterly winds, bands of bad weather sometimes develop into hurricanes.

Miami Daily News, October 5, 1954

CHAPTER FOURTEEN

It was on a Tuesday in early October when Charlie's luck finally changed, though that's not how the day began. Having had to return home to retrieve a forgotten homework assignment, he was late for school. That mistake resulted in him standing uncertainly outside the door to Room 14 where the class of 9D was already immersed in a struggle with French grammar. He dreaded the sudden classroom hush, the collective stares from thirty pairs of eyes, the inevitable snide comment from some bold joker. The journey across the front of the class would seem a mile long before he reached his seat in the back corner. It would be more merciful to spin around and go home.

Instead, to Charlie's own surprise, he grasped the doorknob, took a deep breath, and made his reluctant entry. All he had feared was quickly realized in the next few seconds. Even Mr. Marky added to his discomfort with a scornful comment about buying a new alarm clock.

Period two was gym class. And the bad day got worse. On a typical morning in early October, the grade nine students would be outside, with the boys learning about football techniques and the girls playing soccer, each gender segregated at their own end of the field. Today, the rain had forced them back indoors.

Brock Collegiate was proud of its huge gym. It had a twenty-foot sliding partition that divided the space in two halves, enabling separate classes for males and females. Today, however, things were different.

Mr. Tavener directed the 9D boys into the usual three squads, six in each row, spread across the gym and lined up from tallest to shortest. As the tallest boy, that put Charlie, in the front squad, at the far end of his row. They all expected the teacher to announce a game of floor hockey.

"Gentlemen, in a moment we'll be joining Miss Filder's class for volleyball." He was instantly interrupted by raucous shouts and hollering. "Settle down, guys, show some respect." Though spoken in a low-key voice, they were immediately obeyed. Mr. Tavener had played football in college, weighed about 225 pounds and was known for banging unruly students against the metal lockers in the change room if he didn't get what he wanted.

Charlie was self-conscious about his thin frame, especially standing next to more muscular classmates. He had never expected to be exposed, in tee-shirt and shorts, to the female half of 9D. But before he had time to fret, the partition slowly opened. On the other side, gradually coming into view were the girls, lined up in their own three squads, also from tallest to shortest. Charlie felt, perhaps irrationally, that each young woman was staring at him.

Miss Filder then proceeded efficiently to pair up the students in boy-girl combinations. Charlie found himself standing next to the tallest of his female classmates, an already blushing blonde pony-tailed girl whose name he still didn't know. She looked equally uncomfortable in her blue bloomer uniform which failed to conceal skinny white legs and a flat chest.

As instructed, each of the twenty pairings proceeded to bump a volleyball back and forth, most enjoying a relaxed familiarity and comfort level. In contrast, Charlie and his partner grimly and silently practised the routine until, mercifully, the whistle blew to signal the end of the class.

Following gym class, most of the boys showered, Charlie not among them. Mingling with a group of loud naked male teenagers was more togetherness than he could handle. He was content to put up with his sweaty body for a few hours.

The school day finally ended, leaving Charlie feeling more morose than usual. The sense of not fitting in was overpowering.

"How was school today?" Katie inquired of her son, trying to make the question sound more routine than it was. In truth, she was still concerned about the boy's obvious lack of friends and social isolation.

"I got there late but it was okay." His answer gave away little of the inner sadness and uselessness he had brought home with his books and an empty lunch bag. "I'm going out, I'll be home for dinner." He put on boots and raincoat before quietly heading out the back door and into the steady drizzle.

He saw her before she noticed him.

* * *

The dark-haired girl was back but standing on the far side of the Humber, gazing at the water by her feet. She too was wearing rain gear: a bright red waterproof cape which shielded her upper body from the elements, heavy brown slacks, and yellow rubber boots.

Charlie was now directly opposite, transfixed and afraid to move a step further in case, like some desert mirage, she might suddenly disappear. In the next moment, she abruptly looked up, startled at the sight someone else sharing her solitude. Then she broke the silence.

"What are you doing walking in the rain?" She smiled.

"Just walkin'." It wasn't until later that night as Charlie replayed the conversation over and over in his mind that he realized with regret how dumb that answer was.

"Do you come here often?" she continued, seemingly not put off by this inane conversation.

"Pretty much every day after school."

"Why would you do that?" Her smile grew broader.

Charlie almost answered truthfully until he caught himself. "Like to walk, I guess."

"Even in the rain?"

"Yeah, rain's okay." This back-and-forth banter was becoming ridiculous. Water was dripping off his nose.

"Well, I have to get going. My parents don't like me out wandering around." Her smile turned almost apologetic.

Out of nowhere, Charlie found a surprising and sudden boldness. "My name is Charlie."

"I'm Maria. I live right over there." She pointed to a half-finished house about 200 yards back from the river. Charlie was startled; it looked as if the above-ground part had been sliced off.

"I haven't seen you at Brock."

"I go to St. Francis. I'm in grade nine."

"Me too. Grade nine I mean, not St. Francis. I go to Brock." He sounded like a three- year-old and wondered if she were humouring him.

Maria then turned toward home and, it would seem, out of his life forever. Motivated by a combination of desperation and a desire for connection, he yelled over the noise of the babbling water.

"Will you come back tomorrow?"

She looked over her shoulder as she continued to move through the tall wet grass. "Yes."

Charlie remained frozen in time and space until she disappeared around the front of her amputated house. Triumphantly, but gently, he carried her "Yes" home with him, like a newly discovered precious gem.

That evening Charlie surprised his parents by sending himself to bed an hour earlier than usual, offering no explanation beyond a vague excuse of being tired. His real motivation was an impatient irrational hope that by advancing his bedtime routines, he could magically hasten the arrival of Wednesday.

* * *

The next day arrived on schedule but then proceeded to advance more slowly than he could have imagined. Getting to school early didn't alter the reality of having to sit through class after class, listening without absorbing a single word of wisdom dispensed by his teachers. Even the supportive Miss Manton noticed his preoccupation, though let it go without comment.

Charlie tried staring at the large clock mounted on the wall, telepathically willing it to move its hands faster. But each hour remained a full sixty minutes!

At 3:30 p.m. came the long-awaited dismissal bell, and Charlie left so quickly he was dodging slower pedestrians as he broke into his practised jog along Bloor Street. He moved as if pulled by an invisible force over which he had no control. That same energy soon propelled him through the back door where its sudden bang announced his breathless arrival to Katie.

"What's the rush?" she wondered aloud.

"I promised to meet someone after school" he offered vaguely, all the while eying the stairs which he must immediately ascend to change his clothes.

"Can't they wait a few moments 'til you have a snack?" She chose the neutral "they" to avoid the appearance of prying into whether the object of all this fuss might be a girl.

"No, we're meeting right after school."

"Are you going for your usual walk by the river?"

"Yes, that's where we're meeting." Then he was gone, up the stairs, his big feet banging on each step and into the bedroom. She heard the door slammed in haste.

Charlie then faced an unexpected dilemma. The sun was shining for a change, and the day was warm for October. What should he wear—though surely anything would be an improvement over a raincoat and boots. He finally decided on a pink long-sleeved shirt and new charcoal grey pants, fashionably baggy at the knees and drawn tight at the ankles.

Ten minutes later, he had crossed Westdale on a run, then cut through Jackson Park before arriving, breathless with excitement, at the high bank overlooking the Humber. He spotted a few younger boys walking slowly along the river's edge, looking for frogs, but they soon disappeared around the bend. Charlie was alone. The water moved steadily southward, indifferent to his vigil, its calm, steady flow in sharp contrast with his racing heart and growing worry.

What if I've missed her? Maybe she changed her mind. What if she had a detention and is stuck at school? No way would she not come otherwise.

As the minutes passed and late-afternoon shadows began to darken the water, his hopes faded with the setting sun. He gave no thought to the passing of the supper hour. Finally, as the bullfrogs chorused a mocking serenade, he accepted the bitter reality that she wasn't coming.

Defeated, he turned slowly toward home and the inevitable scolding he would receive for being late.

It didn't matter. Nothing did.

CHAPTER FIFTEEN

K atie waited nervously in Pastor Hanson's office. The small room was lined with maple plywood, creating both warmth and coziness, an atmosphere she was unable to appreciate at that moment. Dominating the room was a large solid-looking walnut desk with a photo of his family prominently displayed. Scattered pieces of foolscap on which he had scribbled notes, presumably the beginnings of next Sunday's sermon, lay strewn across the desktop along with three different hymn books and an opened Bible. On the opposite wall, a tall bookcase seemed to sag under the combined weight of other thick Bibles, a set of Commentaries on The Scriptures, several Biblical dictionaries, and a well-worn copy of *Roget's Thesaurus*.

A small window, bordered with lemon yellow, cotton curtains—Mrs. Hanson's handiwork—brightened the space considerably even in the early morning light.

Katie fought a recurring impulse to slip away. She dreaded the pending conversation, which she knew would be awkward and embarrassing. She could be gone before he arrived. Or, more politely, await his appearance, then announce some immediate situation to which she must attend without delay. Or schedule another meeting, which would buy her more time to gain some courage—or invent another excuse to avoid the conversation altogether.

Katie's decision was made for her by the sudden entrance of Pastor Hanson, accompanied by his wife.

Although initially surprised by Gloria's unexpected presence, Katie found herself immediately at ease, as she was extremely fond of this kind gentle lady. She also took note of the pastor's informal appearance. Today, he wore a white short-sleeved dress shirt, without a tie and suit jacket. She glanced at his bare arms, sinewy and tanned, then quickly looked away.

"Mrs. Thompson, I hope you don't mind my bringing Mrs. Hanson along with me. I always value her perspective when it comes to situations involving our church ladies." Katie thought his choice of the word "situations" was diplomatically neutral—as was his use of "ladies" instead of "women." It occurred to her that he also might feel awkward alone with a woman in his office. She then realized that the large family picture served to remind any female parishioner sitting in his office—maybe even the pastor himself—that he was a married man.

"Not at all, I'm glad to see you again, Mrs. Hanson."

"Please call me Gloria. May I call you Katie?" There was no suggestion of extending this familiarity to her husband. "Pastor Hanson" he would remain.

"Yes, of course, and thank you for agreeing to see me on such short notice. I know how busy your schedule must be." Of course, Katie had no idea if it were, but it seemed the right thing to say.

"No problem at all. We're always happy to see folks. That's an important part of the ministry here at Faith. What was it that you wished to see us about?"

Now came the dreaded hard part. "You remember about a month ago when you preached on how sin gets in the way of having a relationship with God?"

Pastor Hanson looked a bit puzzled. He had thought he preached about sin most Sundays.

Then he remembered the sermon that Katie was referring to. It had centered on the idea that unconfessed sin contaminates our relationships with both God and other people. He had used the Biblical story of King David, who not only had committed adultery with the wife of a soldier, but had then sent the unsuspecting husband out to battle, having pre-arranged that he would be killed in combat.

Katie remembered his graphic description of King David's plight: bones melting with guilt, unable to sleep or eat. Then, the best part of the story; David's cry for God's forgiveness as recorded in Psalms—"create in me a clean heart"—which had instantly resulted in a wonderful sense of freedom and release. Pastor Hanson often struggled inwardly over how David could just dump all that sin and wrong behaviour so easily, but always rebuked himself for questioning the Biblical account. Katie's theology however was unsophisticated; she was unaware that the resultant death of David's infant son was a scriptural reminder that wrongdoing, even if forgiven, could still lead to tragic consequences.

Cleansing not consequence was on Katie's mind.

"Yes, I was talking about David, wasn't I?" He leaned forward and nodded, inviting her to continue. There was a time when he would have continued with a lengthy summary of that sermon, but, over the course of their ministry together, Gloria had gently taught him how to listen as well as preach.

"It happened during the War. Doug was away and something happened, something I'm not proud of, something I still regret." Katie looked at Gloria for understanding and reassurance. "There was a bachelor whom Doug occasionally brought home for dinner before the war. They worked together, and Doug felt he could use some good home-cooked meals. When a job suddenly opened up in Penticton, he left; he couldn't join up like Doug because of his eyesight. Later on, he was back in Toronto and came to visit me and Doug. Of course, Doug was already at training camp, but the friend didn't know, and I guess I was still angry that Doug had signed up..."

Katie stopped at this point, wiping away a tear which was slowly sliding over her cheekbone. She hoped irrationally that the rest of the story would tell itself so she wouldn't have to say it aloud.

"I know this must be hard for you." Gloria offered both a Kleenex and support in the same motion. "Can you continue?"

Pastor Hanson waited patiently. In his earlier counselling ministry, he would have bombarded her with questions to get to the heart of the matter more quickly.

"This man—I won't say his name—we spent some time together that evening and one thing led to another. Neither of us intended to, but I was lonely and so was he." Although it lasted only a moment, silence then filled the room for what seemed forever.

Now the hardest part. Gloria realized she would have to be the one to move them forward. Katie was obviously stuck, and her husband would never initiate talk with a female about intimate sexual matters.

"Katie, how far did you go with this man?"

"We… we… had… relations. He touched me where only Doug had touched me… and I let him do it." Her face reddened and she felt a sticky sweat on her body. But the worst was over.

Pastor Hanson finally spoke. "I'm glad you felt trusting enough to share this with us. It must have been hard to carry such a secret all these years."

"After it happened, I wanted so much to tell Doug when he was home on leave, but that would have destroyed the little time he had with Charlie. Then after the war ended, he was home for good and we started a new chapter in our lives. I decided that it was better left unsaid. But coming to church these past months, I realize something like this doesn't just go away."

"So Doug has no idea about what happened?" Gloria phrased the question carefully, ensuring no condemnation accompanied her words.

"No."

"And what about this other man? Did you see him again?" asked Pastor Hanson.

"No. I felt so guilty, the least I could do was make sure it never happened again."

"So you never saw him again?" asked Gloria, inserting herself back into the conversation.

"Never. In fact, he went right back to British Columbia. I think he felt as badly as I did."

"I see two issues here," said the pastor, after a pause. "The first is to seek God's forgiveness. We can do that right now if you want to."

"Yes, that's why I came! I want to make things right with him."

Pastor Hanson felt decidedly more at ease, now that he was walking on more familiar ground. Over the next few moments, he confidently led Katie through an explanation of what the Bible said about sin. Only when he was assured she understood what he called "God's Word," did he move toward prayer. He would begin a prayer of forgiveness, then she would repeat his words, but only if she felt they reflected her own thoughts and wishes.

The three adults moved their chairs into a circle so they could join hands. "O God, your son said—" (For an instant Katie pondered why God needed reminding about what his son said but quickly checked herself.)—"for where two or three are gathered together in my name, there am I in the midst of them." Katie dutifully, but genuinely, repeated each sentence. As her contribution Gloria added a heartfelt "Yes, Lord" or "Thank you, Jesus" whenever she felt moved to do so.

In a flash, it was done. The pastor reassured his parishioner that, indeed, God had forgiven her sin; past wrongdoing no longer blocked her relationship with Him. Like David, Katie felt a weight had been removed from her shoulders and, wiping tears of relief, thanked them both. It was a deep release to have shared most of that long-buried secret, to no longer be carrying it alone. And to know that God could still love her was a miracle in itself. She allowed herself a secret moment of doubt, wondering if divine love would be sustained if she told the rest of her story, but quickly set it aside.

"One more thing, Katie, Remember I said there were two issues to deal with."

Surprised and confused, she had forgotten. She felt so much better, wasn't that enough for now? Or did Pastor Hanson sense she had more to confess?

"Katie, what about Doug? You said he doesn't know." Pastor Hanson had moved them to new uncharted waters and, suddenly, she wasn't sure she wanted to go along. A quick glance in Gloria's direction told her the other woman was as unsure of where they were headed as she was.

"No, we just moved on with our marriage. Isn't the past the past, especially after what we've done today? Thank you again, both of you." She was definitely feeling uncomfortable again, wanting this renewed discussion to end right then.

"Katie, you need to think carefully. Don't you think that part of this new beginning should include a confession to Doug? No, I don't expect you to answer right away, but will you promise to think about the fact that there is still a deep secret between you and your husband."

"Of course, Pastor, but really I just want to thank you for the advice and the prayers— both of you."

With that, Katie formally shook his hand and received her usual warm hug from Gloria. Then she stepped back into the bright daylight and felt a fresh breeze envelop her as she started down the sidewalk. Behind, she had left part of the dark secret which had haunted her for twelve years. Ahead was the unresolved question raised by her pastor about telling Doug, not to mention that other unconfessed part of her story she still carried and which still burned deep. Had what she'd done resulted in God taking Sarah's life? And there was yet one more secret she had not even fully admitted to herself.

Gloria and Frank Hanson sat quietly for a moment in the tiny office, each inwardly reflecting on the past hour's conversation. The pastor's wife was the first to break the silence.

"You were very gentle with Katie this morning, Frank."

"I suppose. But who am I to judge?"

"You're thinking of your own past, aren't you?"

"Gloria, you know as well as I do the story of the woman who committed adultery. Jesus stepped in and told that group of men who were going to stone her: 'Let he who is without sin cast the first stone.' I am certainly not without sin in my own life."

"You've come a long way since then. I'm very proud of you."

"I've got you to thank. And God too, of course."

And with that, they each fell silent.

* * *

In the late 1940s, the city's self-proclaimed *"Toronto the Good,"* and its carefully cultivated image was shaken by gang violence. Arguably the most notorious of these groups were the Beanery Boys. Dovercourt Road was their home territory, and rival gangs knew to stay clear. Frankie Hanson had been at Wasaga Beach during the worst of the riot which saw blood spilled and limbs broken by baseball bats and fists. Too young for the war service which might have given him maturity and purpose, Frankie had dropped out of Southdale High school, worked part-time, and spent the bulk of his leisure hours hanging out on street corners. While jobs and training opportunities were plentiful, they were primarily reserved for returning veterans.

Frankie prided himself on looking cool in his black drape pants, held up by a belt with a large silver buckle. In summer a white cotton tee-shirt with sleeves rolled shoulder-high displayed his bulging biceps while conveniently storing his pack of Export A cigarettes. His large flat feet, fashionably ensconced in white buck shoes, completed the swaggering look he had spent an hour trying to create. His most treasured possession was his dead grandfather's round silver-embossed pocket watch, safely stored in his left pants pocket and attached to his trousers by an equally flashy gold chain. He enjoyed pulling it out, more for show than to check the hour. In winter, he shivered beneath a black leather jacket more designed for appearance than practicality, and prowled the corner with a menacing presence designed to hide how he really felt.

Before abandoning his family, Frankie's father had taught him that violence got fast results, while his mother pushed herself into exhaustion trying to raise five rowdy kids. Even in the midst of a chaotic household, Frankie soon found himself lonely and alone. The gang offered belonging and stability—and a model of rough masculinity that matched his father's way. Which is where Gloria Jansen had found him.

Gloria was nineteen years old, and a faithful member of the large active youth group at a United Church down the road from the Beanery Boys home turf. Her minister, Rev. Caldon, was a visionary with a heart of compassion for the wider community beyond its red brick walls. His young people were challenged every Friday night to reach out to that larger world with the "Good News" of God's love—especially for outcasts: the drinkers, the families living off their welfare cheques, the homeless. Even troublemakers like Frankie Hanson. So when Gloria and Frankie first met, well-meaning but naïve idealism ran headlong into a crude reality.

It was a snow-blowing Saturday afternoon in January, 1947, a day when cumbersome winter coats, woollen toques, knitted mittens and rubber galoshes were donned like a knight's armour to protect against the raging elements.

"Hi, my name is Gloria. What's yours?" she asked, extending her gloved hand and with a wide smile. She was accompanied by two well-groomed young and nervous men from the church, in keeping with the minister's directive that they stay in small groups for encouragement and protection.

"I see you brought your bodyguards with you," replied Frankie, taking a menacing step closer to them. Instinctively and in unison, all three took a prudent step backward.

"Do you think I should need bodyguards?" she asked sweetly, hoping the scary stranger wouldn't hear her heart pounding in fear.

"Depends on what you want." He slowly let his eyes wander up and then down her body. Gloria was thankfully well hidden under loose-fitting brown slacks, a thick white woollen knee-length coat and sensible ankle boots. When his lascivious scrutiny eventually returned to her face, he was startled to encounter blue eyes resolutely staring back at him, her smile unchanged. She again politely asked for his name.

"It's really Frank but they call me Frankie." He softened for a brief moment.

Gloria handed him a colourful brochure describing the youth group and its Friday evening programs. "We thought you might be stopping by for some fun."

"What the hell do you consider fun?" He scoffed, mimicking her gentle voice.

"Well, whatever you and your friends want to do, I suppose." And as that unfiltered sentence left her lips, Gloria wished with all her heart she could take it back. Like toothpaste, though, once out of the tube there was no return.

Frankie of course pounced on her words. "Well, me and my friends have lots of things we want to do. Are there any other good-looking dames to entertain us?"

By then, one of the "bodyguards" had heard enough. He stepped forward aggressively to stand protectively in front of Gloria. "Watch your language in front of a lady."

"And if I don't?" Frankie jabbed a finger into his antagonist's chest. This supposedly community-friendly outreach was rapidly going in the wrong direction. Gloria intervened.

"Look, all we want to do is to let you know our group meets Fridays, you would be welcomed. Or we can open our recreation facilities on Saturdays or in the evening, if that's better. You can play basketball or volleyball, or you could bowl."

Despite his large size, Frankie shunned most sports in fear of looking clumsy and unskilled. However, bowling was a different story. The Beanery Boys had frequented Tom's Bowlerama on Dovercourt, until they were permanently kicked out for bad behaviour. Despite a reflexive suspiciousness whenever anyone seemed to care about him, Frankie felt himself slowly drawn in by Gloria's invitation.

The following Saturday afternoon, he decided to check out these church folks and their building. In a lower level, under the impressive sanctuary, several older adults were playing a gentle version of volleyball, more intent on fun than competition. An even older group was enjoying a leisurely game of shuffleboard. A table of euchre players occupied one corner of the huge room. Frankie stood awkwardly, unsure whether to back out or stroll casually around the room. He didn't like this anxious feeling of not being on his own turf. Still, it was a lot warmer than outside. Then he saw Gloria making coffee in a well-equipped kitchen. A few seconds later, she noticed him. After whispering a silent prayer to find the right words, she took off her apron, hung it carefully over the back of a chair and came out to greet the nervous newcomer.

"I'm glad you came, Frankie," she simply said with a genuine smile.

In response, he shuffled his feet, rocked back and forth on his heels and, frighteningly, found himself lost for words. Crude street talk or sexual innuendo was suddenly off the table. And she had remembered his name.

"Hi, Gloria, I'm glad I came too." And he surprised himself by meaning what he had just said.

* * *

Frankie's journey to faith began that afternoon but, like many of life's paths, the trail led through hilltops and valleys, with a few detours added along the way. He resisted the believability of the Bible stories, struggled to give up cigarettes and cussing, and found the expectation of Sunday morning church decidedly less preferable to sleeping in. But he couldn't resist falling in love with Gloria.

For her part, and despite being initially intrigued by his bad boy image, Gloria primarily saw Frankie as a project, someone who needed to "get saved." Gradually that changed. As he began to let down his guard and risk being more transparent within the safety of her friendship, she discovered that under his swagger and assertiveness was a hunger for love and acceptance. It wasn't long before they found themselves in a committed relationship.

It was January, 1949, when Frankie finally "got saved." Gloria was overjoyed when he agreed to be part of a young people's group attending a Youth for Christ rally in Chatham, Ontario. During that day-long ride from Toronto on a bumpy chartered bus, Gloria's mood alternated between a growing excitement over finally hearing the Canadian evangelist, Leighton Ford, and a gnawing anxiety that Frankie would reject his call for salvation. Already famous and successful in leading large crusades across North America and England, Ford was the same age as Frankie. It was this youthfulness as well as his powerful sermons, that drew crowds of the younger generation to hear his message of hope.

Ford's advance team had long ago contacted local clergy in this small southwestern community. As it was necessary to secure a venue which would fit the occasion. A church sanctuary would certainly have enough seating but might not appeal to the expected unchurched crowd. The high school auditorium was rejected as being too closely associated with academics. But every Ontario town had a hockey arena and that's where the crusade would be held.

When the long but upbeat service wound down to the inevitable altar call for salvation, Frankie went forward without hesitation, knelt with several young men and women beside Ford, and accepted Christ as his saviour. Of course, he hardly knew what most of the words really meant, but he did know that something or someone was calling him to that spot.

Throughout the altar call, Gloria sat transfixed in the arena's uncomfortable bleacher seats, her prayers for Frankie answered literally before her tear-filled eyes. Riding on the bumpy bus back toward Toronto, she remained deep in thought. She and Frankie had talked of marriage, although she was fully aware of the Biblical warning against the "unequally yoked," i.e. marriage between a believer and a non-believer. Rather than violate that directive, she would wait for God to guide him toward belief, so that they might follow Jesus together.

But while her prayers were answered, a heavy doubt remained: what if this were a "conversion of convenience?" What if it were his desire to marry her that motivated him, not the love of the Lord? Was his conversion real or simply a ploy to soften her reluctance?

"You've been really quiet, are you tired?" asked Frankie, with a look of undisguised concern.

"No, I've just been thinking..."

"About—?"

Gloria paused, then decided to risk their relationship by sharing what weighed heavy on her heart. At first, Frankie listened without comment, as an inner frustration built. Finally, he could hold it in no longer. "How can I prove to you that what happened tonight was real, something I did for me? Yes, for us as well. But for me, even if there was no us."

"I'm sorry. I know it was real, and I'm overjoyed." While Gloria's admission of regret was sincere as well as her sense of joy, both she and Frankie knew it was more a statement of faith than of certainty.

Over the next few months, however, faith slowly grew into fact. Frankie continued to evolve in his religious journey, joining Gloria in church every Sunday and meeting regularly with Rev. Caldon. While she was obviously pleased that he was receiving spiritual guidance and counsel, Gloria was genuinely shocked when Frankie excitedly revealed a second reason for those meetings: he was considering the ministry.

"I know it sounds crazy for someone like me to be talking this way, but Rev. Caldon says it's a 'calling,' that God draws certain people to be preachers, no matter what's in their background. Like the Apostle Paul, who started out persecuting Christians and ended up being their best missionary."

"So you might become the latest Apostle?" Gloria's wide smile betrayed the fact that she was kidding; but to ensure there was no mistaking her words, she added more seriously, "Frankie, I really am proud of you and will support you all the way."

Six months later, on a glorious Thanksgiving weekend in 1949 the happy couple was married. In September of the following year, Frank (as he now preferred to be called) began studies at Pambrooke Bible College and moved with his bride into the married students residence on campus. Given his lack of a high school diploma, a door to acquiring a university degree, followed by seminary studies, would not be open for him. By contrast, Pambrooke's more open admission standards allowed them to accept a few older mature students on a one-semester trial basis, If successful, he could then move on toward earning a Bible College diploma and eventual ordination.

With Gloria working full-time at Loblaws, the couple just managed to support themselves. Despite past disdain for studying, the highly motivated Frank worked hard to maintain his passing grades. In June 1951, with his proud mother and Gloria's parents in attendance, Frank Hanson graduated with a diploma in theology.

Faith Tabernacle had been prayerfully seeking a pastor after their beloved and long- serving Rev. Manniter retired. The Church Board took a chance on the new graduate and invited him to preach for a call.

Frank Hanson lacked any pastoral experience beyond the three-month internship during his last semester plus two summers running a youth camp in Haliburton. But it was his life on the streets of Toronto that attracted the Board's attention. For a congregation with a deeply held vision for outreach to the city's disadvantaged and marginalized, who better than a former street person to lead this ministry? And when Frank then stood in their pulpit to deliver a powerful, (albeit still rough around the edges) sermon, the congregation unanimously voted to invite him to be their pastor—and ultimately, Katie's confessor.

HURRICANE HAZEL'S PATH UNDETERMINED

The storm was moving in a west-north-westerly direction at about 19 miles an hour at 6 am today, practically parallel with the Venezuelan coast. It is about 1200 miles southeast of Miami. Movement toward the west or northwest is indicated during the next 12 hours.

Miami Daily News, October 7, 1954

CHAPTER SIXTEEN

I t was on Thursday, the day after Charlie's lonely vigil by the river, that the rain returned.

As he trudged along Bloor to school, water trickled down his cheeks, giving expression to the hidden tears he was barely able to suppress. Against his mother's advice, he had refused to wear his long, black rubber raincoat. Somehow, the cold wet deluge pounding on his unprotected back and shoulders served as a kind of self-flagellation, a fit punishment for indulging in such impossible expectations.

By midday, his mood had lifted somewhat. Even gazing occasionally, and surreptitiously, at Miss Manton's crossed legs displayed under her desk was only a temporary distraction. He wondered, should he risk even more rejection by trying to like someone else, another girl like Maria, if one could even be found in his school?

Right away, this yearning, almost physically painful, was offset by a self-protective urge, an overwhelming need to avoid further disappointment by staying away from girls, the source of that last painful experience.

Last evening, Charlie had begun his homework, a writing assignment on The Merchant of Venice, only to find himself scribbling *Maria* all over the notepaper. In his mind, he replayed every second of their encounter. He envisioned the shy smile framed by her long dark hair, her bright red, rain cape which reminded him of Little Red Riding Hood alone in the forest. He would save her from the wolf—any danger in the world—if only she had come back.

By the time the dismissal bell finally rang, Charlie had made up his mind. Maybe it was not too late to give up hope. He would return to the river that very afternoon. Two hours later, it was the same story. Once again, Maria had not shown up. That evening, he retreated to his imaginary world of comic books, a place where he was never disappointed. There he could rescue an endangered Amazon princess, win her grateful admiration and, more critically, her love.

Friday promised to be a better day, since it was almost the weekend, giving him a much-needed break from school. He had seen more than enough student couples, flaunting their happy connectedness in the halls and cafeteria.

As it turned out, Charlie's distraught condition was not totally disguised. On arriving home, wet and miserable, the boy was surprised to encounter Doug already home in the kitchen, enjoying a cup of tea with Katie.

"Dad, is everything all right?"

"Of course. Work on the Planter home was shut down with the rain. I don't mind an early start to the weekend." He looked fondly at Katie.

"And this gives me someone to share my 4 o'clock tea with," Katie added brightly. "Goodness knows my son never stays around long enough after school to keep me company," she teased with a smile.

"Will you be off again this afternoon on your mysterious adventures?" Doug joined his wife in the fun.

"Mind your own business, both of you!" Abruptly turning his back, Charlie fled up the stairs, slamming his bedroom door a moment later.

Both parents exchanged looks of surprise. Doug stared at Katie, dumbfounded. "What set him off so quickly?" But while Katie usually had greater insights into their children's behaviour, this time she was equally baffled.

"I don't know, Doug, he's not been himself these past few days. One minute sky high, the next down in the dumps. Maybe you should go up and try to speak with him."

Doug didn't relish the idea of this brand of conversation. He and Charlie were more comfortable sharing a ball game or a trip to the farm. Nevertheless, he was not one to shirk parental duties, especially if either of the children was in pain. He followed the path his son had just travelled, albeit less dramatically, and gently knocked on the door, half expecting a barrage of anger to come crashing back at him.

"Charlie, can I come in?"

"Yeah, if you want."

"Your mom and I are worried about you. You seem upset about something."

"I'm sorry I yelled at you."

"I'm not concerned about that but I really do want to know what's going on. Is everything okay at school? Are you in trouble with a teacher?" Doug sat down on the edge of the bed. Charlie lay with his head propped on a pillow against the headboard, his face half-hidden behind a comic book.

He had never before been tempted to share this deeper part of himself with his parents. Though of course, he had never before felt such inner sadness and loneliness. When Sarah died, it was different. The whole family shared the pain and the loss. And though their common grieving remained unspoken, Charlie had never felt isolated. Now he did. Now, for the first time, he yearned to break free of his emotional exile; he wanted to let his father carry part of the burden. Maybe he could even offer some advice about getting past this emptiness. He took a deep breath.

"I met this girl." In spite of himself, Doug instinctively and instantly pictured a pregnancy, then just as quickly realized that was not where this story was going. He also felt a sudden sense of vicarious pleasure knowing that his son had finally discovered the opposite sex. He knew to say nothing, his silence and attentiveness encouraging his boy to continue.

"I met her on Tuesday at the river; I really liked her. She promised to come back on Wednesday but never showed up. Yesterday was the same thing, I went back and she wasn't there. Now I don't know what to do. She obviously didn't want to be friends, if you can be that when you've only met once." Charlie was red-faced, and Doug feared he might begin to cry, making it more awkward for both of them.

Katie was usually stoic in dealing with whatever life brought her way. When she would occasionally express some troubling feelings— sadness or fear, especially—Doug had a tendency to offer some bland reassurance. It usually came out as "You shouldn't feel sad because—." Over the years, through Katie's gentle help, he had learned that by denying the reality of someone else's feelings, he was inadvertently minimizing the validity of what that person was experiencing. Now, with Charlie, he was able to avoid that trap, and was careful to let the boy know he'd been heard and his hurt understood.

"It sounds like you really got your hopes up and got badly disappointed in the process."

"Yeah, it hurts. I wanted to have a girlfriend, like everybody else at Brock."

Doug was known as a "fixer" at home and on the job. If the washing machine broke or the cement truck was late, he didn't stand around sharing sadness with Katie or the guys at work. He found a solution. His impulse now was to shift the conversation toward advice-giving. But again, years of marital experience with Katie had also taught him that people who hurt don't always need advice right away so much as to unburden themselves. While it went against his grain "to do nothing" he depended on her insights when, like today, he found himself wading through a minefield of emotions. Laying bricks was definitely more straightforward.

The conversation continued a bit longer, but its goals had already been achieved: Doug had provided a shoulder to cry on as well as a gentle listening ear. Charlie had been unusually transparent and now felt less alone with his pain. Nothing had changed in terms of his situation, yet somehow he felt better.

Still, by the end of their talk the "fixer" had managed to squeeze in a little advice, suggesting to Charlie that he venture to Maria's home instead of waiting—perhaps forever—for her to reappear.

Saturday was a good day to implement this strategy. Maria would not be in school so he could choose the best hour to knock on her door. Saturday would also turn out to be a bad day to implement the plan; Charlie had forgotten that her father would likely also be home.

CHAPTER SEVENTEEN

Friday evenings were Doug's favourite part of the week. The weekend stretched before him like an inviting oasis, promising rest, family activities and maybe even a bit of time for him to watch television. Only the customary half-day of work on Saturday impinged somewhat on this scenario. Lately, though, his boss was relaxing that demand, anxious to fend off the overtures of the outside union which had been wooing his workers with promises of a shorter work week if they would sign up.

And this particular weekend he would not have to work, thanks to the intermittent rain showers which had been soaking the ground all week.

On the television, the war news from Indo China was depressing as usual. In May, the garrison at Dien Bien Phu had finally surrendered. According to the news anchor, French troops had valiantly mounted a strong defense against a relentless siege by the ragtag Viet Minh army of 50,000 determined to liberate their country from unwanted colonizers. Now, these same troops were about to enter Hanoi itself. In their wake, a million refugees, mostly Roman Catholics, had streamed south toward the new demarcation line and the safety of South Viet Nam.

Doug typically avoided war news. He had seen enough carnage in Europe. Yet tonight, for some reason, he allowed himself to revisit those painful memories.

* * *

The Canadian First Division's campaign in Sicily had gone surprisingly well. Its First Brigade was made up of three regiments: the Royal Canadian Rifles, the Hastings and Prince Edward and Doug's 48th Highlanders. These two other units, noting that most of the 48th were from Toronto, quickly labelled them the "Glamour Boys." Together, the three regiments doggedly fought their way across the island's mountainous terrain, supported by the heavy guns of the First Armoured Tank Brigade. He remembered with a rueful smile the goat paths that served as roads. He recalled building Bailey bridges to traverse steep gullies. He shuddered at the memories of those Canadian thirty-seven-ton Sherman tanks. Their crews morbidly called them "Ronsons"—like the cigarette lighter—since their thin armour plating afforded little protection against incoming anti-tank shells. Doug saw firsthand too many fiery and fatal explosions, the men trapped inside as if in a miniature crematorium. He could still smell the horrific sticky odour of men burned alive.

After only thirty-eight days, the battle for Sicily was won. Mussolini, the boastful dictator, was deposed by his own citizens on July 25. On September 3, 1943, the Allies crossed the narrow Straits of Messina and invaded Italy.

The next day, home in Downsview, an anxious Katie read the headline in her Toronto newspaper:

ALLIES INVADE ITALY CANADIANS IN SPEARHEAD

After crossing the narrow Strait of Messina which separated Sicily from the Italian mainland, Doug found himself in a new and vicious war. The fighting began at Reggio di Calabria. He recalled wading ashore, leaving the relative safety of their flat-bottomed landing boat to struggle slowly through the warm salty water. For a bizarre moment on that rocky beach, he found himself remembering a huge unrolled map that long ago his grade ten geography teacher had displayed to the class, on which he'd pointed out the boot-shape of Italy with its extended "toe." Doug was now standing on that toe, with Italian guns trying to chase him back into the placid neutral sea.

The land around Reggio di Calabria was hilly and speckled with fragrant-smelling orange groves and neat rows of olive trees. On higher elevations, the tamed farmlands were replaced by thick forests of pine and poplar. As the Canadians advanced warily through the town, they encountered frightened residents—mostly old men, women and children.

The younger men had already been conscripted by Mussolini in his quest to spread the green and white flag across the world—a dream now replaced by white towels and sheets, flags of surrender protruding from windows along the winding cobblestone streets.

Without Mussolini, the Italian government had quickly collapsed; and by September 8, an armistice followed, ending that country's participation in the war. Many of Italy's soldiers who had not already been taken prisoner joined bands of Communist-leaning partisans, now actively fighting alongside the Allied invaders. Others, their fascist minds unwilling to abandon the dream of conquest, were absorbed into the German war machine to continue what was now Hitler's campaign alone. But most of the Italian soldiers, weary of war and disillusioned by its false promises, simply tossed aside their uniforms and returned home to family and trade.

Among them was Donato Lupozzi.

Doug's regiment swept northeast across Calabria. Their recent Sicilian encounters with mountains and river crossings had taught them how to move quickly through the countryside. The Germans had systematically and strategically retreated, leaving behind them a series of blown bridges to slow pursuing Allied armies. When it was impractical or too time consuming to build Bailey bridges, bulldozers of the Royal Canadian Corps of Engineers simply pushed rocks and dirt into deep gullies and created their own crossing points. As they moved steadily inland toward Cantanzano, soldiers of the 48th were kept fueled on bully beef, hardtack, cheese and tea. A monotonous diet, and one unable to prevent the ravages of disease. In those first weeks of fighting, jaundice, malaria and dysentery which had plagued them in Sicily followed like pursuing angels of death into Italy.

Allied planning decreed that Canadians and British forces would move up the east coast of the boot while the Americans fought their way on the west side of the peninsula, heading toward Rome. Between them and their goal stood twenty divisions of battle-hardened elite German troops.

At this point, Doug chose to leave his memories behind and returned to the television news. The war in Indo China seemed safely far away.

— tracking the movements of Hurricane Hazel, a very dangerous storm now thrashing westward across the Caribbean Sea.

Daytona News-Journal, October 10, 1954

CHAPTER EIGHTEEN

On Saturday morning, Charlie crossed the Humber Bridge at James Street, about half a mile north of the spot where, almost two weeks ago, he experienced his first riverbank encounter with Maria.

Pausing in the middle of the span, he leaned on the rail and stared down at dark murky water rushing under his feet. Earlier in the day, as he impatiently awaited the appointed hour, everything seemed to move in slow motion. Now, as the reality of his momentous scheme was upon him, events were moving too quickly.

If he ventured but a few more steps, he would be out of his cocoon and into her world. Safety lay behind him. On her side lurked the possibility of danger and risk. His old enemies—embarrassment and fear of rejection—were surely waiting to ambush him and would put to rest any hopes for a relationship with Maria.

Yet he was compelled to continue across the bridge which divided them. West of the Humber was a broad, flat expanse, where scattered clusters of new bungalows were gradually supplanting abandoned weed-infested pastureland. Maria's house stood apart, isolated at the end of a muddy, still-unpaved road. A black '48 Chevy sedan was parked beside a half-built garage. Upon spying the car, he was once again overcome with indecision. Already anxious and uncertain over the whole idea of dropping in, he now faced the prospect of meeting with an understandably suspicious father.

I hadn't planned on her dad being home. Should I turn around before I make a mess of things? No, I can't stop now. This is my one chance to see her again, and I'm almost there.

Though actually, it's not my only chance. I might see her at the river again."

Charlie considered, but soon admitted he was not prepared to wait in the rain for another month.

Besides, she's not going to walk down there once the weather's cold. This is my only chance So, what will I say if her father answers the door? Pause. I'll say I'm a friend of Maria's. I was just walking by and wanted to say hi—if she isn't too busy. And not forget to introduce myself and call him 'Sir'.

It wasn't that Charlie had come totally unprepared. He'd been up before the sun. He'd carefully selected a new pair of dark pants and a pink, long-sleeved dress shirt under a maroon cardigan, now half buttoned against the cold wind. He'd applied Brylcreem to slick down his unruly hair. He'd brightened his smile with Pepsodent toothpowder, which also promised to sweeten his morning breath. Most importantly, he'd carefully polished his black oxford shoes with the flat horseshoe-shaped cleats implanted on the bottom of their heels.

Cleats were the thing, promoted by the manufacturer as helping extend the life of the shoe. For Charlie and many of his male school mates, though, the biggest benefit was the resultant authoritative clanging sound they made. Today, as he walked on the cement part of his journey, Charlie felt like Marshall Matt Dillon on *Gunsmoke*, with cleats instead of silver spurs.

He had also planned an activity for his date, should God grant him this opportunity. (Last night, in a rare moment of prayer, he sent his request into the universe.)

He would invite Maria to go with him to a movie that very after-noon. The matinee would start at 1 p.m., giving them time to walk to the Bloor streetcar, followed by a short bus ride to St. Clair St. He'd even selected the theatre, subject of course to Maria's approval: the Royal George for a double feature—the more time with her the better!—*The Bowery Boys Meet the Monster* and *The Boy From Oklahoma* starring Will Rogers Jr. The only unfinished detail was whether he should offer to hold her hand on their walk home. He quickly decided that the risk of rejection and embarrassment was too high. Though if she initiated contact, he could hardly refuse.

It was this image and the excitement it conjured that fueled his final steps up the walk.

Charlie took a deep breath and knocked, not so gently as to remain unheard, not so loud as to be rude.

"*Buon giorno.*" A short, heavy-set woman in a long black skirt, dark woollen stockings, sturdy black shoes and a white blouse, opened the door. Her chocolate-brown hair was long, speckled with grey and neatly tied in a bun.

"Um, is Maria home?" He almost added "Sir" just like he had been rehearsing.

"*Come ti chiami?*"

She sounded annoyed or suspicious, he couldn't tell which. "Maria." He repeated louder, hoping that might help.

"*Come ti chiami?*" Although he spoke not a word of Italian, Charlie knew that whatever she was saying, it was important.

"Maria!" He tried one more time, more desperately than loud.

A sudden burst of laughter from inside the house came as a welcome interruption. "You just told her twice that your name is Maria. What a coincidence! Same as me." And Maria appeared, emerging from what appeared to be the basement. Her white apron failed to conceal rounded hips and a slender waist. His eyes took in that now-familiar long hair and glowing olive complexion. Her naturally red lips framed two rows of perfectly white teeth.

"My *Mamma* is asking your name." She didn't seem at all surprised to see Charlie at her door.

"It's Charlie." He couldn't think at that moment of a suitable feminine equivalent for the practised "Sir."

The older woman continued in Italian: "*Come stai?*" This time Maria was quick to intercede. "Just say '*bene*'." Charlie did as he was told, hoping he was not offending the lady of the house. Mrs. Lupozzi smiled politely but her ample girth still barred his entry. Then came the sound of heavy footsteps coming from behind. Marshal Dillon, thought Charlie, would never have been caught in this vulnerable situation.

"Who this boy?" The father spoke with the same air of authority as Mr. McGiver, the school principal—and former tank commander. Mr.

Lupozzi was shorter than Charlie but twice as wide, all of it seemingly composed of muscle. He wore a faded red plaid lumberjack-type shirt. His face was whisker-stubbled and, despite the season, still wind-and-weather-tanned.

"*Babbo*, this is my friend Charlie—from school," she added the last two words quickly, knowing that any reference to educational activities would diffuse any possible outburst.

"Is nice to meet you, boy. Come in, come in." So far, so good for Charlie.

He was led downstairs into what he assumed would be the basement, which generated an anxiety-provoking vision of them all sitting around a coal furnace. Instead, he was pleasantly surprised to find himself in a comfortable living room, dominated by an overstuffed couch and matching chair, all in a gaudy brightly-coloured floral pattern. A small television set sat in the opposite corner. Above it loomed a large gilded framed portrait of a small man in a red robe, sitting placidly on a golden throne. He held a long ornate staff in his right hand. Keeping him company on the wall was a plaster statue of Jesus on the cross.

Babbo soon produced two fancy goblets which he proceeded to fill and introduce as his best homemade wine. Charlie assumed the second glass was destined for Mrs. Lupozzi, so was taken aback to find it headed his way. Alcohol was not a part of the Thompson household, although he'd spotted a bottle of rye whisky in his grandparents' pantry. Nor had he had even a sip of O'Keefe's Beer, which the other local teens regularly consumed, under safety of darkness, in the ballpark.

Charlie received the glass with a weak smile and a murmured thanks. He snuck a desperate glance at Maria, seeking direction or deliverance, but none was forthcoming. *Babbo* then raised his glass with what the boy assumed was a toast—a toast in honour of the visitor.

"*Per cent'anni!*"

Maria politely translated: "He is wishing you a hundred years of luck."

Charlie raised his own glass and nodded while the others looked on approvingly.

Inwardly, he pondered what kind of luck this formidable man had in mind. He took a sip. The others watched expectantly.

The wine burned all the way down, such that Charlie was sure his esophagus and stomach would soon begin to smoke. How could he possibly finish? Then Maria unexpectedly saved the day!

"Let me show you our garden. There are still a few tomatoes and onions, you could take some home for your mother. Oh, and bring your wine," she added casually, almost as an afterthought. Charlie followed obediently, secretly rejoicing in the rescue. Away from paternal scrutiny, Maria encouraged him to make a libation of it on the damp ground, like some sacrificial offering to the Earth Goddess Charlie had once read about in a comic book

"How did you know?" he murmured gratefully. "Your face—" she began but ended up laughing. "It was so funny!"

"Do you think your dad saw?" Charlie couldn't tell if the churning in his stomach was due to anxiety or the wine.

"No, don't worry about it. In fact, when we go back in, I bet he'll offer you another glass."

"What should I do?"

"Don't be scared. I'll handle it."

Emboldened by the wine, Charlie pressed ahead with his plan.

"Maria, would you like to go to the show with me this afternoon?" And with that, the words he had shaped and practised over and over were out. The seconds of silence that followed, however, were like grains of sand dropping one by one into the bottom of an hourglass. Then she spoke.

"Sure." And with that one little word, Charlie's heart was off to the races, the blood rushing to his brain. He prayed he wouldn't faint.

The garden harvest long forgotten, Charlie and Marie returned to the house. Sure enough, *Babbo* was lying in wait with a second glass. Maria was quick to intercept.

"Charlie's parents allow him only one glass a day. I don't want him to get in trouble."

On cue, Charlie twisted his face into a visage of bitter disappointment at the harsh rules set by such obviously cruel parents. The ruse worked. A momentarily subdued Donato put away his homemade wine and invited the honoured guest to sit down. Yet another awkward silence followed, during which Charlie found himself the object of rather intense scrutiny from both Donato and Rosa. Their watchful demeanour told him that, behind their friendly near-effusive welcome were two very suspicious and protective parents. His fears were confirmed when Donato finally broke the silence.

"What you want with my daughter?"

"I would like to take her to the movies, Mr. Lupozzi—Sir."

Donato patiently translated Charlie's words for his wife whose English was limited. Rosa replied in a torrent of Italian, none of which sounded very promising to the guest. Then Maria joined in, followed by her father who added his hands into the discussion. Charlie increasingly felt himself to be at the mercy of this family. Then as quickly as it began, the volume of the voices lessened. Donato even managed to smile at Charlie.

"My *Babbo* says he will drive us to the Jane Junction. Otherwise, it's a long walk to the streetcar."

Charlie's strategy had actually included that "long walk," giving him more time with Maria, but he knew better than to decline Donato's offer. They would have plenty of couple time later. He rolled the word "couple" around in his inner voice. It sounded good.

* * *

Charlie and Maria soon found themselves in the backseat of Donato's car, which would have been a welcome event save for Rosa, who had planted her ample self between them. The ride over the Humber Bridge and along Bloor to where the streetcar looped seemed to take even longer, no doubt due to the enforced closeness. Donato kept a watchful eye on Charlie's hands through the rear-view mirror.

Finally, the old Chevy reached its destination and pulled up to the curb. Maria opened her back door and jumped out, then reached in to help her mother exit. This made sense, thought Charlie, since this way he could slide out the passenger side rather than risk opening the driver's side door into the heavy Saturday traffic. He too jumped out, then politely stuck his head back in to thank Mr. Lupozzi—Sir. But Donato brushed the gesture aside and, instead, directed a torrent of rapid-fire words toward Rosa and Maria, now standing on the sidewalk. In return, they nodded in agreement.

In a clever effort to demonstrate his good manners—and to initiate the rest of his dating schedule—Charlie opened the front passenger door for Rosa, only to be surprised when Maria aborted his chivalry by closing it, then blowing her father a kiss through the glass.

"*Mamma* is taking the bus too" she explained. Charlie was puzzled but absorbed the news without panic. It made sense for Mrs. Lupozzi to take advantage of a trip into town to do some shopping. She would probably rendezvous with them later for the ride home. Good planning!

But when the bus dropped them off near the Royal George movie theatre, Charlie's plans began to unravel.

While he lined up for tickets, Maria and her mother scanned the stills of the two movies which were posted on display beside the ticket window. They engaged in another loud and animated discussion, then Marie beckoned to Charlie to leave the lineup.

"*Mamma* doesn't want to see these movies. She says there's a better one down the street at the St. Clair. She noticed it on the bus when we drove past." Charlie's heart sank. The news that *Mamma* was going to accompany the young couple to the show converted anxiety to sheer panic. His inner monologue kicked into high gear:

I don't have enough money to buy three tickets unless we don't get popcorn and a drink.

I'll look cheap.

Then *What if someone from school sees me? What kind of cool guy brings a girl's mother with them on a date?"*

The worse. "*Now I won't be able to hold Maria's hand."*

Charlie had fantasized all night about the armrest in the space between their seats. He had figured out how he would strategically place his right hand there first, like a restaurant's glowing neon sign hoping to attract customers. Then, with a shy sideways glance and just a hint of a smile, she would gently lower her left hand over his. Just the thought of its expected warmth and softness on his skin had caused him to toss and turn until midnight.

Rosa was a devoted fan of Mario Lanza, so there was no question in her mind that they would see *The Student Prince*. The three of them were escorted down the long, sloping aisle by a uniformed usher, a teenager about Charlie's age. Charlie thought the boy looked his way rather scornfully as the trio marched single file behind him, but hoped it was only his overly sensitive imagination at work.

The usher's flashlight directed them to the row which Rosa had chosen as they entered the darkened space. Sure enough, on arrival, she ordered Maria to slide in first. Then, with a glance of triumph directed at Charlie, she followed, leaving the forlorn young man to trail behind.

Again, he thought he heard a snicker or two from the row behind, but was too embarrassed to look. After a Looney Tunes cartoon and a preview of coming attractions, the movie began, in gloriously coloured Cinemascope.

Edmund Purdom looked dashing as the titular Prince. Ann Blyth was Kathie, the beautiful recipient of his ardent love. And when Prince Karl stood beneath Kathie's balcony, singing in Lanza's glorious tenor, Charlie was moved in spite of himself. As his serenade slowly melted the shy young woman's reluctant heart, Charlie couldn't resist sneaking a stealthy glance toward Maria, scarcely visible behind her mother's sizable barrier

Beloved, with all my heart I love you,

With every breath I pray, some day You will be mine.

To his surprise, Maria was looking at him as well! And in that moment, despite the darkness of the theatre, Charlie's world instantly became radiantly brighter.

Hazel's Toll is 200 Dead 500 Hurt in Ravaged Haiti

Leaving a death toll in Haiti of more than 200 and an injured list of at least 500, according to unofficial reports reaching here, Hurricane Hazel moved toward the island of Mayaguana in the Bahamas late today.

Miami Daily News, October 13, 1954

CHAPTER NINETEEN

B etween the concrete and asphalt-covered city of Toronto and the northern granite rock and pine forests of the Canadian Shield lie the fertile farm fields and small towns of Central Ontario, with a multitude of creeks and rivers crisscrossing the land like veins on a hand. By the second week of October, that land was now saturated with rain and unable to absorb another drop. It then became runoff, flowing obediently into the nearest waterway which, unlike the land, received it without complaint.

Charlie's afternoon with Maria quickly spilled over into similar streams of conversation in the homes of both the Thompson and Lupozzi families.

Donato had met the moviegoers, as planned, at the Junction loop. Charlie had voiced his decision to walk home from there, the fantasy of holding Maria's hand post-movie shattered by Rosa's hovering omnipresence. But Maria insisted he accept a ride, despite the fact that *Babbo* had made no such offer but who, with only a few muttered words to himself in Italian, reluctantly turned the old Chevy toward Lawson Avenue.

This second drive with the Lupozzi family would have proved equally awkward if *Mamma* wedged herself once again in the back seat between the two young people. This time, Maria directed her date to take a front seat. As the noisy muffler precluded any attempt at conversation with anyone in the back seat, Charlie turned to the driver who was staring grimly and over-intently at the road ahead. Charlie did quite well in geography class, so it seemed a safe bet to break the silence by asking where the family had lived in Italy.

"Calabria." Donato gruffly replied without turning his head.

"That's near Sicily, in the toe of the boot, right?" Charlie was pleased he knew this and hoped Maria was suitably impressed.

"Was a beautiful place to live. With own grapes and orange trees." Mr. Lupozzi looked momentarily wistful.

"My dad was there during the war," Charlie continued innocently. At that, Donato's wistful expression was instantly erased by an expression of pain which radiated from the man's clenched teeth to his flushed cheeks and furrowed brow. Realizing he had unknowingly blundered into forbidden territory, Charlie was desperate to extricate himself from the minefield without blowing up the entire day into pieces of shattered dreams. Again, it was Maria who saved the situation.

"You would have loved to see our fruit grove. Can you imagine getting orange juice from a tree not a bottle? *Babbo*, tell him about the grapes and how you made the wine."

The conversation limped along, as everyone in the car agreed grapes were a better topic than the War. Each clung to it like a life raft until, mercifully, they arrived at Charlie's house.

* * *

This unintentional triggering of painful memories would, later that day, evolve into two streams of deep reminiscences. For Maria's parents, the hastily aborted car discussion resumed after dinner, but only after their daughter had withdrawn to her bedroom and her confidante, a pretty blue diary. Although rarely patterned in their long relationship, Donato did most of the talking this time, his words fueled by a glass of his homemade wine. Rosa was content to listen, inwardly relieved that her husband seemed finally ready to talk about what had happened. It was as if he were surgically cutting open his own chest to reveal the pain inside.

Donato Lupozzi had been repatriated home from Africa in 1941 after the defeat of Italy's battered armies in Abyssinia. Donato gratefully returned to his beautiful Reggio di Calabria, only to find it occupied by four divisions of German troops. For the next few months he was allowed to farm his land, the Germans wisely realizing he was of greater value growing food than shipped off to Libya, where he would have been thrown into Rommel's hopeless fight and eventual defeat by the British self-styled "Desert Rats."

All that changed when the Allies invaded Sicily in 1943.

Private Lupozzi was once again thrust into battle. The Italians were rushed to the Sicilian front alongside the German defenders to resist the rapid eastward advance of the British 8th Army where, once again, he found himself caught in a hopeless cause. The Nazis' huge Tiger tanks were of little value in mountainous terrain. American bombers rained down tons of explosives on dug-in Italian positions. British heavy artillery drove the Axis allies back toward the Straits of Messina. In Rome, the Italian political leadership saw the peril of continuing to support fascism and Mussolini's fanciful dream of empire. *Il Duce* was arrested in July by the orders of King Emmanuel.

The Axis troops, outnumbered 10 to 1 by the combined American and British/Canadian forces, wisely determined to withdraw from Sicily. Somehow, German general Kesselring managed to haul out with him most of his heavy guns, tanks and other vital equipment, rather than abandon them to the invaders.

Twice, Private Lupozzi had survived an encounter with the enemy. With a sense of relief or at least resignation, most of his compatriots in Sicily had surrendered. In the middle of August, he was evacuated to Italy along with 100,000 fellow German and Italian soldiers.

Yet, it wasn't those troublesome memories of war that Donato revisited with his wife and his wine. It was the terrible weeks that followed.

On September 3, 1943, two weeks after his escape from Sicily, Canadian troops landed in Calabria. Within a week, Marshall Badoglio's Italian forces had surrendered. Donato could go home; the Lupozzi family was once again reunited.

But Donato's beloved farm had been ransacked by the retreating Germans: crops destroyed, fruit trees and grape vines picked clean and, mostly alarmingly, his chickens, sheep and cows were gone. His wife and little daughter were without food. And he had brought nothing with him, except his life.

He clearly remembered the Canadians. They came quickly through Calabria, meeting little German resistance as they pushed eastward across the bottom of Italy's boot.

He remembered walking with his family into the village center, hoping to find flour or eggs. Even nine years later, he could recall standing on the edge of a road as the invaders—or were they now liberators?—roared up the hill and down the main street. First the speeding olive-camouflaged jeeps bouncing along the bumpy street. Then the heavy armour, a long column of slower-moving Sherman tanks, with belching smoke and oily-smelling fumes; he could still hear the rhythmic clatter of their metal tracks, a grinding crunch over the cobblestones. Next, a line of troop-carrying trucks, each crammed full of men in brown uniforms, their faces peering at the silent villagers with a mix of curiosity and wariness. When, suddenly the whole procession stopped.

Up ahead, the lead jeep had made a fast U-turn and was now back in the center of the village. A tall strongly built officer alit, his eyes quickly scanning the crowd. A meeting had obviously been pre-arranged. The mayor and village police chief emerged from among the curious but anxious villagers lining the road. A priest quickly joined them. Donato knew all three. Together, they proceeded to warmly greet the Canadian, reassuring him through broken English and much gesticulating that the last German troops had pulled out a week ago. As tensions eased on both sides, the Italians and the Canadian moved their discussion into the parish church. The remainder of the convoy then slowly rolled ahead to the far edge of town, where the rest of the Canadians stopped to rest and refuel their vehicles.

The next day saw the result of that church conference. Canadian army rations were distributed to the hungry Calabrians. Donato and Rosa, with little Maria clinging to her mother's leg, stood patiently in line with the other desperate families. As they inched closer to the distribution tent, Donato took note of their benefactors. Like the officer, they were big men, several inches taller than the townsfolk. They wore red patches on their sleeves, (a mark of the 48th Highlanders, he later learned.) Most were unshaven and rough-looking in appearance. Yet, unlike the Germans, they behaved in a relaxed and casual manner. Stile, like any soldier far from home, they gazed at the younger Italian women. Donato instinctively put his arm around Rosa.

Within two days, the Canadian First Infantry Division had moved on. Continuing to meet little German resistance along the way, their rapid advance continued eastward to the Adriatic coast. Doug's Division, which merged the 48th Highlanders with the Royal Canadian Regiment and the Hastings and Prince Edward Regiment, then swung north, heading up the Italian coastline toward the town of Ortona. There, the Germans paratroopers were no longer in a planned retreat, but preparing for a final bloody standoff with a rapidly oncoming and overconfident enemy.

For the Lupozzi family, the war brought further unexpected horror. French Colonial troops followed the British and Canadians. Then came the Moroccans, not with food but marauding intent.

It happened when Donato left for the village for seeds, so that he could plant and replace his pillaged crops. No sooner had he left than the Moroccans arrived. Rosa barely managed to hide Maria before she was assaulted.

When she was older, Maria asked her parents why, when her friends all had large families, she had neither a brother nor a sister. She never knew the terrible truth that her answer lay on a barn floor.

It was those unbearable memories that Donato and Rosa resurrected, amid tears and mourning, the evening after they met Charlie.

* * *

Charlie's innocent remark to Mr. Lupozzi also reverberated in his own home that evening.

After reminiscing about the Sicilian Campaign a few weeks earlier, Doug Thompson was determined to put aside his war memories. Now, the mention of Reggio Calabria set them once again in motion.

He remembered the hungry Italians and their gratitude. He recalled pushing further inland, up then down over endless hills which eventually gave way to rugged mountainous terrain. Doug smiled briefly as he recalled the Division's label, "Monty's mountain goats."

By mid-October, they had reached Campobasso where, to his relief, there was no major encounter with the Germans, who had already withdrawn. The Division set up administrative headquarters, and the town was quickly nicknamed "Maple Leaf City" by exhausted soldiers on recreational leave. He briefly smiled again, remembering the bagpipes, the pick-up baseball games with his buddies, some of whom would never return from the winter mud of Italy. Rested and reorganized, the troops of the First joined with the Canadian Second Division, and moved steadily northeast toward the Adriatic coast. There, at the town of Termoli, they turned north, moving carefully up Highway 16.

Doug was amazed at what happened next. Allied traffic was quickly snarled as thousands of troop-carrying trucks, tanks and jeeps clogged the road, all heading toward a battle zone 70 miles ahead. Word spread among the 48th that the Germans had set up a defensive line across the middle of Italy, determined to stop the Allied armies from reaching Rome.

With a shudder, he recalled the carnage he passed. Burned-out carcasses of tanks scattered in ditches where they had been pushed by road-clearing bulldozers. Dead horses and mules on the side of the road. Worst of all, though most of the human casualties from previous fighting had been removed, an overlooked fly-encrusted corpse, incongruously surrounded by white daisies and other wildflowers.

Then Torella, where the Germans made their desperate last stand. The men of the 48th were ordered to replace the exhausted Royal Canadian Regiment and push the enemy further north. About fifty ground-attacking kittyhawks and warhawks roared overhead to soften up German defenses. The long-awaited and dreaded order to advance came the morning of October 25, 1943. He could still hear the squeaking treads of the Sherman tanks supporting the attack. His platoon moved forward, their coiled anxiety replaced by a gut-deep fear of being shot. He occasionally glimpsed the dust-covered grey-green uniforms of enemy paratroopers crouched behind the concrete rubble of flattened houses. He fired again and again, at first hoping that he wouldn't kill anyone. Then, as he passed the torn and bleeding bodies of his friends, a primal rage welled up inside his stomach. A German suddenly sprung like a jack-in-the-box from a pile of broken concrete and ran zigzag between two shattered buildings. As he had been taught, Doug aimed for the body mass of his moving target. He slowly pulled the trigger. He wondered now, all these years later, if he had hit the soldier. Then thought no further.

It was the Regiment's only real encounter with the Germans that month, but it still cost the 48th a bitter loss of twenty-six dead and seventy wounded.

In November the rains came. Air cover provided by the Canadian Spitfire squadron brought over from Windsor now became irregular, depending on good flying weather to get the fighter planes off the ground. The fighting grew more intense. While the First Division had already suffered almost 700 dead and 1,700 wounded after the Battle of the Moro River, the worst carnage lay ahead. To the north of the Moro was Ortona, a deep seaport on the Adriatic coast and a prize deemed by the Allied generals to be strategically important.

The ten thousand Italians living there found themselves trapped between the oncoming Canadians and the entrenched German First Parachute Division which was dug in at strategically placed positions throughout the town. Most civilians wisely and hurriedly fled to the surrounding hills and caves, muttering curses against the *tedeschi,* Hitler's soldiers, whose stubborn resistance would surely lead to the wanton destruction of their homes and beloved church.

Doug paused in his reflection of grand strategies and battle planning, as his thoughts turned personal. How could he have carried all that gear mile after weary mile? He tried to recall every item and where it was placed on his body. For starters, he was one of 4,000 riflemen in the Division so there was the Lee Enfield rifle and bullets. And the "pineapple," a grenade he had learned to throw with accuracy. His bayonet, food rations, water canteen, bandages and gas mask. In total, it weighed seventy pounds. Still, he remembered with a smile, that was lighter than the Thompson submachine guns some of his buddies grudgingly lugged with them.

"The Gully" was the name affixed to their next objective, a wide valley between 200 and 300 yards across, with a steep slope on the German side. General Vokes had ordered a creeping barrage of heavy artillery to precede the advance of his 48th Highlanders. On the morning of December 16, the regiment successfully attacked behind the cover of the big guns. A week later, they were across the gully and preparing to move on to San Nicola and San Tommaso.

Here, Doug paused. Harder memories lay directly ahead.

The Canadians moved against the towns on the moonless night of December 23, walking slowly and soundlessly in single file along a path which had not been scouted in advance. It was so dark that each man was guided by grabbing on to the shoulder of the soldier ahead. Now, all these years later, Doug began to sweat with reawakened fear.

Doug's unit soon stumbled upon a houseful of Germans casually opening Christmas presents. He could easily eavesdrop on their raucous chatter, and found this sudden intimacy with the enemy both frightening and exciting. As directed by Sergeant Macklin's hand signals, the Canadians quietly surrounded the weather-beaten stone dwelling and crouched down, rifles pointed at the windows. Macklin, who knew a few words of German, called for the celebrating soldiers to come out.

"*Komm Raus! Komm Raus!*" Inside, a few seconds of sudden shocked silence. Doug once again found himself again involuntarily holding his breath. If the Germans came out firing, he would have to make his first kill. Instead, the shocked and frightened paratroopers stumbled out the door, hands raised high as they walked uncertainly toward the gun barrels. "*Ich ergebe mich.*" They were surrendering. Nineteen were taken prisoner without resistance.

That marked the end of the good news, as Kesselring immediately ordered a vicious counterattack. Moving in behind the advancing Canadians, a company of Panzer Grenadiers cut Doug's company from their supply lines. The Highlanders were trapped, unable to retreat or move ahead. It was now December 25. Cold and wet, the day was spent trying to reserve their remaining munitions and food. Doug recalled their collective sigh of relief when several foragers from his unit brought back three sheep, their grilled meat helping to abate the gnawing hunger in his belly. He wondered what his family would be doing. It was their tradition to open gifts on Christmas morning. By now, Sarah and Charlie would have ransacked their stockings. Was his own big woollen sock hanging empty and forgotten by the fireplace?

Now safely at home, looking at that very fireplace, Doug reflected on other Christmas mornings, when there was no distance of war separating him from Katie and the children. And he smiled, remembering that even while he was overseas, Katie had made sure to fill his stocking.

In the bedroom directly above, Katie lay awake, waiting for Doug to join her in bed. As soon as she heard his footsteps on the stairs, Katie planned to roll on her left side and pretend to be asleep. Charlie's story about the Lupozzi family had distressed her deeply. All the half-buried feelings of guilt and shame, emotions she thought she'd left behind weeks ago in the safety and acceptance of her pastor's office, were unleashed. Once again, she felt unworthy of being Doug's wife. And for that reason, she needed to avoid his touch.

CHAPTER TWENTY

The small white piece of paper was carefully folded in half, safely sheltered from outside eyes. Maria had written her phone number and quietly passed it to Charlie as they exited the theatre.

He had always found in movies a refuge from the outside world. He could recall the first movie his father had taken him to see. Afterward, on the way home, Charlie asked how the people on the stage could change their clothes so quickly behind the screen, and was somewhat disappointed to learn that the gun-toting hero and his crusty old sidekick were actually filmed in far-away Hollywood.

Once he turned twelve, Charlie was allowed to go to Saturday matinees by himself; and on most weekends, that was exactly what he did. There was usually a serial and cartoon in addition to the main double feature. The serials were aptly called "cliffhangers." Their thin storylines stretched like an elastic band anywhere from twelve to fifteen chapters, each week's drama ending with the rugged hero or helpless heroine in mortal peril. Seven days and a ticket later, the audience would find out if and how they survived.

* * *

In the first year or so of his matinee-going, Charlie preferred the cowboy serials. A favourite was *Gunfighters of The Northwest*. He was surprised to see the Lone Ranger, Clayton Moore, playing an entirely different role without his horse Silver. *The Fighting Mounties* soon followed, but by this time, Charlie was on the lookout for matinees which included a female lead. Cowboys and Mounties apparently had little time or inclination for romance. Science fiction, on the other hand, was more promising, especially Flash Gordon and his faithful and beautiful girlfriend Dale.

King of The Congo was even better. Here, Buster Crabbe was rescued by the lovely and bewitching Gloria Dea as Princess Pha. In Chapter 8, *The Mission of Evil*, he returned the favour, saving her from the fearsome sacrificial rituals of the treacherous Rock People. The rest of the time, she was in charge, something Charlie found surprising, but strangely comforting.

When it was over, he was always reluctant to exit the dark warmth of the theatre into the harsh glare of a bright sun, traffic noise and a sidewalk overflowing with people. All of it a far cry from the escapist fantasy he had just been a part of. It always took him a few moments before he could remember in which direction to walk.

* * *

Today, Charlie was starring in his own cliffhanger, as he rehearsed a phone call to Maria. The resulting emotional rollercoaster—fear, excitement, hope, anxiety—was more intense than any movie serial.

What will I do if Mr. Lupozzi answers? What if he hangs up as soon as I say who I am? Maria wouldn't know I called. She'll think I'm not interested. If I call again after that, it might make him even madder at me. But let's say Maria picks up. Should I invite her for a second date? It's been 24 hours since the movie, the school week starts tomorrow. Is it too early to suggest next weekend? Could she go out during the week? What if Mrs. Lupozzi answers? We didn't do so well last time. I wish I weren't such a chicken. I gotta do something or I'll miss out for sure.

Then the smell of a pot roast cooking in the oven enticed him from his dilemma.

The routines of a typical Sunday were familiar and comfortable for the Thompson family. Katie and Mary went to church—Sunday School at 10 a.m. for children and adults, the worship service an hour later. Since Sarah's death a year ago, Katie had made church-going part of her Sabbath routine. Of course, at Faith Tabernacle, very little was routine. Even what to call the preacher was a learning experience for her; though an ordained clergyman, he preferred "Pastor" to "Reverend". He often said jokingly: "I'm not perfect enough to be 'revered,' but I do want to care for my flock like a shepherd. Which is what 'pastoral' means."

Nor were his services the least bit predictable. Some Sundays, the congregation sang so well and were getting so blessed with the old hymns that Pastor Hanson led songs until it was time for a final prayer and then they were out the door. Other times, he preached so long that the teachers who were caring for children in Kids' Church downstairs had no choice but to turn them loose in the sanctuary, which never failed to bring sermon and service to an abrupt conclusion.

Then there were the Sundays when he would have an altar call, not at the end but plunked right into middle of the service.

"I feel God would have us get on our knees right now and let Him know we are thankful for His love. This altar is open. Come with your gratitude; come with your thanksgiving. Gloria, play that beautiful hymn of faith, *How Great Thou Art* as God's people come forward. If you feel that gentle tug of the Holy Spirit on your heart, listen to that still, small voice inside and walk up this aisle right now."

* * *

Mary loved church. The Sunday School was well-run: strongly supported financially by the congregation, blessed with experienced teachers and boasting large age-appropriate classes for kids 3 to 15. There were even two nurseries, one for infants, the other for toddlers. In the infant room, the service was piped in audibly so mothers could listen while feeding or changing their babies.

Mary particularly liked the flannel graphing. Tiny cloth lambs, Biblical characters, even a miniature Noah's Ark, when added to a background board, brought scripture to life and made her feel as if she were a part of it.

Charlie on the other hand had attended only a few Sunday gatherings. He found the teen class a bit overwhelming. Apart from two boys who were clearly there under parental edict, most of the group knew their Bible, whereas he had no clue where to find Ecclesiastes or 1 Peter. Most of them could also pray out loud without notes, and he lived in dread of the inevitable occasion when he might be called upon to open the discussion with "a word of prayer."

There was always that one awkward moment in the opening of each class, when Mr. Chemdo would scan the faces of his students before finally locking eyes with one of them and inviting him or her to pray. Charlie made sure his eyes would never meet Mr. Chemdo's inquiring gaze.

But it was the discussions he feared the most. Each time he was there, the class had engaged in a lively conversation around the Bible passage being studied. The first time it was about the Trinity. Although he had a question or two in his mind, Charlie hung back. The next week, Mr. Chemdo presented what he called "the only way to salvation:" the need to confess one's sins, to ask God's forgiveness, to accept Jesus as saviour then become Christ's willing follower. Loud-voiced and dramatic, he announced with conviction that "It was the death of Jesus that made God's forgiveness possible. Thank You Jesus! Hallelujah! Glory to God!"

For Charlie, the class always led to more questions than answers. He was still grappling with believing in Jesus as God's son everyone else was being saved. He needed time and solitude to ponder these ideas, and would do so alone, as he always had. The group was no place for him to find answers.

So that first Sunday in October, the day after his date with Maria, Charlie chose to stay home with Doug. Despite her disappointment, Katie said nothing, for to do so would have made her appear critical of her husband's non-attendance; and that was a mutually agreed-upon taboo in the Thompson household.

* * *

Mary knew she should take her worries to the Lord. In fact, she had been told just that in her Sunday School class. Having no clue what that meant—where exactly would one find the Lord, to give him those worries?—she decided to do the next best thing: ask her mother after lunch.

Mother and daughter returned at 1 p.m. Katie immediately washed her hands, exchanged her gloves for oven mitts, and opened the door of the reliable Westinghouse stove to check on the progress of Sunday dinner.

Preparations for the noon meal were begun in the morning before church. The roast was floured, browned and placed in a large blue-speckled enamel pan, and surrounded by an honour guard of carrots, onions and potatoes. The oven was set for 250 degrees, water added, and the mixture left to cook for three hours. This meant Katie and Mary had barely a moment to take off their hats before the lady of the house summoned her hungry family to the table.

"God, bless this food to our bodies and us to thy service. Amen" Though it was Doug's quiet voice saying the blessing, he found no contradiction between this weekly show of devotion and his long-standing opposition to the church. Growing up, he had heard the same prayer uttered by his own father, and he was not about to change this ritual in his own house. It was tradition, not a doctrine requiring further examination.

With a bit of prompting from the children, Doug would sometimes recite the more traditional Scottish blessing, adding for the occasion a thick Glaswegian dialect:

Some hae meat and canna eat,
Some nae meat but want it,
We hae meat and we can eat,
And sae the Lord be thankit.

Today, however, Katie noticed something unusual. This time, he seemed to linger a few seconds before saying "Amen." Had he intended to add something? The moment passed, but her curiosity lingered through the meal.

As usual, Mary kept the family entertained with colourful descriptions of that morning's Sunday School class. Doug always respectfully refrained from challenging the literalist teachings around Jonah (residing in a whale's acidic belly for three days?) and Noah's Ark (surely ridiculously manure-filled after forty days afloat.)

"Miss Gardiner says she wants to go to Jerusalem to see where Jesus was buried. I'd rather see where he was born."

"Maybe one day you will," said Katie with a reassuring smile. "We could all go, as a family. You too, Dad."

"There are a lot of places in the world we could visit, Mary. Maybe we should see some of Canada first. Scotland too, one day."

"Do you know where Grandpa and Grandma used to live in Glasgow, before they came to Canada?" asked Charlie, sensing the Jerusalem trip could prove an awkward conversation for his father.

"I have an address, but I don't know if the house survived the bombing. It was right near the docks."

"Daddy, did you get bombed when you were in the war?" Mary was aware her father fought in the war, but she knew little else about his experience.

For an instant Doug appeared startled, as if she had opened a door that he had no desire to enter.

"That was a long time ago and I'm here now. That's all that matters."

But of course that wasn't all that mattered. Both children, but especially Charlie, had often wondered about their father as a soldier shooting a real gun. But, the same as conversations about church and Sarah's death, the topic of war seemed to be off-limits where their father was concerned.

Maybe that awareness of Doug's discomfort led to Charlie's impulsive and out-of-character next sentence which changed the subject and took the conversation to a whole new and surprising direction.

"I want to ask a question about dating a girl."

Both parents glanced at each other in surprise. Mary immediately started to giggle, both hands over her mouth in a hopeless effort to hide the sound. Doug immediately gave her a withering glance.

"Go ahead, son. What are you wondering about?" Doug recalled the conversation he had shared with Charlie only two days ago.

"Remember I told you we went to the show?" He avoided mentioning that embarrassing part about their parental escort. Mary had by now replaced her giggles with open-mouthed unabashed curiosity about her brother's first romantic adventure, and eagerly awaited more revelations.

"Yes, Maria, right?" Doug replied helpfully, while Katie nodded encouragingly. Both were anxious to learn as much as possible from their normally reticent and very private son.

"Well, I'm not sure what I should do next. When do I call her? How many days should a person wait?"

"Did you tell Maria you had a good time? Did you thank her parents for the ride?" Katie waded in with the beginnings of an idea.

"Not really. I guess."

"Well, that would be one good reason to call her. You could do that today and see how the conversation goes. Maybe even ask her when you might see her again."

Charlie knew the next phone call was a more complicated situation than his parents realized. *Who might answer the phone call? What if Maria isn't home—will my message get passed on? What if she doesn't want to see me again? What if she isn't allowed to see me again?* What was different is that they had given him enough information and motivation to step forward. And after a second helping of meat and potatoes, Charlie got up to the call.

Then his father asked him to sit down for another minute.

"I had planned to say this during grace but felt it might not be the right time." He paused, struggling to control his emotion. The rest of the family froze in place, uncertain what would come next.

"We all know Sarah's funeral happened a year ago. I also know that we've not really talked about Sarah's death since the funeral. It's not as if we don't think of her every day, or miss her smile and her laughter." Fighting against his tears, Doug struggled to continue without falling apart.

"I wanted to let you kids to know I realize how hard it's been on you to lose a sister. And Katie, to lose the little girl that you carried for nine months and loved for another twelve years. Maybe we could make that loss more bearable if we talked about it as a family."

And with that, the barrier was finally lifted. Once Katie was past the shock, she immediately began to talk about Sarah and her journey through grief. This in turn gave Charlie and Mary the confidence to share their own.

Gradually the conversation shifted from the pain of loss to a celebration of Sarah's life and the bittersweet memories they held forever close in their hearts. Tears became laughter, as story after story emerged, until Doug once again surprised them by asking that they bow their heads. For an instant Charlie wondered if his father was planning to say grace again.

"Lord, you know I'm not a praying man. I just want to thank you for giving us the gift of Sarah in our lives for those twelve years. We will never forget what we lost, please help us remember what we had. Amen."

Katie was the first to go to her husband in a loving tearful embrace. The two children were close behind. Even normally reticent Charlie felt himself drawn as if by an invisible magnet. In response, Doug's long strong arms enveloped them all and, for as long as he could, refused to let them go.

* * *

Lunch over, Mary finally caught up to her mother, desperate to unburden herself of the guilt she had been carrying for weeks. One look at her daughter's stricken face and Katie quickly set aside the dishwashing, took off her floral-patterned apron, and directed her daughter to sit beside her at the kitchen table.

"What's the matter, my little one? You look upset."

"It's about Sunday School." She paused. "Do other religions go to heaven when they die?"

"I think you mean do people who are from other religions go to heaven."

"Yeah, people like Rachel."

"That's a really good question, honey. Have you been talking about this in Sunday School?" Katie's non-answer reflected her own confusion about this question, and she hoped Mary wouldn't notice. Since attending Faith Tabernacle, Katie was aware the congregation held Christianity to be the only true religion. This was not something she had ever heard growing up in the Presbyterian church.

"Yes, Miss Gardiner says we're to share the Gospel with non-believers. I'm not sure how you're supposed to do that, but I told Rachel she needs to believe in Jesus."

"What did Rachel say about that?"

"She just kept playin' crokinole."

"And how did that make you feel?" While Katie posed her question as gently as possible, it was still enough to cause a trickle of tears to spill from her daughter's eyes.

"Mom, if Rachel doesn't believe in Jesus, does that mean I won't see her in heaven and we won't be friends anymore? Who would I have for my Double Dutch partner?"

"That would really be sad, though maybe people don't skip rope in heaven." Katie suppressed a smile, not wanting to appear to be making light of Mary's worries.

"But it's still my fault if Rachel doesn't get to heaven. I should've made her listen."

"No, no, Mary, it's not as simple as that."

"Sometimes at night I have scary dreams about Hell and Rachel's there." And amid Mary's deep sobs, Katie grew increasingly alarmed. Her innocent daughter had now been thrust into the turbulence of a theological controversy spanning centuries, arousing strong convictions among learned church scholars. But these were grown men and women, not an eight-year-old child whose life should remain free of such struggles.

Katie knew this issue required input from someone with much greater religious knowledge.

"Mary, I have an idea. How be I take you to talk with another pastor, someone who might be able to help us figure this out, someone who knows more about God that you or I do?"

"You mean someone even smarter than Pastor Hanson?"

"No, not necessarily smarter, but someone who might have a different point of view." At least, that's what the now-desperate mother was hoping to find for her guilt-burdened little girl. Katie resolved to phone her parents' minister, Rev. MacDougall, first thing Monday morning.

For the time being, all she could do was hold Mary close and tell her not to worry.

$$* * *$$

Downsview Presbyterian Church was typically quiet on Monday, traditionally the minister's day of rest and relaxation after busy Sunday services. Today was different; Rev. MacDougall had unlocked the heavy wooden doors to the old building promptly at 9 a.m. and, with a tired sigh, settled himself in his office. He had planned to spend the day hiking on the Bruce Trail, his favourite part of Ontario since it most reminded him of beloved Scotland.

Instead, despite the short notice, he had readily agreed to meet Katie and Mary.

Rev. MacDougall remembered Katie from when she would join her parents on the odd Sunday and, more recently, when he had officiated the funeral for her elder daughter. Not surprisingly, he assumed they needed to work through some lingering grief. But why would Katie bring her daughter, and on a school day? When his visitors arrived at 9:15, and following a few moments of ice-breaking chatter, the minister found his answer.

"Rev. MacDougall, I know our family is not part of your congregation," she began tentatively, "but I hoped you might still be willing to help us."

"Of course, Katie, a church's caring doesn't stop at the front door." She was touched by his comments and by the dialect which instantly reminded her of her Ranwick kin, who had visited from Scotland a few years back. "Is this about Sarah's death? It's been about a year, hasn't it?"

"Actually, no, although we still miss her terribly. And thank you for remembering."

"Then what brings you to see me today—and with Mary?" Turning toward her, "You were a wee one last time I saw you, you've grown into quite a young lassie." Mary smiled shyly.

"In fact, Rev. MacDougall, Mary is the reason we're here. Dear, can you ask the minister your questions?"

Without hesitation, Mary shared her concern about Rachel, her Jewish faith and her "need for Jesus." Rev. MacDougall listened intently without comment or question. Inwardly, he was besieged by a mix of emotions. He felt a growing anger, that any child should be expected to carry such a burden for her little friend's soul. At the same time, he had to be careful so as not to intrude upon another denomination's teaching. A dozen local clergy from diverse faith traditions and beliefs met monthly for mutual support, fellowship and planning. The group deliberately tread cautiously around issues which might divide them, focusing instead on their common ground as Christian ministers who presumably worshipped the same God and preached from the same Bible.

Once Mary had finished sharing her worries and confusion, Rev. MacDougall loosened his tie, took a deep breath and sent skyward a silent prayer for guidance. During that brief pause, Katie explained how her daughter had come to her only yesterday.

"Mary, I'm really glad you let your mother know that this was bothering you. And, Katie, I'm honoured that you chose to ask for my 'wisdom' as little as there may be on this very complicated question of who will get to heaven." As usual, Rev. MacDougall presented himself as a modest man, ever ready to deepen his understanding of his own faith. He brought this same approach to his sermons, frequently posing more questions than offering simplistic pat answers.

"Mary, let me try to explain it this way: Do you know the Lord's Prayer?

"Of course," she replied proudly. "We say it every morning at school—and at Sunday School in my church." Katie squirmed a bit at the reference to another church but Rev. MacDougall continued unperturbed.

"Can you remind me how it begins?" The minister smiled encouragingly.

"Our Father, which art in Heaven," she answered confidently.

"Do you know why we call God 'our Father'?"

"I know that he really isn't my father. He isn't even really a man. He's a spirit and invisible."

"I can see you're paying attention to your Sunday School teacher. But let's think a little more about this, okay?" Mary leaned forward, responding eagerly to the minister's gentle approach.

"I learned at my school, which was called 'seminary' that he is 'Father' because human beings can't see or understand an invisible spirit. So we say God is like the best-ever human father or mother in the world, and even better than that, better than we can imagine."

"Wow! That makes him really special."

"Mary, your father and mother have two children here on earth, right?"

"They used to have three, though."

"I remember. Do you think your father loves one of you more than the others?"

"No, of course not." Mary looked quickly at her mother who nodded just as quickly in agreement.

"Who are God's children?"

"Everybody, 'cuz God the Father made everyone. I learned that too."

"So if you and Rachel and everyone is a child of God, and if he loves all his children like a human dad does, even more so, would he love Rachel or Charlie any differently from you, even if she or he has a different religion—or no religion at all?

"Nooo, I guess he wouldn't do that. My dad likes me and my brother and we're *really* different." Mary smiled up at him.

Rev. MacDougall went on to explain, at a child's level of understanding, that Jesus himself was a Jew and a minister just like he was, except Jesus was called teacher or "Rabbi." Then he took a deep breath before proceeding.

"Mary, Miss Gardiner and I each try to understand God and the Bible as best we can. But we are only human, and often people see things differently. No one has all the answers! All you can do right now is to listen to grownups when they talk about religion and ask lots of questions. When you are old enough, you can decide what you truly believe. In the meantime, isn't it enough to know that God loves both you and Rachel and wants you to love her like He does? If you can do that, you won't have any more nightmares."

Mary thought for a moment, then looked as if she had something to say. Accepting his smile of invitation, she asked in a hopeful voice, "Is Sarah in heaven even though she didn't know Jesus?"

"Perhaps she never knew about Jesus the way Miss Gardiner does, but Jesus and God certainly knew her. Imagine if you had a very loving father whom you never met but who knew about you from the day you were born. Wouldn't he still love you and want you safely at home with him if you had to leave your home in Toronto? Well, that's just like what happened to Sarah."

"Of course he would." For the first time, Mary noticed her mother silently crying and went to her. "Mom, it's alright. Sarah is with God and Grandma and Grandpa Thompson. Don't be sad."

"Mary, these aren't sad tears. They're thankful ones." As mother and daughter embraced, the minister added one final thought.

"Remember when you said God is invisible? Well, He is but there is a way to actually see Him. Would you like to know how?" Surprised, Mary and Katie turned to the minister simultaneously.

"The Bible says that 'God is love.' That means I just saw God right now." Mary couldn't help but scan the room, wide-eyed and open-mouthed. "Mary, I saw you go and hug your mother as soon as you saw her tears. That space that drew you to her was filled with love. God was in that space and in that hug. That is where you will always see Him—wherever there is love in our home and in our world."

CHAPTER TWENTY ONE

The Humber was flowing faster than usual for this time of year. Recurring heavy rain had infused the river with energy force, giving it new life and purpose. The steady downpour caused the boy standing alone on the riverbank to huddle gratefully inside his black raincoat.

Charlie watched the muddy water swirling around half-submerged rocks that protruded from the river like the heads of curious hippopotamuses. On the downward side of each rock, momentarily protected from the current, foamy bubbles formed and frolicked for an instant before being carried away to an unknown destination around the next bend.

Yesterday's phone call had gone easier than anticipated. Maria answered after seven carefully counted rings. Before accepting his invitation to meet at the river, she placed her hand over the receiver while apparently seeking and getting parental permission.

As arranged, he was there at the dot of 4 p.m., hardly daring to believe he was about to see her again. A moment later she appeared, clad in a bright red slicker. Charlie did not even have time to feed his fear, that like before she wouldn't show up. The only problem now was that she was on the wrong side of the river!

"I thought you said we would meet over here," she called across the noise of the water. "I thought you were going to be over here," he shouted back, pointing downward to where his black rubber boots were firmly planted.

Charlie was rarely impulsive. He knew that Maria's school was on his side of the Humber, on Dennis Road, and that she always walked home. It made practical sense for them to meet on his side—at least that was the plan he thought he made clear on Sunday. It had been thoughtfully designed and pre-played in his head as almost all his actions invariably were. Now here they were, gazing across an impassable 70-foot-wide stretch of water, separated by fate like Romeo and Juliette which, coincidently, he had been studying in English class.

But when the occasion demanded it, Charlie could be spontaneous. He began to pull his feet from the protective confines of his boots.

"Charlie, what are you doing?" asked Maria, her voice a mixture of concern and amusement.

"I'm coming across." And with those words, he felt as if he were in a Tarzan movie, minus the crocodiles, about to ford a formidable river to rescue his Jane.

"Charlie, it's too deep. You'll get soaked—or drowned."

So much for Tarzan. "Well, wait there until I cross at James Street. I'll run."

"I can't. I have to be home by five. There isn't enough time. I'll be in big trouble if I'm late." Her face confirmed the worry was legitimate.

Charlie was prepared to break Roger Bannister's world record covering that mile: the distance to James Street, across the bridge and back down the far side of the river. But the reality was more sobering. If he selfishly asked Maria to wait, it would likely result in a curfew for her, or worse. Today's meeting would then become their last, and he would forever languish in Mr. Lupozzi's bad books, banished from Maria's life forever.

After an agonizing pause, the would-be friends so close and yet so far, the decision was made. They would linger no longer that day. Rain-soaked, cold and frustrated, Maria and Charlie turned away from the rushing waters and reluctantly set off on their separate ways. After only a few steps, though, Charlie knew he had to turn around and shout her name across the river, like tossing a lifeline.

"Maria, what about tomorrow but this side of the water?"

"Okay, sure" She tossed back a dazzling smile and resumed her trek home.

On Tuesday, the sun made a rare but most-welcome appearance. Its warmth matched Charlie's mood. He and Maria would meet again, this time on the same side of the river. Still, it seemed odd that despite their old-world ways, her parents were so casual about letting her spend time alone with him. A moment later, he didn't care.

Charlie floated through his classes. He strode more purposefully down the long corridors from room to room. He made eye contact with students sitting near him and joined in their banter before the teacher arrived. He even volunteered an answer or two in history class. Yet, with all his newly positive attitude, the school day dragged until the final bell—and freedom.

He refused to waste a precious second by stopping at home to drop off his books. That morning, he had forewarned his parents that he would be visiting "a friend" after school but would certainly be home by six for dinner.

"I bet your friend is a girl," Mary innocently teased after hearing her brother's casually presented announcement. Charlie's withering stare quickly silenced her.

"You mind your business, young lady. Charlie is old enough to choose his own friends without your help." Inwardly, Katie hoped Mary was right but dared not spook her maturing son.

By 4 p.m. the sun had stopped resisting the heavy clouds intruding from the west and disappeared from view. But Charlie's mood remained sunny as he carefully climbed down the slippery bank to reach their riverside point of rendezvous. And there she was! Even if the now-lost sun had forcefully pushed its way back through that cloudy barrier, the day could not be any brighter.

Maria had left yesterday's white raincoat and red rubber boots at home. What remained was something altogether different, her school uniform. Topped with a white, long-sleeved blouse under a dark green woollen sweater, her black pleated skirt came to mid-calf. Her black socks were knee-length (the Catholic school's way of ensuring not one inch of bare female leg was revealed.) Her black laced patent-leather shoes were mud-spattered from her descent down the steep incline.

Charlie had stuck with what he hoped was his winning combination: pink shirt, charcoal grey baggy pants, lightweight beige-coloured jacket and beloved cleated brown shoes.

"You made it." Even as she stated the obvious, it was both heartfelt and sincere.

"You did too. You even got here ahead of me." Just as obvious.

"I couldn't wait to get here. I've never walked so fast. I'm still out of breath." Her dark cheeks, tinged with a slight pink flush, proved the truth of her words.

Charlie too was breathless—though from delirium not exertion. "Yeah, I was watching the clock all day."

"So what was your day like at school?" she inquired.

"Same as most days—too much homework and some of my classes are boring." He was certainly not going to present his true self, the one that rarely spoke in class and who still ate lunch alone in a patch of muddy grass off school property.

"What's your school like?" The only thing Charlie knew about Catholic schools were the teachers were nuns, who wore long black gowns and sturdy laced-up shoes, and the kids had to be in uniform.

"I like my classes and we don't get too much homework." She was certainly not going to talk about how the boys were always making comments about her in the cafeteria. So unlike Calabria, where there were no boys in her class.

Over the next few seconds they stood silently facing one another, a few feet apart, keenly aware that this was the first time they had been together, without her parents and on the same side of the river. It felt scary and exciting at the same time.

"Do you want to walk?" asked Charlie, breaking the silence.

"Yes, but let's go south." Below them, the river curved left around a sharp bend, its dancing water no longer visible."

* * *

As they followed the bend, they were soon out of sight of Maria's home. It was new territory for Charlie, who rarely ventured past the solitude of the Humber. Sometimes, for a change of scenery, he would follow the riverbank north, toward the bridge at James Street—but never around that bend to the south.

Downstream, the Humber cut through marshy land. Over the years, several maple and willow trees had fallen across the eroding and crumbling bank and into the river. Despite their upper branches drowned beneath the rushing water, their shore-rooted trunks defiantly blocked the narrow trail. It quickly became tough going for the young couple, who stopped and rested, side by side, on a thick log.

"Have you been this way before?" asked Charlie, wondering why Maria had chosen this direction.

"No, I just wanted to see what was down here. Have you?"

"No. It's new for me too."

"Then I guess that makes us explorers," laughed Maria, turning her face toward Charlie. Her laughter came easily and once again revealed perfect white teeth attractively framed by her full red lips. He had remembered every detail of her face from her first appearance as the dark-haired mystery girl. But now she was no longer an apparition. She was here beside him, close enough to touch.

And sure enough, Maria gently placed her right hand across his long fingers, leaving it there as if it had found a home. In shyness, she didn't look at Charlie. They sat like that, still as statues, except for the four legs which rhythmically swung back and forth in the space beneath their wooden perch.

They talked about school and family, gradually sharing more openly as trust and comfort developed. They spoke of dreams and ambitions, of fears and hopes. Within an hour, they had become true friends. But, like Cinderella, the stroke of midnight was fast approaching for Maria—except in her case, midnight was 5 p.m.

"I have to get going; I'm supposed to be home by five."

"OK. Let's start walking." He jumped down and turned to catch her as she leaped off the log. His timing off, their bodies bumped together, and she threw her arms around his neck for balance. Throwing his habitual caution to the winds, he circled his arms around Maria's waist. Neither moved. Neither possessed the will to let go.

Finally, Charlie's logical mind caught up to his aroused emotions. "Maria, we better get going. You know I don't want to, but—"

Maria laughed. "Okay. You lead the way."

"Maybe we can find a shallow crossing, so you don't have to go all the way back to the bridge. It would be a lot shorter." Now Charlie was beginning to grow anxious. He had been pleasantly surprised that Mr. Luppozi had allowed her to spend two whole hours with him. He wasn't going to give him any reason to erect any barriers concerning his relationship with Maria.

"Your father was pretty good about letting us spend so much time together." He half-turned, throwing his words over his shoulder as she followed in his footsteps. In return, she threw back only silence.

A few moments later, they finally found a suitable spot for crossing: a maple tree trunk sprawled part way across the water. Just beyond and closer to the far shore protruded several rocks, which could act as stepping-stones.

"What do you think?" Charlie didn't think he'd be brave enough.

"I can do it." She hardly hesitated.

Efficiently removing socks and shoes, Maria stood before him, her bare feet half-disappearing into the muddy ground but not so deep that he couldn't take notice of her polished bright red toes. With one final hug, she turned and scampered, agile as a squirrel, across the log. Then, upon reaching the first half-submerged rock, she hesitated. The odd shaped granite was covered in slimy green moss. Even worse, the next rock lay at least three feet beyond the first—and was equally slippery.

"Be careful," he shouted, as if she weren't already.

"This is harder than it looked from the shore." She looked down as the rapidly moving stream flowed angrily under her feet.

Then to Charlie's open-mouthed astonishment, she began to roll up the hem of her skirt. "I don't want it to get wet."

Charlie paid no heed to her explanation. He gazed with mounting excitement as Maria's brown thighs were gradually exposed, inch by inch, as her skirt was lifted. He marvelled at seeing tanned legs in autumn until he realized that, unlike his Scottish light-complexioned background, her olive skin would reflect her Mediterranean heritage, regardless of the season.

"Wish me luck," she shouted over the roar of the current, and leaped nimbly on to the first rock.

"You did it," Charlie watched with admiration. "Keep moving, just two more to go." His words were swept away in a sudden gust of wind.

"I didn't hear what you said." Maria carefully turned around to face Charlie.

"I said you are doing good." He leaned forward to push his words cross the watery space between them. He saw her nod, confirming the message was received. Then her brown eyes darted to the path directly behind Charlie. This time, she was the one in open-mouthed astonishment. She stood motionless as a marble statue.

Charlie turned quickly—there was Mr. Lupozzi staring back at him with murderous intent.

To Donato Lupozzi, the scene before him stirred both a father's heartbreak and a protective anger. What he saw was his beloved Maria posing provocatively on a rock, her hair blowing freely in the wind, her long legs exposed for the pleasure of a man who watched with lustful intentions. The enraged father spoke first.

"What you doing to my daughter?" He roared, advancing on Charlie who was back-pedalling as quickly as possible toward the river's edge.

"Coming back from a walk." As soon as he said it, he knew it wasn't enough to cover the current situation. He tried again.

"Maria was trying to get home on time and we thought this way was faster. She didn't want to get her shoes wet." Charlie now realized how bad the picture looked from Mr. Lupozzi's perspective.

Not surprisingly, Maria's father was in no mood for explanations. He moved closer to Charlie who had by now backed himself into the water. The boy pondered for an instant whether death by drowning might be preferable to a fatal beating. Then Maria spared her new friend from having to make this impossible choice.

"*Babbo*, it was my fault. I lied and told him you gave me permission to meet after school." Maria now desperately attempted a return to Charlie's side of the river. She clambered back on to the fallen log, her petrified voice preceding her—"*E colpa mia.*" She hoped the guilty plea, this time in Italian, might spare Charlie's life.

"*Vieni qui!*" shouted Donato in return, as Marie finally reached him. As commanded, she approached, looking like a wet fearful puppy. For the moment, Charlie was a forgotten spectator. Though he couldn't understand the words, there was no mistaking their meaning.

With dramatic gestures, Maria explained that she had not only lied to Charlie but arranged for their walk. Charlie now understood why they had not taken the easier northward path; it would have risked their being spotted from her parents' house. With tears slowly trickling over her high cheekbones, Maria insisted they had done nothing wrong—only sat on a fallen tree trunk and talked.

* * *

For Donato Lupozzi, nothing was more sacred than family honour. Protecting his only daughter from men was a solemn duty. He had failed to protect his wife from the foreign soldiers. He would die before failing to protect his innocent child. He turned toward Charlie, still standing in the river as if mired in quicksand, water streaming past his thin white ankles.

"*Fuori di qui!*" he pointed toward the path leading up the steep bank and the road beyond.

Charlie needed no translator. He quickly did as he was bade, afraid to give even a single backward glance at Maria. If he had, however, he would have seen her leaning against the huge log for balance, as she gracefully dipped one foot then the other into the flowing water, washing away the accumulated mud more easily than she could rid herself of an overwhelming sense of guilt and desperation.

CHAPTER TWENTY TWO

Still in a daze, Charlie stood at the top of the riverbank, a few steps from Westdale Avenue. Rush hour traffic streamed by, ignoring his anguish. For an instant Charlie had an impulse to throw himself under the wheels of the closest truck. His breathing was laboured, not so much by the climb as the emotional intensity of that frightening confrontation with Mr. Lupozzi.

Charlie had already accepted that he would never see Maria again.

We messed it up; I should have known her father would never have approved of us meeting like that. Why didn't I question it? I suppose I can write her a note once in a while. But no calls. No dating. I never even got to kiss her.

At least I didn't get beat up. At least now I've got time after school for track. That's one thing I can get right, just not this girl business.

A minute later, as he waited for a break in the traffic, to cross Westdale, Charlie felt the sudden presence of someone directly behind him, looming like a shadow of death. Maria and her father had quickly climbed the steep path, the man half-dragging his daughter up the slope. As Charlie braced himself for a second attack, Mr. Lupozzie roared, "We go to you house. See you father, you mamma." And pointed toward his car parked beside the baseball diamond. Charlie glanced at Maria who shrugged helplessly.

Maria climbed in beside her father while Charlie, like some arrested bank robber on his way to jail, was ordered into the back seat. Kicking up gravel, the old Chevy roared out of the riverside parking lot and moved recklessly toward Charlie's house.

Doug had just washed up for dinner when an insistent pounding on the front door interrupted their meal preparation. Fortunately, as Mary was away at Rachel's, she would miss the drama which was soon to follow.

He quickly answered the door and was confronted by the sight of Charlie standing behind a powerfully built and obviously irate middle-aged man. The stranger spoke with an accent Doug immediately recognized as Italian. Completing the scene was a pretty dark-haired young woman who remained on the top step of the verandah as if she dared not come any closer. Both she and Charlie looked equally chastened by whatever had brought their irate companion to his porch.

"You the papa?" He was almost in Doug's face.

"What's going on?" Doug felt his own anger rising at the confrontation.

"You boy and my girl—" The man could go no further, his heart pounding and breathing rapid.

"What happened?" asked Doug, turning to Charlie.

"Nothing happened, Dad. We were just walking along the river. This is Maria." It seemed like an odd time for introductions but poor Charlie didn't know what else to offer by way of explanation.

In the instant before Charlie spoke, Doug had given credence to the frightening thought that his son and this young girl had been caught by her father in some sexual encounter.

Fortunately, Charlie's innocence was both obvious and reassuring and, for the moment, believable.

"Pleased to meet you, Maria." Like his son, Doug felt ridiculous, as if the awkward situation were just another social situation.

Katie's timely arrival broke the tension. Mr. Lupozzi's loud voice had reached the kitchen where she was setting the table. She now appeared at Doug's side, still wearing her apron. As further introductions seemed irrelevant, she smiled.

"Why don't we all come inside?" she said, motioning toward the living room. No point putting on a public show for the neighbours, she thought, keeping her growing embarrassment firmly hidden behind her fixed smile.

The group moved into the house, and Doug offered the couch to Maria and her father before his family sat down. Doug and Katie settled into the two matching stuffed chairs, while their visibly distraught son sat in an arborite chair hastily carried in from the kitchen. Thus Maria and Charlie found themselves facing one another but dared not exchange more than an occasional furtive glance. Both knew it would be the adults who did the talking.

"Now, tell us again what happened." Doug calmly initiated the conversation, though inwardly he experienced a mix of concern and annoyance over this sudden intrusion into their supper hour.

"My Maria and you son"—he had forgotten Charlie's name—"they were at river—no permission from me. Nobody tell me. I find them together. I bring him here to tell you. No more they be together." As anger rose up in his throat, causing him to pause and catch a breath, Katie took advantage of the moment.

"What do you mean 'they were together'?" she asked, fearing the worst but not really believing her son could be that involved with a girl he hardly knew.

"He watch her on the tree. She wear no stockings, no shoes. Dress high up. Very wrong." His description, while pronounced with much force, made no sense to Doug or Katie. They turned to Charlie for clarity.

"What happened, son?" Doug asked, hoping the boy's answer might sound more reassuring than this vague inappropriate behaviour

"We were walking along the Humber. Then Maria tried to cross the river to get home on time. She took off her socks and shoes so they wouldn't get wet." He looked at his father, his eyes making a silent plea for understanding.

"And nothing more happened—between you and Maria?"

"Nothing happened. We were walking and stopped to talk for a while. But nothing happened."

As none of the others was prepared to ask for an interpretation of "nothing happened," Katie stepped in.

"Didn't you ask Maria's father for permission to see her today?'

Charlie immediately thought of *Terry and The Pirates*. This past Sunday, the wicked Dragon Lady was about to extract vital secrets from Terry's girlfriend Gail, using torture as a tool. Just in the nick of time, the American pilot bravely jumped in to rescue her, not through strength but through words:

"I'm the one you want. Gail knows nothing. It's my plan. Go after me if you want but let the girl go."

But before Charlie could implement Terry's strategy and take the blame, Maria rescued him.

"*Babbo*, it was my fault. I told Charlie we had your permission. Don't be mad at him or his family. I'm sorry, *Babbo*." Her eyes moistened with unexpressed tears.

Mr. Lupozzi stood silent, the red of his angry face slowly draining until it pooled at his thick neck. Katie now chose to rescue him.

"Come into the dining room and sit down—all of you. Dinner is almost ready."

* * *

The formal dining room, with its round oak pedestal table, fancy Wedgewood china, her grandmother's sterling silverware and heavy, sturdy high-backed chairs, was seldom used except on special occasions. Charlie and Doug inwardly marvelled that such a painful situation could be magically transformed into a "special occasion," right up there with Christmas and birthdays.

In Donato's southern Italian tradition, refusing hospitality was not an option, despite the awkward circumstances which had brought them together. In fact, he now had another reason to continue his visit. Donato called Rosa to let her know where he and Maria would be for the next while. The full explanation would have to wait until they returned home.

Cutlery and silverware were quickly transferred to the new venue—Charlie and Maria eagerly helped; anything to reverse the damage they had caused—and the two families sat down. Katie had roasted a fresh chicken, intending it to last two days. Now it would be just enough to feed their guests., Still, she considered no leftover chicken sandwiches or homemade soup to be a worthy sacrifice under the circumstances.

Donato Lupozzi was not a man given to facile apologies. Yet even on the porch, he realized he had misjudged Charlie. He needed to pull an apology from deep within, and it needed to be voiced before the meal began.

"I speak wrong to your boy"—he obviously still hadn't remembered the "boy" had a name. "I am sorry."

"Mistakes happen," Doug chose to be conciliatory, sensing Donato's effort to set the situation right.

"My Maria, she get punished, but at home, not now."

"Mr. Lupozzi, Charlie has told us your daughter is doing well at school." Once again, Katie adroitly shifted the conversation. Maria smiled shyly but kept her eyes away from her father's glare.

Dinner conversation quickly led to the common ground of Italy and September, 1943.

Doug would not have introduced the subject, being unsure of the other man's personal experiences with the Canadian invaders—or did he remember them as liberators? But his guest didn't hesitate.

"You were with Canadian soldiers in my country?"

"Yes, I was there with the 48th. In September, 1943. Charlie tells me you are from Calabria?" Not wanting to presume, it was directed as a question, not a sentence.

"My family—we are there when you come. The four and eight give us food." Maria was shocked to see her *Babbo*'s eyes moisten.

"I remember going into your town. The mayor was there. We didn't know what kind of welcome we would get, but everyone was really nice to us. I remember---" His voice trailed off, as memories took him far away.

The rest of the meal was punctuated by politeness, smiles and occasional laughter and more storytelling. Even Charlie and Maria felt it was safe enough to relax and enjoy the food and conversation, though they still didn't dare exchange more than a covert glance.

For the three adults, any repercussions from the riverbank confrontation lay dormant but not safely buried. It wouldn't be until later, when each of them had exchanged the day's busyness—kitchen cleanup, evening routines and homework—for the dark quiet of night and bed that old demons were stirred and memories flooded back.

CHAPTER TWENTY THREE

D onato Lupozzi adjusted his thick feather pillow for the tenth time but achieved the same result. Sleep continued to elude him. His thoughts had taken him back to Calabria. Rosa was in that sunny little kitchen, stirring her pot of pasta and singing softly. The fragrant sauce—tomatoes, peppers, beef and onions—were happily bubbling on the wood stove, two loaves of bread rising in the oven below. Maria would soon be home from school—a girls' school, safe from the prying eyes of boys. She was seven years old, her innocent eyes alive with life itself, her raven hair neatly braided.

Earlier that night, when he and Maria had returned from the Thompsons' dinner, Donato had sent Maria to her room so he could explain to Rosa the troubling events of the past few hours. Her initial reaction was like his, instinctive anger at her misbehaving daughter. She too agreed some punishment was warranted. But when Rosa learned their host was a former Canadian soldier who had actually been in Calabria during the war, her attention turned to her husband. Any time Donato was reminded of those terrible years, he became distant and dark for days. Now, as she lay beside him, Rosa could tell this time was no different.

But it was neither roving marauders nor pervasive hunger which was robbing him of sleep this time. It was neither the roar of English cannon nor the stench of death. It was the realization that his little girl was becoming a woman, and far too soon. For the first time, he began to accept that one day she would be gone. That one day some other man would claim her. Of course, he had always known she would marry. As *nonno*, he looked forward to bouncing a tiny bambina or bambino on his knee. As long as it remained in his head, none of it was troubling. But today he had witnessed a boy staring at her half-exposed woman's body on that rock. Try as he might, Donato could not expunge that image from his thoughts. The dark night rolled on, unconcerned with his plight.

Now the riverbank incident claimed its second victim. For Rosa, memories of Calabria shifted from worries about Donato to her own long-buried pain. In the dark of midnight, after sleep finally claimed her, she once again encountered the Moroccans. They came up the road, but not in the orderly formations of the Canadians or Germans. They came in groups of two or three, covered in dust and grime. Some carried chickens and vegetables stolen from homes along their route. A few came seeking to satisfy other needs.

A tall skinny soldier with a wild mat of dark hair, a torn tunic and a rifle casually slung over his shoulder filled the doorway of her home. Donato was away. As he pushed past her and into the house, Rosa screamed for her husband—and woke up bathed in sweat and calling his name.

Donato groggily rolled over and pulled her into his warm body, his strong arms encircling her with protection and sanctuary. He too remembered, with a heavy weight of guilt, what his absence in Calabria had cost.

"*Non temere*," he murmured gently over and over until she once again found refuge in sleep. "*Non temere*." Don't be afraid.

* * *

Doug Thompson's night was equally troubled, albeit with different memories. Seeing this new immigrant from Italy had opened the floodgates to thoughts of the war. Once his family had gone to bed, Doug sat quietly in his maple rocker, hoping the steady back-and-forth rhythm would slow his racing mind.

It was only a few days ago that Charlie's off-hand comment had reluctantly returned him to Calabria. Today's unexpected visitors had once again transported him to 1943 and Italy.

The epic battle for Ortona ended on December 28, with the town liberated but battered into rubble. The 48th was in action further west, being ordered to take San Tomasso. British artillery covered the Canadian attack with its heavy guns. Four massive Sherman tanks led the way, the thirty-five-ton vehicles clanking ahead of battalions of slowly advancing troops and offering shelter from German snipers. From behind the Allied lines, two-pound mortars lobbed smoke bombs to conceal the advancing Canadians.

Doug's company was moving steadily up a muddy road when the men suddenly came under a barrage of artillery fire. As shells landed in their midst and jagged chunks of shrapnel filled the air, they dove for cover in roadside water-filled ditches. In dismay, they quickly realized the shelling was coming from British guns which, somehow, were firing short of their targets. The beleaguered soldiers screamed and cursed at the sky but to no avail; the deadly rain continued to pour down.

Among the Canadian casualties that day were raw recruits, newly arrived on the front and rushed into battle. Doug pulled two bodies off the road, their uniforms stained red—a dead man's badge of honour? When the errant barrage was finally stopped, the attack on San Tomasso resumed. The Highlanders soon took the village, but only after vicious house-to-house fighting. The dead remained in the ditch.

As Doug relived those hours, he felt the familiar fear rise again in his stomach. He could see himself crouching to enter a half-demolished house, but not until he had pulled the pin and rolled a grenade through the open door and down the hall like some deadly bowling ball. Even after hearing the ear-shattering blast, you could never be sure the building was clear. The platoon moved slowly, room by room, hoping no Germans were squatting in some darkened corner, waiting to kill them. They also prayed they had slaughtered no innocents, who might have huddled inside.

By December's end, the Canadian First Division had suffered 2,339 casualties, including 502 dead and 152 missing. As the German 1st Parachute Division and Panzer Grenadiers grudgingly yielded territory, the struggle slowly moved northward up the eastern flank of Italy. By September, 1944, the 48th Highlanders were poised to attack German defenses stretched out across the Rimini Line all the way from the city of Rimini on the Adriatic coast and the higher ground of San Fortunato to the west.

Back home, war dispatches from the Italian front no longer claimed the front page of the Telegraph. Katie anxiously awaited word of the 48th. But the reality was that other news was making headlines. Dramatic events were rapidly unfolding elsewhere.

On June 6, 155,000 Allied troops stormed ashore in Normandy. Western Europe's deliverance had begun. The Third Canadian Infantry Division and Second Canadian Armoured Division, with some 14,000 soldiers, landed at Juno beach. Offshore, Royal Canadian Navy ships provided support from its heavy guns. Back home, both the Star and the Telegram proclaimed a successful Canadian assault against German coastal defenses and, later, their capture of Caen. Canadian troop columns would soon be driving inland, pushing the Nazis back toward Paris.

Meanwhile, Canadian forces in Italy soldiered on, despite the lack of headlines. Italy had become the less important "second front." Rumours spread among the soldiers that they were suspected of having avoided the invasion of Western Europe on purpose, and were supposedly waiting out the end of the war in much safer Italy. The furious Canadians wrongly blamed aristocratic English politician Lady Astor for calling them "D-Day Dodgers" and so belittling their battlefield struggles against "Jerry," their formidable German adversary. With a wry smile, he remembered how they and the British had concocted their own set of lyrics, set to the tune of "Lily Marlene":

We landed at Pachino, a holiday with pay
Jerry brought a band out, to cheer us on our way
Showed us the sights, and gave us tea
We all sang songs, the beer was free
We kissed all the girls in Napoli
For we are the D-day Dodgers, over here in Italy.
Now Lady Astor, get a load of this.
Don't stand up on a platform and talk a load of piss.
You're the nation's sweetheart, the nation's pride
We think your mouth's too bloody wide.
We are the D-day Dodgers, in Sunny Italy.

A later stanza reflected the anger and venom felt by the men:

When you look 'round the mountains, through the mud and rain
You'll find the crosses, some of which bear no name.
Heartbreak and toil and suffering gone.
The boys beneath them slumber on
They were the D-Day Dodgers, who'll stay in Italy.

He was roused from his half-sleep by Katie's gentle voice summoning him to bed. She was well aware that, come tomorrow, he faced a long's day's labour. Yet she too would find that a good night's rest also eluded her that night, as she pondered the day's events. Any mention of the conflict in Italy brought her own wartime memories into sharp relief, and this time was no different. In the middle of that long night, she resolved to see her pastor and his comforting wife tomorrow.

* * *

Not only the adults were troubled.

Maria Lupozzi knew full well that by being alone with a boy, she had dishonoured her family. Worse, she had publicly embarrassed her proud *Babbo*. But worst of all, by lying, she had committed a sin against God.

She accepted her father's punishment without argument; being confined to home for a month (apart from school) would help alleviate the guilt which hung around her slender neck like the dead albatross she read about in English class. Besides, if she were still in Calabria, she might have received a whipping. Fortunately, now that they were in Canada, her parents accepted that corporal punishment was considered inappropriate—to Donato's secret relief.

In bed that night, Maria felt pulled between the constraints of her family's culture and the lure of freedom calling to her from this new world.

Charlie was equally restive. His parents had assured him there would be no punitive consequences for his Humber escapade. Nevertheless, there were consequences of a different kind. He could not stop thinking about Maria. By itself, this was nothing new. She had been on his mind since that first moment when she pranced along the riverbank, into his sight and into his life. What was different was a primal hunger that raged throughout his body.

As before, he desperately wanted to see her again, for friendship and conversation. But now he fantasized about kissing her, about pulling her body close to his and never letting go. He could almost smell the fragrance of her long dark hair as they drew close, the warm softness of her back as his arms encircled her.

In those hours of sleeplessness Charlie had replaced the comic book images of jungle heroines with the memory of Maria on that rock, her brown legs splashed with river water, her hair pushed by the river breeze and blowing wildly across her face. She was now his Wonder Woman.

* * *

Everyone who had sat around the Thompson dining room table eventually found some measure of comfort that long night. But of all those affected, only Charlie—shy and timid Charlie—would find resolution in a plan of action. He would see Maria tomorrow—somehow, somewhere!

CHAPTER TWENTY FOUR

Maria's high school was about a twenty-minute walk from Brock Collegiate. For Charlie it would have to be a ten-minute run. His plan was simple: He would leave school right at the bell and intercept Maria as she walked home. He knew the route she would be travelling and, if he was fast, he could catch her on Albert Street near the corner of Lomax Avenue. They would then have ten minutes before reaching the Humber Bridge, at which point he would slip away lest Mrs. Lupozzi be looking out her window. Charlie knew her mother would be especially vigilant after only twenty-four hours.

Charlie's scheme overlooked one small detail when, at school's end, he found himself burdened by three weighty textbooks in addition to the usual notebooks. Three different teachers had independently assigned chapters from their texts to be read by next class. There was no time to drop them off at home. He would have to carry them as he ran.

At 3:11 p.m., he rushed through the heavy dark-stained wooden doors with their wired window glass and onto Bloor Street. He ran up Princess, then Palmer and Lismer before reaching Albert. Just a few more blocks to Lomax and he would be there.

Charlie's arms were aching from the weight of the books. His lungs were burning and his feet sore from the constant pounding on the concrete sidewalk. He should have worn sneakers, not thin-soled leather dress shoes. His pace slowed to a walk.

With two short blocks to go, Charlie noticed a trickle of sweat rolling down his rib cage, leaving behind a residue of body odour. He knew that his face was covered in perspiration. His handkerchief took care of his face; the underarm wetness and stink would prove more of a challenge.

Just then, Charlie saw Maria one block away and heading straight toward him. He noted with instant relief that she was alone. Last night, he had wrestled with two possible scenarios. In the first, she was surrounded by a cluster of female schoolmates. How could he find time and space to talk with her without having to share his almost-girlfriend with onlookers? But the second scenario was much worse. What if she was with some boy from her school, some tall, muscular football player—and Catholic? That last part would undoubtedly please Mr. Lupozzi, but could forever relegate Charlie to second place.

His almost-girlfriend recognized him. He saw her mouth open with surprise, then transform into a wide smile. As she drew nearer, Charlie admired again the attractive school uniform, its white blouse contrasting against her olive skin. He couldn't keep himself from checking her bare knees to see if the Humber riverbank mud had been scrubbed off. For an instant he felt a compulsion to open his arms, inviting her into an embrace. That was what had happened in *The Student Prince*. Instead, when they finally came together, Charlie playfully and gently punched her in the arm, as if he were greeting a buddy at summer camp. He instantly regretted it, but Maria's smile never faltered.

"What are you doing here?"

"I came to meet you and maybe walk you part way home"

Now her face tightened for a moment. "You know I'm grounded. I'm not supposed to see you. Even though I want to."

That last phrase triggered such a pounding in Charlie's heart that he feared it might burst through his skin.

"I wanted to see you too. That's why I'm here." He was being redundant but for some reason it didn't matter.

Neither knew what to say next. So Maria resumed her walk toward home, her shining brown eyes silently inviting Charlie to come along. He quickly moved in step beside her, then impulsively offered to carry her books. He had seen the more popular guys make this move with their girlfriends. Maria paused and then, extending both arms, carefully placed her texts into his eager grasp. Her escort quickly balanced this new added weight. By repositioning his own books on his left hip and arranged hers on the right. Almost immediately, he realized the next blocks would be an endurance test.

Though the schoolbooks were now anchored between his hands and hips, their positioning caused Charlie to walk with a most unnatural gait, his shoulders rigidly fixed, his long skinny arms pulled lower than what was comfortable and locked into place. He felt new rivulets of sweat roll down his dampened forehead and cheeks but this time had no means of wiping them away. Salt began to sting his eyes, and he blinked desperately in an abortive attempt to flush it out.

What if Maria thinks I have some kind of facial tic? Or even worse, that I'm winking at her, like a creepy person. Maybe I could shake my head wildly and get rid of it that way. Except then she'll wonder why I keep saying no when she hasn't asked me anything.

All he could do was soldier on, hoping she wouldn't notice his dilemma.

Next, since the walk was his idea, Charlie felt it was up to him to initiate conversation—to demonstrate an intelligence of mind or perhaps a subtle bit of humour. Unfortunately, he could think of nothing smart or funny. Even worse, between Maria's unusually fast walking pace and his increasingly weighty book burden, he was getting out of breath. Would he even be able to complete a sentence without gasping for air and sounding weak?

Instead, Marie began to talk about her day at St. Francis's. Charlie inferred that she was an excellent student, despite her dismissive comments about English and algebra tests. While certainly not bragging, she didn't hide the fact that she found schoolwork easy. She went on to describe her involvement in the school band where she played the violin. She also liked basketball and hoped to make the Junior team when tryouts began in November.

As Charlie listened with genuine interest, he was also filtering her chatter to determine from her free-flowing description of school life if there were interest in any of the boys in her class. So far so good!

After a few minutes Maria suddenly stopped, leaving her companion striding on ahead for three steps before realizing she was no longer beside him.

"Hey! I've been doing all the talking. How was your day?" Up to this point he had been content to simply enjoy listening to her soft warm voice while trying to deal with the increasing numbness in both arms and the pungent smell lurking underneath them. But Marie hurried to catch up and looked up expectantly.

"Pretty much the same as always," he replied with a weak smile, hoping the latter would compensate for the paucity of his answer. In reality, he was indifferent to school, had no extracurricular involvements (now that he had abandoned his cross-country coach) and knew he was at best a mediocre student. What else could he find to say?

"Then tell me more about your family. I enjoyed meeting them yesterday. Where does your dad work?"

"He's a stone mason and bricklayer. Building walls for new houses and making fancy decorations for their porches."

"And your Mom? She seems really nice, having us for dinner and all, despite—."

Charlie felt decidedly more relaxed, now that the conversation shifted away from school to home. No one had ever asked him about his family; and as he shared spontaneously and with some pride, he realized how much he liked them. For the first time, he voiced feelings he had never articulated: about how his dad worked hard to support them, and his mother often made special desserts. He even talked about Mary in positive terms, remembering the many Saturday afternoons, when he had no friends knocking on the door, that they'd played make-believe or checkers together.

Though he was tempted to mention his other sister, it seemed too soon for that. Instead, he turned the discussion back to Maria.

"I liked meeting your dad too." He instantly remembered with an internal shudder Mr. Lupozzi's red face and realized "liked" was not quite accurate; but he persevered. "What does he do?"

"He helped build the subway. He's in construction. My mom stays at home and volunteers at our church."

They were almost at the bridge. For Charlie, the time was passing far too quickly— although his throbbing arms silently disagreed. But they couldn't risk being seen. What if Mrs. Lupozzi was at the window with binoculars? Or her father happened to drive home early? It was already past 4 p.m. So much remained to be said.

"I'd better give you back your books and get going," he said, more casually than he felt.

"Yes, we don't want my father to see us together." She smiled, giving voice to the unspoken worry they both carried.

"I could walk with you tomorrow. If you want," he added hopefully.

"Same time? Unless I get a detention" Given her school performance, it was clearly a joke.

"OK. I'll be seeing you then." How do you say goodbye to an almost-girlfriend in public, he wondered.

Once again, Maria made the decision for him. With a quick "see you then," quickly retrieved her books and, with one final dazzling smile, turned toward home, leaving the almost-boyfriend staring at her retreating figure.

CHAPTER TWENTY FIVE

K atie had awakened that morning, but only after the alarm clock rudely exchanged its timid ticking for a raucous ringing in her ear. She habitually arose at 6 a.m. before any wake-up alarm was needed, but last night's ghosts had drained her of all energy.

Yesterday's unplanned dinner conversation with Mr. Lupozzi and Maria had resolved the issue of that clandestine river meeting, but did nothing to put to rest the dormant memories reawakened by her husband's talk of the war. Despite lingering grogginess, she managed the routine morning demands of launching her family off into their worlds, fueled by a particularly nourishing breakfast of porridge, toast, juice and eggs and fully presentable for outside scrutiny in their freshly laundered clothes.

The only respite from her conscience was to promise God and herself that she would see the pastor as soon as he was available Which is why, at 10:00 a.m., she was sitting on a hard wooden pew near the back of the sanctuary in Faith Tabernacle.

In a few minutes the door to the sanctuary opened and Gloria Hanson greeted her with that full-body hug which always felt more like a squeeze of religious enthusiasm. Then the two women moved to her husband's office and sat across from the pastor's cluttered desk.

Pastor Hanson was already seated but rose quickly to offer his visitor a simultaneous smile and firm handshake.

"How are Doug and the children?" he asked, hoping this qualified as the kind of "small talk" he had learned about in Professor Johnson's Pastoral Care class, a little chatter designed to relax the parishioner before entering into the "meat of the matter." Even so, seemingly innocent questions would sometimes elicit an unexpected burst of tears if they inadvertently hit upon the reason for the visit. Fortunately, not this time.

"They are all fine, Pastor. I'm here today about me." She paused for a moment to muster up her courage.

"You remember that I came to see you earlier this month and told you about my involvement with Doug's friend."

He nodded encouragingly. "Yes, of course. As I recall, you were going to pray about whether or not to tell Doug about"—he searched carefully for the right word— "about your situation."

"Except that's not why I'm here today," Katie hurriedly added, before the discussion strayed in the wrong direction. "I still haven't decided about Doug, but now I have a bigger problem."

The Hansons maintained an attentive silence.

"I must tell you both that I was not completely honest last time." Unbidden tears began to well up and, despite her efforts to hold them back, spilled out of her eyes and rolled slowly downward over her flushed cheeks. Katie found herself stuck in mid-confession. Gloria gently came to her help.

"Maybe you could share the thing you were unable to talk about last time?'

"It's still hard to talk about that, but I need to deal with this more or it will tear me apart. Last night we had company for dinner. An immigrant man and his daughter." She then explained the reason for the sudden and upsetting circumstances surrounding that meal.

"Anyway, Doug and the man got reminiscing about the war years. That stirred up a lot of emotions I thought I had left behind. They weren't buried all that well, I guess. I tossed and turned all night." Katie turned to Pastor Hanson. "Which is why I decided this morning to ask for a meeting with you."

"I'm glad you came, Katie," he assured her, then waited with an inviting silence.

Inwardly, he wondered whether this dinner guest might be the man with whom she had been romantically involved. Could he have resurfaced more than a decade later?

Katie sensed his unspoken question and quickly moved to clarify the situation. "This man is Italian, from one of the towns in Italy where

Doug served in 1943. That got me thinking about what I did the first month he was away."

"You mean with Doug's friend?"

"Yes, I told you part of the story last time but there is more you need to know, I'm afraid. He and I... we went too far... it got intimate... and I, I carried his child. Doug doesn't know." At this point Katie broke down into sobs which seemed wrenched from the depths of her soul. Her thin shoulders shook uncontrollably, her face buried in both hands. Between sobs, she struggled painfully for each breath.

Pastor Hanson glanced anxiously at his wife, who immediately rose from her chair, knelt beside Katie, and enveloped her in her arms. The two women remained locked together as the sobbing gradually eased. Offering any such physical assurance to women was not an option for the pastor. He was grateful for both Gloria's presence and her genuine compassion.

"Like I said, Doug was away, had been since October of '41 when he enlisted at Newmarket." Katie had found a white linen handkerchief deep in her purse and was wiping away tears as she resumed her story. As the details of this long-buried painful chapter in her life slowly emerged, she found herself shifting from recounting the event to reliving it.

Greg Ramidal had knocked on the Thompsons' front door a couple of weeks after Doug left. He was surprised to learn that his work buddy had enlisted and would be spending the rest of the fall and winter training at Camp Pender in New Brunswick. At best, he might get one short leave before being shipped out to England.

Katie reminded the Hansons that she first met 35-year-old Greg in 1939 shortly after her marriage. Over the next several months, Doug would occasionally bring him to the house for dinner. Afterwards, while she did the dishes and prepared Doug's lunch for next day, the two men smoked and talked in the living room.

By 8 p.m., she was always tired. Her first pregnancy (which resulted in Charlie) was proceeding without complication, but still left her fatigued by day's end. So she would stop by the living room and, conscious of her bloated and tired-looking appearance, offer a warm goodnight to their guest. Doug would routinely see him off an hour or so later.

From their bedroom, Katie would lay awake and listen. Over time, she found herself focusing more on Greg than her husband. She easily pictured him sitting in the overstuffed easy chair. He was taller than Doug, more wiry than muscular, with the dark tanned face of a man whose days were spent outdoors. His hair was long and needed cutting. Had he ever married?

Was he maybe now courting a girl? As soon as her thoughts turned in that direction, she dismissed them as inappropriate, rolled over as best she could during that long pregnancy and was asleep before Doug joined her in bed.

Just before Charlie was born the following July, Greg moved to British Columbia. The start of the war in September a year earlier meant new and better-paying work for him in the farms and orchards of Penticton. Over the next eighteen months, they never heard a word from him—until the day he suddenly stood on her doorstep and Katie invited him in.

As she paused again in her story, bringing her thoughts and emotions back into the pastor's office, Katie wished that she was Catholic. They had confessional booths, where a person could get the guilt out without having to look into shocked and disapproving eyes. But when she reluctantly met their gaze, Katie was surprised to see only concern and caring.

Inwardly, both the pastor and his wife had a good idea where this story was headed, but they felt the same compassion as Jesus with the woman caught in adultery. For the moment, all other emotions were wisely locked away.

Pastor Hanson gently encouraged her to continue. "Tell us again what happened, after he came in the house?"

"I made coffee and we talked. Charlie—my son—had just settled so we had the whole evening. Greg wanted to know what had gone on while he was out west. And I was curious to know why he was back east. He said it was for his mother's funeral, that he'd be leaving in two days for a job in Vancouver. I felt sad for him. He hadn't seen his mother since last Christmas. She was in good health then but keeled over with a massive heart attack about ten days earlier. He couldn't get here before she passed. That was hard on him. I guess we were both going through a rough patch."

"What was your rough patch, Katie?" Gloria asked with a tone that suggested more than curiosity.

"I don't like to complain about how things were at home back then. It wasn't anyone's fault." That was certainly true. Although she didn't know the word "stoic," she lived her life that way—as did her mother before her.

"The truth is, I didn't want Doug to enlist. We already had a little boy to look after and Doug was twenty-seven years old. The army was for younger men, the twenty-year-olds. I knew there was a war on but why did my husband not see that his family was the real priority?"

"Why do you think he did?" Pastor Hanson tried to put himself in Doug's shoes—what would he have done?—and thought it might be helpful for Katie to do the same.

"I don't really know." She looked puzzled. "I know he believed strongly in being a good citizen and supporting your country in times of need. He loved Canada. I also know two or three fellows from work enlisted, though mind you they were younger. Now that I think about it, I do recall that he was very proud of his father. Grandpa Joe served in the Great War—he joined up in 1917—and he and Grandma Sadie had Doug by then. He was two, the same age as Charlie was…" Katie's voice trailed off.

"It sounds as if you were carrying some resentment by the time this other fellow came back into your lives."

"Of course I was!" She suddenly became visibly angry. "Here I was with a toddler to look after and trying to survive on his pay cheque which certainly wasn't much. But more than that, it was the way the decision was made. He just waltzed in the door one evening and told me he had a surprise. I thought he might have got a raise or maybe a lead on a car. We had been talking about buying a car now that we were a family of three. Instead, he tells me he's been to Newmarket and joined the 48th. Just like he had stopped to buy hamburger from the butcher." Katie realized how silly she sounded, and her mood softened a bit. Gloria used the opening to shift the focus of the conversation.

"What kind of reaction did Doug expect from you? Didn't he suppose you might be upset?"

"In fact, no. He told me later that he thought I'd be proud of him. He knew it would be hard for me as a single parent—and maybe a widow, God forbid—but assumed I'd support his decision. After all, Doug knows I love this country too."

"Then I see why that evening was difficult for both of you. You each were disappointed in the other's reaction." Katie nodded silently in agreement. After hearing herself out loud, she saw more clearly how their talk had been equally hard on Doug. Back then, she'd been too shocked, angry and hurt to see past her own emotions.

"How does this other fellow fit into the story?" Gloria gently steered the other woman back to the issue at hand. Neither she nor her husband referred to Greg by name. To do so would give the man unwarranted legitimacy.

"Greg just came along at the right—or I guess I should say the wrong—moment. I was angry at Doug. I felt rejected, abandoned, that my feelings and situation didn't matter." As the tears began again to flow, she fished in her purse for another handkerchief until Gloria came to the rescue with one of her own.

"It sounds crazy, but the other thing is I really was caught off guard by Greg. I never knew a woman could be attracted to another man once she got married. When I felt myself being drawn to him I didn't know what to do. I mean, of course I knew what I should have done. Stop and kick him out. But I never expected my emotions and physical desires to take over so strongly. My 'should' just went out the window." All she could do was shake her head, as she should have done that day.

She continued. "Like I said, Greg and I had relations, and I got pregnant with Sarah. By the timing, I knew it was not Doug's baby. Greg had already gone back west so he didn't know. Not that it would have mattered, I had no intention of continuing the relationship. And I was able to pass off the baby as Doug's, since he was still living with us at home in early October. You should have read his letter from New Brunswick after I phoned him just before Christmas with the news. He said he'd always hoped we could give Charlie a little sister or brother but that we'd have to wait until after the war. When he was home on leave for her birth, I decided against telling him the truth. If I'd told him, it would have killed him before the Germans could."

"And after he returned in '45?"

"I should have but I didn't. Not after seeing Doug walk right over to Sarah's play pen and lift her up and into his big arms. I can still see him walking around the living room, telling her he was her daddy and would always take care of her. I just couldn't. Guess I was afraid he wouldn't love her the same if he knew she wasn't his."

Pastor Hanson and his wife remained silent. Neither had any desire to condemn Katie's decision. But each knew the Bible's teaching on honesty, let alone its condemnation of adultery. And so they prayed inwardly for divine wisdom and spiritual guidance.

"Katie, you have been honest with us and we can appreciate that this hasn't been easy.

"You have been carrying guilt over this for years, and there's no need for you to hear more about that from us.

"Remember, the Bible condemns adultery, but it also speaks about God's readiness to forgive. When the woman was caught in adultery and the crowd was about to stone her, Jesus challenged them. 'Let the one of you who is without sin cast the first stone.' And they all went away chastened. Our Lord also spent time with another woman, a Samaritan, at the well. She was living with a man who was not her husband. Jesus also treated her with compassion without ever condoning her behaviour."

Gloria knew from experience that her husband was at risk of shifting into preaching mode and gently interceded.

"Katie, what is it that you are most of all struggling with today?"

"I think God punished me by taking away my child eleven years later." She began to sob, her tears shedding both guilt and anger in equal measure.

"Why do you feel that way?" Gloria asked somewhat hastily, before her husband could continue with his reassurance. While she shared her husband's sense of compassion, she also knew that what was needed now was insight, not reassurance, that Katie needed to dig deeper. Why was this distraught woman sitting in their office so convinced God was punishing her?

Katie remained silent for another moment while she inwardly grasped for the right church language to explain her fear. She was obviously no theologian and still only a novice in this congregation, but possessed a good memory for her minister's sermons and teaching.

"Pastor Hanson, you gave me a copy of the Ten Commandments when I joined your congregation. When I read that God punishes children for the sins of their fathers, I figured there would be no better consequences for the sins of their mothers." Katie envisioned the little card she had stuck on the pastel fridge door. She had tried to memorize one commandment each morning, after the family had left the house and while she quietly enjoyed her coffee.

"I never noticed those words until I looked more closely at the Second Commandment.

And there it was, literally right in my face! Pastor, what else can it mean except that God punished Sarah because of my sin?" Hidden within Katie's query was the unspoken deeper issue of what kind of God would inflict that punishment—polio—on an innocent child.

"Ah, but in John Chapter 10, we read that Jesus explained that a man's blindness was not the fault of either of his parents. You see—"

"Pastor Frank." Even as she cut her husband off, she referred to him by title as she always did in front of others. "Maybe we should avoid getting too theological. I think Katie and I might get further ahead if we took a walk together. That is, if you have a bit more time, Katie."

Pastor Hanson was momentarily caught off guard. Gloria rarely interrupted when he was offering spiritual counselling. But it didn't take him long to realize she had seen something he hadn't. He closed their meeting with a prayer that God would give "wisdom and guidance" as they continued working together to help Katie. As the two women then left the room to put on their raincoats, Pastor Hanson eagerly sought a second cup of Sanka.

* * *

The rain had temporarily eased in strength, reduced to a light shower of droplets gently tumbling on Katie and Gloria's shared umbrella as they walked through quiet neighbourhood streets.

"Katie, I know you can find verses in Scripture to hit yourself over the head with. I've done it myself, lots of times, but I've also learned to not take bits of the Bible in isolation."

"What do you mean? Isn't all the Bible true?"

"Yes, God's Word is true, but the Bible is meant to be read as a book, not picking out one page to read and making that the whole story."

"But I read in another story that David's son died as a baby, because he committed adultery with Bathsheba and had her husband killed." Katie glanced at her friend, hoping to make sense of why Gloria was trying to wash away those troubling passages.

Gloria returned the glance with a warm smile. "Let's consider this from a different perspective. How often have you heard Pastor Frank speak about God's love?"

"The first Bible verse I ever heard from him was 'God so loved the world that he gave his only begotten son—'" Katie was eager to demonstrate that she did listen to the minister's sermons. But, for a brief moment, her thoughts strayed to her recent conversation with Rev. MacDougall, who had essentially made the same point.

"Well," continued Gloria, "that is the kind of God I believe in, the loving one, not a God who can't wait to kill babies or—" she paused to consider her next words "—or take away your Sarah."

"But you know how much we prayed for her to get well. Lots of children with polio have gotten better even if some were left disabled. Why couldn't we have her back home, even with crutches and braces? Your church, I mean our church, prayed a lot for Sarah. Mrs. Goodwan used to tell me how much you all did."

"Katie, your question is a good one and I admit I don't understand why some prayers are answered the way we ask and some are not. It's a question the church has struggled with since it began almost two thousand years ago. Right now, we only 'see through a glass darkly' as the Apostle Paul puts it. One day we will understand more clearly. I believe with all my heart that God promises to always be with us to help us get through these hard times, even if he doesn't always stop them from happening."

"Yes, I know I have felt that He is close especially when I am sad. I can't really explain it in words. I just know it helps me to get past that darkness."

"Katie, your words did say it perfectly." Gloria stopped and hugged her friend under their shared umbrella.

Later that morning, Katie made her way home through the now-driving rain, her red umbrella straining to hold itself together against a strong east wind. She felt cleansed by the water splashing in her face. She replayed her conversation with Gloria. That time together had helped Katie to lay down the last of her burden, the heavy boulder she had been dragging behind her on a chain these many years. She no longer felt that some huge past mistake—her adultery with Greg—had caused her daughter to be sacrificed to appease the wrath of an angry God.

Gloria had gently led her toward a new understanding of the Creator she worshipped every Sunday. Once Katie had learned how to let go of the chain, the boulder was left behind.

But one troubling question remained. To complete her journey toward redemption, should she tell Doug about her long-ago affair with his trusted friend?

SPECIAL WEATHER BULLETIN

Hurricane Hazel moved inland near Myrtle Beach, South Carolina, this morning. Highest winds are estimated at 100 miles per hour over a small area. Hurricane Hazel is expected to continue at 35 to 40 mph toward the Northwest for the next few hours.

hat this could lead to premature strokes

Dominion Weather Service, October 15, 1954, 9:30 am

CHAPTER TWENTY SIX

Doug half-listened to the weather report while he worked on repairing the family's old four-slice toaster. This morning's breakfast production had turned out to be burned on one side and not even brown on the other. Charlie and Mary had mildly grumbled about the situation but managed to overcome their temporary annoyance enough to start a vigorous debate. They decided that what was staring back at them on their plate should be given a new name. Mary suggested "toa-bread" a label which Charlie found inexplicably amusing. They proceeded to banter back-and-forth; who would be brave enough to eat bread made from toes? Charlie even emitted a rare giggle at the joke.

But Charlie had another far more important reason to be happy. Despite its disastrous start, the week had been the happiest of his young life. The confrontation with Mr. Lupozzi and Maria's subsequent grounding had miraculously blossomed into pleasurable after-school walks the last two days. Today would be even better.

By lucky coincidence, a football game between their schools was scheduled Friday afternoon at Brock. Maria had been granted permission to go to the game, as two of their neighbours had beefy boys who were linebackers on the St. Francis team. Maria's parents saw nothing wrong with her showing them some support. Doug and Katie were similarly happy when Charlie casually informed them he wouldn't be home until after the game This would be the first time in the school year their typically shy son had shown any interest in an after-school event.

Of course, neither of co-conspirators planned to be there.

During Thursday's now-familiar walk toward the bridge, amid animated conversation and laughter, Charlie and Maria happened up this fortuitous scheduling of sports events. Classes would be dismissed at 1 p.m. Both principals had been on the intercom all week drumming up support. The student body was expected to show their loyalty by being in the stands in time for the game.

The early school release would give Charlie all afternoon to spend with the girl he thought he might be in love with. Their plan was to meet at the river. Maria, of course, would be breaking a parental-grounding edict and was risking more onerous further punishment; Charlie was in danger of incurring the wrath of Mr. Lupozzi, should they be caught. He also would have to endure the disappointment of his own parents, should they discover his deceit.

Both fathers would be at work all day. Both mothers would be at home all day. This time around, unlike Tuesday's disaster, there was no danger of being caught. Moreover, Maria's guilt was gradually being displaced by rationalization. She had finally convinced her inner conscience that she and Charlie were doing nothing immoral or wrong, just walking and talking. It also conveniently bypassed the fact that this time she would be lying to her parents.

As the school day droned on toward the magic hour of freedom, Charlie found his excitement becoming contaminated with concern. It began with the morning's weather report. Of course, hurricanes never blew into Ontario. Still, a forecast of rain interfered with his vision of a blissful, sun-filled afternoon cuddled together beside the gently flowing water.

Sure enough, the day had begun with a steady downpour. It seemed to have rained every day for the past two weeks. On their walks home, apart from that first warm sunny day together, the young couple had been content to splash through the puddles, like Gene Kelly in *Singin in the Rain*. Their bodies, like Kelly's torso in the movie, were well protected by heavy black raincoats and rubber boots.

But a different routine was required for today, one that required good weather. Maria had made them picnic treats disguised as her regular brown bag lunch. She would borrow her family's bright red, picnic blanket—"just something to sit on at the game, better than those hard wet bleachers," if her parents asked. Charlie would bring a canvas tarpaulin.

He told his parents a similar story, that he could sit on it during the game if the seats were wet. Along the way, they would pick up pop and candy bars at Logan's corner store.

Charlie's only hope was for the rain to stop. By dismissal time, however, it had intensified.

* * *

The same rain was keeping Doug from going to work. His boss had phoned shortly after breakfast to tell him they couldn't wait any longer for the weather to clear, giving Doug a rare day off. McMaster Construction was not easily fazed by poor working conditions. But today, the building site on Ramsden Avenue was deep in mud, preventing the heavy trucks from bringing in supplies. With a shrug of acceptance, Doug turned back to his toaster repair.

"Who was that on the phone?" asked Katie, who had been upstairs changing bedsheets. "Don closed down Ramsden. Too muddy for the trucks."

"How nice you don't have to go out in this weather. What will you do with all this free time?"

"Once I get this old toaster back in shape, I'll probably start on the bathroom tap." Doug was not one to waste a day.

Katie had learned in church that God doesn't always answer prayers according to her schedule. Yet here was a clear exception. Since her meeting at the church, she had been wrestling with when to tell her husband about the affair. Unable to resolve the matter one way or the other, Katie had once again turned to Gloria, the one person with whom she felt comfortable confiding her ambivalence. Her husband, whom she would normally consult, was not an option. And while Pastor Hanson was always supportive and non-judgmental, she liked being able to talk with another woman. Not her mother, though; this was one dilemma she would never understand. So yesterday, alone in the house, she had phoned Gloria.

"Katie, I know you are struggling to do the right thing." Gloria stood with her phone as she did with many of the church's calls which came her way. Their small congregation at Faith could not afford a real paid secretary. An extra length of telephone cord enabled her to listen while silently preparing a meal or rinsing a dish. Today, however, was different: Katie would require her full attention if that delicate issue about disclosing her secret was to be resolved with limited damage to her marriage.

"I know honesty is usually the best policy, especially between husband and wife, but I just don't know in this case. Is Doug better off knowing or not knowing? What do I gain by telling him now, all these years later?"

"Maybe you should answer that yourself, Katie." Gloria allowed the moment of silence which followed.

"I suppose I would feel better knowing there were no secrets between us. There are still many times when I feel guilty for not saying anything. But it's not getting in the way of our relationship. Doug and I are honest with one another in what we *do* say. Isn't that enough?"

"Katie, you are making an important observation. Being truthful in what we say is essential in any relationship built on trust. But does that mean that we have to share everything we carry inside? Is what we don't say the same as lying about what we do say?"

"I can see the difference when you put it that way."

"Another thing to consider is Doug's reaction. You describe your marriage as being good, right?"

"Yes," Katie answered quickly and easily.

"What would likely be the greater threat to your relationship—Doug's knowing about the affair or you holding on to this secret?"

Katie was shocked. She had been so concerned about what Doug would think of Sarah, it occurred to her that he might feel differently about her.

"I guess if I knew he'd forgive me, I'd tell him for sure. God's forgiven me—you've helped me see that. I think I even have forgiven myself. But I couldn't bear it if things changed between us, because of a secret I could continue to keep."

"Do you think he would forgive you?"

Katie thought of her husband in Italy, his friends being blown up all around him while he's being shot at, and faced a hard truth. "I wasn't loyal enough to wait for him. I wouldn't forgive me."

"But Katie, setting aside that one night, didn't you in fact wait for Doug for many months? It wasn't as if you ran off with another man the first chance you had. Some women did, sad to say."

"No, I never loved Greg, not even for a moment. That was never a part of what happened.

Like we talked about, it was more about the anger and the hurt. I felt ignored and abandoned. And it was only that one time. Next morning, he was out of my door and out of my life. I've never missed him since—not one day's worth"

"Katie, if you choose to tell Doug. You need to explain it just the way you said it now. I think that would help him understand."

"That is what I'd say, and it would be the truth."

"There is one more factor to consider. Is there any chance someone else could tell him, even if you didn't?"

"No, no one else knows." "Except?"

"Do you mean Greg? But we're not in touch." Katie's answer sounded more confident than she suddenly felt inside. What if he suddenly reappeared? What if he had told other people about their illicit relationship? Would this forever be a sword hanging over her head, waiting for that knock on the door or some snippet of gossip to reach Doug's ears?

After her talk with Gloria, Katie spent the rest of the afternoon replaying the conversation. She accepted that Donato Lupozzi's visit had reopened a chapter of her life which she thought successfully closed if not forgotten and might never slam shut again. Since Monday, her sleep had been fitful and troubled. Night had become the enemy. In the quiet blackness, there were no distractions to provide busy work and take her mind off that long-ago incident.

In the dark hours before dawn, Katie decided her only option was to tell Doug and hope he would understand—and eventually forgive. When this would happen was anyone's guess.

Certainly not while the children were around. Nor in the late evening when he was bone tired from work, for there would be no sleep, and he would have to go to work just the same.

So Katie turned to prayer. If God wanted her to confess, He would have to arrange the right time.

An hour later, Doug's boss called.

ed

l are

't

eir

she

SPECIAL WEATHER BULLETIN

The present Northerly motion of the hurricane is causing considerable apprehension in Southern Ontario. In this respect, it should be remembered that the Allegheny mountain range lies between us and the storm center. The mountain range may break up, or materially weaken the storm's intensity, or cause it to veer off toward the Northeast.

A
m
aga
H
Ly
in
lin

that

es to

cord breaking teen

Dominion Public Weather Office, October 15, 1954, 9:30 am

CHAPTER TWENTY SEVEN

C harlie walked quickly along Bloor Street. A moment earlier, he had deliberately assumed a nonchalant pose and strolled out through Brock's heavy wooden front doors. On School Spirit Days, athletes wore their game sweaters to class, drawing admiring glances and toothy greetings from the girls, while "lesser mortals," the non-athletic boys, watched with a mixture of envy and disdain. For an instant, Charlie second-guessed his earlier decision to abandon cross-country. That could be me, wearing a school team jersey. Then just as quickly, he shook it off.

The Junior and Senior football teams were ensconced behind closed doors in the locker room, putting on their pads and uniforms. The already rain-soaked cheerleading squad was assembled on the red cinder running track which circled the football field. Even before beginning their routines, they had attracted the giddy attention of his grade nine peers, who playfully poked and shoved one another. The other students were already streaming out the back entrances, jumping across parking lot puddles en route to the bleachers. To his relief, no one accosted him, demanding to know why he wasn't staying for the game.

Few shoppers ventured out in the bad weather. Some lingered under the striped awning at Lorenzo's Fruit market, hoping for a letup in the rain. Other, too impatient to wait, protected their brown paper bags of red Macintosh apples and yellow Bartlett pears under raised umbrella canopies and set off with hurried steps toward home. Mr. Lorenzo scurried to cover his sidewalk displays with blue tarpaulins, which immediately began to flap loudly in the strong wind. Passing cars splashed through the water which was fast accumulating on the roadway. Traffic moved slowly along Bloor, windshield wipers frantically clearing front windows in a hypnotic wet rhythm. Even with several hours of daylight ahead, headlights were turned on against the descending gloom of the storm.

Crossing Westdale and trekking through the now-muddy park beside the Humber, Charlie began to doubt Maria would come.

Maybe she changed her mind because the weather is so rotten. Maybe her parents found out about our plans and kept her home. Maybe she's sick. Maybe she thought I won't show up with all this rain. As if that would happen! The worst thing is that there's no way she can let me know. Doesn't matter. I'm sticking with the plan!

* * *

Maria rushed to her green metal locker the moment Latin class was dismissed with a final reminder from Mrs. Samuels about the game at Brock. She hastily gathered her raincoat, boots and food packages, discarded her school texts, slammed the door shut and clicked her Dudley lock. This would have to be a weekend without homework, even at the risk of her parents' inevitable questioning and anger. But in this weather, there was no way she could drag her notebooks and heavy texts all the way to the river. Raising a red umbrella over her head, Maria felt hidden from the world, like the little child who covers her eyes and believes no one can see her.

Charlie reached the river. He was surprised to find the water flowing faster than normal for this time of year. North of Toronto, meadows and farmland were already saturated by the unusually heavy October rains. Today's added deluge could not be absorbed by the ground, and was instead finding its way as runoff into the dozens of creeks and streams which in turn fed the Humber. A few miles upriver, unbeknownst to him, a small dam near the village of Woodbridge was beginning to strain against the added pressure of the unexpected volume of water.

He slid his way down the muddy slope, as if he were gracefully balancing on skis down some challenging course at Blue Mountain. In real life, Charlie had never even strapped on a pair of skis, but today he felt he conquer the world. Reaching the water's edge, he found his old log, where he watched the river swirl past. Back then, his own life seemed to be going nowhere, stuck in a swamp. He remembered being alone and lonely yet at the same time accepting of how the Humber ignored his pain.

Despite the gloom and rain, things seemed so much brighter today. Family had to love him; that was family. But now, for the first time, he had someone with whom he didn't share a last name who liked him anyway. Charlie knew that Maria would be a true friend, even if the romantic connection didn't exist. She would still be someone with whom he could unlock the person hiding inside his quiet passive self. With her, he could laugh and talk about himself, tell her his dreams and fears, his ambitions and frustrations. With her, he was an attentive listener, tuned in to her feelings about her family and events happening in life at school.

But Maria was more than a girl friend, she was becoming his girlfriend. Smiling to himself, he remembered her standing on that rock in midstream, and felt an instant swell of excitement within his deepest core, a powerful sensation that was rushing and churning, like the river itself.

CHAPTER TWENTY EIGHT

"Doug, we have to talk. It's really important. Can you set that aside for a moment?" Katie stood behind her husband who, sleeves rolled up to his elbows, continued his attempts to resuscitate the disassembled toaster with a phalanx of screw-drivers and pliers. With his back to her, she could momentarily hide the tension and fear plainly written across her anxious face.

"What's got you so upset, Katie?" Turning his head, he instantly spotted her distraught expression and reached out to embrace her. Just as quickly, she pulled away from his arms.

"You won't want to be putting those arms around me once I've told you what I need to get out" —she hesitated —"about something I've done."

"What in the world are you talking about?" Had she scorched his white shirt with the hot iron or lost the house keys? "It can't be that bad." By now she was crying silently.

"Let's sit down in the living room first." Katie led the way toward their overstuffed plaid chesterfield but remained standing.

"Katie, you're making me worried" He slowly realized this was something serious. "Are you pregnant? Are you sick?" He stood and faced her in front of the sofa.

"I am sick, yes, but I'm sick with guilt—about something that happened a long time ago."

"Well, if it was so long ago, why not leave it there?" He instinctively knew where this was leading.

"I thought I could but after talking to the Pastor—" She quickly stopped when Doug's shoulders stiffened and his face clouded over. But with anger or disgust, she couldn't tell.

"I thought we agreed that your church-going was a closed issue. It's fine for you and the kids, at least until they are old enough to decide for themselves. I just don't want any part of it. What has he got to do with why you're upset? Has he been preaching more hellfire at you?"

"Doug! It is nothing the pastor said or didn't say. It's just that when I talked to him and Gloria, I came to my own conclusion. They didn't influence me one way or the other, just gave me a chance to hear myself sort things out by talking."

"Okay. So why don't you tell me what's bothering you, and I'll shut up and listen." "You know that I've loved you, since the beginning," Katie began. Doug nodded with a reassuring smile.

"You know we've believed in the importance of being faithful to one another." Now the hard part. "But there was a time... long ago... when I wasn't." One more sentence and it would all be out. A painful memory of childbirth flashed by just for an instant, followed by a deep intake of breath and a silent prayer for God's help.

"You remember Greg."

"Katie, you don't have to say any more."

"But I do. You need to know this or it will kill me if I—."

"Katie, I already know!"

Silence. "You know? What do you know?"

"I know about you and Greg. I know you slept with him when I was in New Brunswick."

"But do you know—?"

"Yes, I know that Sarah was his child."

"How could you? How long have you known? Why didn't you tell me?" Katie's emotions were in turmoil: waves of dizzying shock over Doug's disclosure; disbelief that he had never confronted her all these years; a growing fear now that her secret was out in the open. And, worst of all, did this mean the end of their marriage? She needed to sit down before she fell down.

On the couch, Doug slid closer to his distraught wife and carefully placed a hand on her knee, a soft squeeze of reassurance before encircling her with the embrace she'd refused earlier. Within the security of his strong arms, Katie listened with a pounding heart, as he shared how Greg had written a letter of confession shortly after the affair, asking his forgiveness and promising to avoid any future contact with Katie. Of course, Greg had no knowledge of her subsequent pregnancy or the birth of his biological daughter.

Doug told Katie that it wasn't until he returned from Germany that he knew Sarah to be Greg's child. He could see his old friend in the strong set of her chin, those ocean-blue eyes, even the curls in her auburn hair. More importantly, he saw in Sarah his wife's impulsive kindness, her Scottish prettiness and her gentle manner of speaking. He loved Katie; it was not difficult to love her daughter—now his child too.

Doug had already seen too much tragedy, heartache and death. Why now bring about the death of his own beloved family? He determined that life would go on, leaving past mistakes unspoken, resting undisturbed in the deepest corner of his remembrance. If, one day, Katie felt the need to talk about Sarah's paternity, he would be there to hear her confession— and then life would flow on just as before.

Of course, that naïve optimism proved far more difficult to maintain than Doug could have imagined.

When he received Greg's letter and later, amid the muddy carnage of Italy, Doug's desperate longing for home and Katie's open arms helped carry him past that inevitable shocked sense of betrayal. That poison- ous anger which initially gripped his gut as he read slowly gave way to a gradual acceptance and forgiveness of her disloyalty; and he convinced himself there was no need to either interrogate or leave her. But then he returned to Canada and quickly realized that Sarah was Greg's child, not his.

This discovery resurrected pain he thought lay buried back in Italy. For several months, Doug waged an inner battle with anger he could easily have directed toward Katie and Greg, though never against his daughter. That she was his daughter was never in question. Over time, that sense of abiding joy pacified the rage and allowed him to move past her betrayal— not forgotten but surely forgiven. Now the porch encounter with Maria and her irate father had threatened to resurrect those emotions.

"But I do have to admit that trouble with Mr. Lupozzi and our boy last week got me thinking about it. What if Charlie really had been involved with that young girl in a wrong way? Then I started thinking about you and Greg—but just for a few minutes, and not after realizing our lad did nothing wrong."

"That was the night I knew I had to tell you. All your talk about the war and Italy stirred up my guilt and anger all over again. How can you possibly forgive me?"

"Katie, what would you have done if I came back from Italy and told you I got some girl over there pregnant?"

"Doug! I'd be shocked and hurt, of course. But I would have forgiven you." No sooner were the words out of her mouth than Katie knew they weren't totally true. "No, it would have taken a while. I would have still loved you, but I would have had trouble trusting you again."

"Do you think that love would have eventually overcome the hurts and the doubts?'

Katie didn't respond at first. Instead, she moved even closer to her husband, her arms encircling his neck. Smiling through her tears, she whispered simply "Of course."

"Now you understand how I could forgive you."

"But weren't there times when you wanted to confront me with what you knew—like maybe when we were arguing or you were angry with me?"

"How could I use that against you, considering all the joy Sarah brought into our home? Our first-born daughter, that little baby where we learned how to parent a girl?"

Husband and wife sat quietly for a few moments, reflecting on these comforting memories and allowing themselves to reopen the pain of mourning their middle child, forever gone and removed from the world even before her life could fully unfold.

"We're still sad because we lost her," Katie spoke softly, wiping an errant tear from Doug's cheek.

"And we're still thankful that she was in our lives—if only for those dozen years."

How Sarah entered their lives had never remained as a barrier for Doug to cross. Now, it was no longer a secret burden for Katie to carry. At last, she was simply a gift to be treasured and remembered forever.

CHAPTER TWENTY NINE

Despite all his almost-frantic anticipation and compulsive glances up the muddy embankment, Charlie still managed to miss Maria's arrival.

It was an increasingly strong north wind which muted every other sound except for the constant hum of the rushing river water flowing rapidly by his feet. The wind and water seemed to be competing for his attention. Then, suddenly, there was Maria, more specifically two wet rain-coated arms wrapping themselves around his neck.

"I didn't see you coming," Charlie happily proclaimed from under his rain hat.

"I almost slid down the path and landed in your lap." Both teens simultaneously grinned at the thought. "Where should we go to get out of this weather?" Like her mother, Maria was ready to allow the man to believe he was in charge even when she knew more than he did. She was quite content to let Charlie assume the initiative.

"I thought we could set up the tarp on top of those fallen tree trunks." He pointed to the same toppled maple where, just a few days earlier, they had sat and begun to know each other. Now it seemed as if they had always been friends. The initial shyness and tentative trusting had quickly been supplanted by comfort and openness—even a vulnerability where each could risk being themselves.

In a few moments, even with the wind angrily grabbing at their canvas tarpaulin, they were able to secure its ropes to branched remnants of the old tree. Now the incessant rain no longer splashed in their faces, though it still played a steady drumbeat on their canvas roof.

Charlie spread Maria's red blanket on the bumpy muddy ground, realizing with a momentary jolt of fear, that Mr. Lupozzi would soon wonder how it got so dirty at a football game. He quickly cast that thought into the river; nothing was going to distract him from this fore-taste of heaven.

Maria then laid out her packed lunch, most of which was foreign to her hungry friend. "I've brought sausage—we call it *'salsiccia,'* it's like salami."

Charlie's mind worked rapidly, not wanting to admit he didn't even know what salami was. "Where do you buy it? I've never seen it in our butcher store."

"You don't buy it; you make it," she giggled and for an instant Charlie assumed she was laughing at him, then shook it off.

"What else have you got?" Maybe something familiar?

"You must know what *macaroni fatti in casa* is."

"I know what the first word is," he offered bravely.

"And I have some *formaggio.* That's a cheese." She realized by Charlie's look of bewilderment that explanations were in order. "And I took some of my *Mamma's* eggplant which she grew in her very own garden. Eggs he knew, but egg plants? It made no sense. On the Ranwick's farm, the eggs came from hens.

"Great! I like cheese." Though in reality, "cheese" was limited to Velveeta spread.

"And for dessert," she paused dramatically.

Please, God, make it something I can eat. Desperate, he even offered a plaintive prayer to the God he wasn't sure existed.

"*Grispelle!*" She waited for some reaction, preferably one of joy. Instead, more blank looks. "Like fritters. You know what they are, right?" More blank stares, now combined with growing red-faced embarrassment.

Maria was kind enough to bail out her friend from his misery.

"Oh, and Dad's Cookies!" Then she couldn't resist —"You *do* know what they are, don't you?"

Charlie saw that behind her gentle teasing was a humorous smart young woman. "I didn't know your dad could bake," he replied, and they both began to laugh. As they started to eat, one diner was taking noticeably smaller bites and chewing a bit more tentatively than his companion. But despite his initial misgivings, Maria's lunch turned out to be delicious. Charlie fantasized for a moment what it would be like if they were married. They would cook together and invite both sets of parents over for Sunday dinner, where Charlie would impress his in-laws with a Calabrian meal. That got him thinking about Mr. Lupozzi's wine and the near-miss that caused.

"Did you bring some of *Babbo's vino*?" Seeing he and Maria would surely be married some day, "Mr. Lupozzi" seemed too formal. In his blissful euphoria, Charlie could even envisage himself down the road a few years, throwing both arms around Maria's father at that special Sunday dinner and kissing him on both cheeks, just like in "Three Coins in The Fountain."

Maria smiled back at Charlie's joke, remembering his contorted face when he took that first sip.

"No, I wouldn't dare bring any alcohol. The laws are so strict in Canada—no drinking outside the home or hotel bar. It's not like that in Italy. And we're not really old enough. Can we have some of your pop?"

Charlie reached into his store-wrapped paper bag, now soggy from the weather. Good thing the bottles didn't fall through the bottom on his way here. With an exaggerated swagger, he produced them, still chilled from Mr. Jarvis's cooler.

"Your choice: Hire's Root Beer, Grape Nehi or Coca Cola?"

"I want the Grape—unless you do," she added quickly.

"Fine by me. I'll take the root beer."

"Have you got the opener?"

"Shit, I forgot!" The curse word was out of his mouth before his lips could contain it. If Maria noticed, she chose to ignore it. In reality, she thought the rough language made Charlie seem more manly. Besides, her father certainly swore in English, though the words sounded more colourful when he raged in Italian.

"Now what? I'm really thirsty, and I don't want to drink river water."

"Maybe I can find something outside that'll open them." He offered that plan more in hope than confidence, having no idea what kind of tool could be found in nature.

"Charlie, it's too wet." The heavy rain continued to pound on the flimsy roof of their primitive shelter. "Stay inside—with me—where it's dry."

Charlie gazed at Maria and forgot about his quest for an opener. She was sitting on their blanket with her back propped against the hard maple of the fallen trunk. Her stockinged legs were tucked up against her body so that her chin could rest on those bare knees that Charlie had been drawn to from that first meeting. She opened her arms wide, inviting him into their embrace. Because of his height, the boy had to crawl across the tiny tent to reach her. There he hesitated, unsure of his next move. This was new territory.

"Come and sit closer." Even in the shadowy gloom of their tent, her smile dazzled, beckoning him like a lighthouse draws some ship toward its safe harbour. He moved into her arms. She drew his head against her breast and held him tightly. Enveloped in her scent, a combination of garlic breath sweetened by some vague fragrance of perfume—or maybe just soap—he found it intoxicating.

The two teens remained locked together, their hearts beating rapidly as if tapping out Morse-coded love messages back and forth, both content and unsure how or if to proceed.

Charlie gradually became aware that his awkward twisted position was causing a painful twinge in his back and growing numbness in both feet. Was Maria feeling just as uncomfortable? Yet he dared not move, for fear the magic spell would be broken.

Should I try to kiss her? Does she want me to touch her breasts? Should I tell her I am in love? He recalled locker room chatter about getting a girl excited by blowing in her ear. Those ears were currently out of reach, but other parts of her were accessible! *Should I ask permission? Do I stroke them or go under her sweater for the bare skin? What about her brassiere? How would I ever get that undone? Am I supposed to? Will she catch on that this stuff is all new to me? None of this seems very romantic. Aren't things supposed to happen naturally, like in the movies?* He now regretted not paying more attention to the love scenes and less to the gunfights.

Maria resolved his dilemma by gently lifting his head from her chest and pulling it slowly toward her slightly parted red lips. The rest of him eagerly followed!

Of course, he had never kissed a girl before. A guy would need to have a girlfriend before that could happen. He had reluctantly kissed his mother on her cheek at bedtime up until a few years ago when it felt too awkward. Then there was Great Aunt Jenny. She was a lip kisser and every Christmas when the Thompson family visited her in the nursing home, Charlie got her seasonal gift of a cold wet kiss planted firmly on his tightly closed mouth.

When he had been occasionally invited to neighbourhood children's birthday parties in the preteen years, the kids sometimes sat in a circle to play "spin the bottle." But when the twirling milk bottle finally stopped, it was always pointed at someone else to be kissed. He had never decided whether to feel relieved or disappointed.

With Maria, the whole experience was far removed from Great Aunt Jenny or party games. She drew him closer and closer until finally their lips brushed. Then she left him there and waited.

By this point Charlie was no longer cautiously and systematically assessing every next move; he was propelled forward by some new and powerfully deep current. He pushed his lips against hers and found them open to his advance. He felt her hot breath entering his mouth as if he were a victim of near-drowning being resuscitated. In that moment his own breathing seemed to have stopped before suddenly returning in a rapid heaving of his chest. He moved his lips over hers, exploring every inch of their moist softness.

With that move, Charlie crossed the invisible threshold between childhood and adolescence. His comic book heroines suddenly faded into dull coloured paper drawings. Other more recent fantasies bound up in movie matinee cowgirls and jungle princesses were exposed as nothing more than visual shadows on a big screen. Girls he noticed at school and even Miss Manton may just as well have been surrounded by barbed wire—they were untouchable. But Maria! She was smooth skin and fragrant-smelling tangled curls of hair. She had voice and form and, most importantly, was in his arms.

Despite her assertiveness, Maria was equally a novice. Parental rules and priestly admonition had combined over the years to implant a rigid standard of saving sex for marriage. These values had been presented negatively: you must avoid the shame of pregnancy; and, no husband wants a wife who's not a virgin on their wedding night. Although the more experienced young women at school had hinted about the vague unspoken delights of necking and petting, no one had actually shared the secret that being entangled with a boy could be exciting and vastly pleasurable.

Even so, enough of the adult indoctrination had stuck with Maria under that canvas in Charlie's embrace. She had strategies in reserve, ready to implement should the situation demand action. Girl chatter in the locker room and cafeteria informed her how best to keep some over-stimulated boy's wandering hands away from straying off-limits.

But, to her relief, there was no need. Charlie lay quietly and content beside her. He was more than satisfied—he was in love.

They felt the wetness under their bodies in the same instant. Pleasantly warm and gently creeping into their make-shift tent, the river's gradual intrusion was surprising but not frightening. Maria squealed and sat up. Charlie moved their remaining food away from the damp blanket. Neither moved quickly. Then Charlie crawled over to peek outside their shelter.

CHAPTER THIRTY

By 4 p.m. the downpour had intensified under a heavy sky canopy, dumping an unrelenting deluge of warm rain upon an unsuspecting city.

Toronto had never encountered a hurricane. Even more deceptive were the bland reassurances from the Dominion Weather Office: heavy rains would continue throughout the day before tapering off by midnight. True, Hazel's hurricane-strength winds had weakened during their destructive northern journey. What had not been foreseen was her determination not to veer eastward, not to follow typical paths of previous hurricanes which travelled up the east coast, sometimes as far as the Atlantic provinces, before wandering harmlessly out into the ocean.

Hazel instead chose to continue her passage up over the Adirondacks, through New York State and straight across Lake Ontario, before setting her sights on the vulnerable Canadian city north of the border. Toronto had no disaster plan for hurricanes. Apart from occasional spring overflowing, both the Don and Humber Rivers were placid, content to live within the confines of their banks like long-domesticated farm animals behind barbed wire fencing. Housing had been built on flood plains, reassured of their safety by developers and builders who had checked historic river flow records. Upstream dams were primitive relics of earlier settlements with their water-powered mills, but they had sufficed over past decades.

By 5 p.m., Doug Thompson and Donato Lupozzi had grown concerned. Each realized his child was caught in this storm, probably seeking shelter with other students under the bleachers of their football field. Each anxiously and separately made a decision to find them.

Shortly after, and almost simultaneously, their two cars rolled into Brock Collegiate's parking lot. They emerged and were surprised to find the other standing in the rain. Neither had bothered to bring an umbrella. They were further surprised then alarmed to find the parking lot empty and the school deserted. Mr. McGiver had sent his teachers home early. The Junior football game had been completed but the Senior game had been cancelled at half-time. There was no sign of Charlie or Maria.

Doug went to find a phone booth to call home, in the hopes Charlie was already there. The only result of that call was to alarm Katie. She had been napping, a rare occurrence for her but a much-needed respite following the emotionally draining intensity of their earlier conversation. Having shed her oppressively heavy blanket of guilt, she had drifted easily off to sleep while the rain drummed loudly on their roof.

Donato waited impatiently for the other man's return, hoping for good news. If Charlie were home, then he couldn't be somewhere with his daughter. He had already wondered that morning whether Maria might encounter him at the game. Now his suspicions grew in tandem with his Calabrian temper. Like Doug, his workday had been interrupted by the wet weather, causing a return home by noon. Rosa was pleasantly surprised, since her hard-working husband could now enjoy a long weekend at home. There was wine to be made from their recently harvested green grapes, and the last potatoes and carrots to be pulled from their soggy garden.

When Doug got back from his unsuccessful mission, they talked guardedly and calmly, keeping a tight hold on troubling emotions bubbling inside. While Doug was anxious for his son, he feared a repeat of Tuesday's front porch confrontation. Donato however was only concerned about Maria. Thinking as Doug did, that perhaps she was already home, he asked for directions to the phone booth. He returned five minutes later with the same answer, accompanied with a growing hostility and accusations.

"My girl she's no home. Maria with your boy, I know."

"You're probably right. Let's try and figure where they are." Doug was used to negotiating with temperamental union members and demanding bosses. He knew he would need every well-honed tool in his diplomatic toolbox to prevent another round of pointless anger and finger-pointing.

"Look, I know you are worried." (Doug thought it best to use that softer descriptive word.) "So am I. Let's figure out where they might be." He repeated his words to shift the focus of their conversation toward problem-solving rather than to begin arguing. With a sinking heart, Doug realized he already knew where they might be. And so did Donato.

"We go to the water. We take my car." Doug obediently followed the irate Italian and silently climbed into the plastic-covered passenger seat.

CHAPTER THIRTY ONE

Charlie and Maria, puzzled and marooned, found themselves on an island newly birthed by the rampaging Humber.

When he had peeked out from their tarp-covered hideaway a moment earlier, the rain splashing into his eyes, Charlie had lost his bearings. Where was the riverbank? Why were they surrounded by swirling muddy water? Initial bewilderment was briefly followed by a moment of amusement. He smiled to himself before inviting Maria to take a look.

"You won't believe this! We're going to get wet, walking through this stuff." Of course, he was already soaked so he happily envisioned his girlfriend hiking across the swirling water ahead of him, shoes and stockings off once again, skirt held high to keep it dry but unintentionally—or otherwise—exposing those long brown legs to his adolescent gaze.

"Charlie. We can't walk through this. It's already gotten too deep." She looked frightened. "Let me try first and check it out." Taking off his shoes, he tentatively stepped into the flood and was almost pulled off his feet by the hidden power of the current. He quickly backpedalled to the sanctuary of their little island and inwardly pondered their situation with growing concern.

No one knows we're here. We might have to wait until the water level lowers. That could be after it's dark. I can't even build a campfire in this rain. If we were dry it would be romantic. We'd lie on our backs and watch the stars. Except it's still pouring. Wait until her father realizes she's not home on time after school—way past her curfew deadline. I'll be blamed, my parents will be mad, and I'll never see her again. Not good! But I'm not going to panic Maria. We'll figure something out.

Yeah, and if we don't, it's bad news all round for everyone.

"Okay. We can wait here until the river drops back to normal." He secretly hoped she'd like that option. "Or we could figure how to get back to shore."

"I've got to get home. I'm likely in big trouble already. What time is it?"

"I don't know. I don't have a watch on me. It must be five by now."

"How can we get across?"

"I think we have to wait until it drops. It might only take a bit longer. I've never seen it get this high so suddenly. What time do you have dinner?"

"At six, but I need to be home before then to help make it and don't forget. I'm not even allowed out after school. I'm in real trouble." To Charlie's shock and concern, she began to cry, her beautiful face reddening, her big brown eyes watering. He moved instinctively to hold her, a gesture more comforting than erotic. Maria sank into his encircling arms and trembled with fear of her father. The young couple remained locked together for several moments, oblivious to the continuing rain.

Reality soon intervened. They reluctantly pulled back from one another and surveyed the scene around their island. Instead of receding as they'd hoped, the Humber was now quickly encroaching on their remaining lump of land as if trying to grab their feet. They retreated to the fallen trunk and climbed on top just as an onrush of water swept over their shelter, angrily washing away their tarpaulin, blankets and remaining food.

Maria blurted out, "We're being punished for lying to our parents and doing what we did in the tent." Maria's Catholicism included on-the-spot divine retribution for transgressing God's laws. Any residual pleasure and sensual arousal she had allowed herself to feel an hour ago was carried away along with the blanket. That was where they had laid together. God had swept away all traces of her sin but left her with self-condemnation. She wished God would wash away her sin as quickly as He snatched her belongings.

"Maria, I'm sorry. It's my fault. I'll take the blame." Charlie wasn't sure if he was thinking of God's wrath or *Babbo*'s, but he knew he feared her father more, even after Maria's quickly offered reassurance: "It's not all your fault. I wanted to be with you. I wanted you to kiss me."

Perched on their tree trunk, the river raging inches below their dangling bare feet, Charlie knew that whatever happened next, Maria's confession had just made it all worthwhile. An hour passed, and the water level was now lapping at their legs. Still, Charlie had no regrets.

Then the old maple, which they had trusted to stay firmly anchored in the mud, began to quiver and with a groan to shift beneath them. The river pushed relentlessly against their precarious perch, determined to carry the trunk and its occupants along like a prized victory trophy. In that moment, he flashed back to the lake and his paralyzing fear of water.

"Maria, we're moving. We've got to get to shore right now." Panicked, Charlie started to climb down from his branch and, before Maria could stop him, stepped into the current, now up to his waist. In an attempt to conquer his fear, he remembered Tarzan and Jane caught in the treacherous crocodile-ridden Congo River; he would hold his ground, grab Maria, and lift her to safety. But this was not a Saturday matinee. And he was not Tarzan. The flooded river quickly pulled the boy off his feet and left him clutching their maple trunk against the relentless current. It was not long before his thin arms began to lose their battle against the river's tug-of-war.

"Charlie, hold on. I'm coming." Maria jumped in and encircled his chest with her arms, just as Charlie's arm strength left him and he let go of the trunk. Both were immediately swept downstream, their bodies still entangled in a macabre embrace.

Charlie's primitive survival instincts now ruled his reactions. His arms flailed wildly, desperately trying to grab at roots and bushes which overhung the riverbank as they were dragged along helplessly in the current. He could hear himself screaming for help until water suddenly splashed into his open mouth and temporarily silenced his voice.

Maria reacted first, as her pool lessons began to kick in. She had been taught that resisting a powerful current would only exhaust a swimmer. She knew they had to ride out the trip until they reached calmer water. She also knew she needed to keep Charlie firmly in her grasp if he were to survive.

"Stop struggling. Just let me hang on to you. I know what I'm doing." Her words sounded more confident than she felt but had the desired

effect of calming his fear. He let himself relax in her arms and, still cough-
ing and sputtering, closed his eyes, silently praying to his mother's God
for deliverance.

* * *

Doug and Donato cautiously climbed down the muddy embankment and almost slid into the river. The entire landscape looked different,
as if it had been replaced like theatre sets between acts. The placid flow of
the Humber was now a raging torrent of dirty water. That old time-worn
winding path beside the stream was gone, as was the fallen tree trunk
where they had hoped to find their children safely sheltered.

"Maybe they're home by now," Doug offered hopefully but without
much conviction. He had to shout over the roar of the flood and the howl
of the winds which were quickly gaining strength.

Donato wasn't listening. He was reaching for a brightly-coloured
floral blanket thrown by the wind into the lower branches of a partly sub-
merged willow tree. Rosa had brought it from Calabria. He held it high
for Doug to see.

"We need look more down here." Donato pointed through the rain
to where the river curved sharply left. They slowly crawled back up the
slick embankment, pulling themselves upward by grasping whatever
branches or rocks were anchored in the slope. Upon reaching the top,
they hurriedly began to walk south through the darkening end of daylight, climbing over scrub brush and fences, vainly scanning the near
shoreline for their missing children."

* * *

Half-drowned and fighting to stay afloat amid torn tree limbs, dislodged bulrushes and other debris, Charlie and Maria had been propelled
further downstream. Having minutes earlier snatched them from their
sanctuary, the Humber just as quickly spit them back to shore. They lay
exhausted, like beached whales, bruised and emotionally drained, on a
tiny sandbar which had somehow resisted the pull of the current.

"Charlie, are you alright?" Maria gently touched his shoulder.

"We made it. I was scared to death." He gasped his words and shook with the cold.

"The whole river has flooded. What's going on?" She raised herself up and surveyed the rampaging water with a mix of shock and wonder.

"I don't know but we'd better get out of here before it gets worse."

They stood up, their legs shaking under them, and began to brush off mud and sticky clay sediment. Their clothes, carefully selected that morning to create a good impression, were torn and water soaked. Charlie reflected on what had just happened.

I was going to drown and she saved me. She held me up when I was sinking. I couldn't have made it without her. I could have drowned. The near-death experience overwhelmed him, he felt dizzy and had to sit back down because he might cry or even faint.

"Charlie, are you sure you are OK?" She leaned over him anxiously.

"You saved me. You saved my life." Charlie reached for her hand but could say no more.

She sat down beside him, recognizing they were not going anywhere soon. Emotional and physical exhaustion had finally overtaken them.

After what seemed a long time, they heard windblown shouts coming from atop of the bluff. It was Doug, rapidly clambering down the steep slope. Donato had run back to bring the car further along Westdale to be closer to their location.

"Are you alright?"

"We're soaked but we're ok." Charlie shakily stepped forward to meet Doug's outstretched arms. Father and son held each other for a silent moment of relief, then Doug impulsively reached out for Maria. She awkwardly and stiffly entered his arms but remained only for an instant.

"Dad, Maria save my life. I wouldn't have made it." He looked in amazement at his bedraggled friend. "The current almost pulled me under. She jumped in and grabbed me and she knew to drift with the flow until we ended up here."

"I took a lifesaving course." She offered shyly by way of explanation.

Moved with gratitude, Doug was about to hug her again, but stopped when she took a backward step.

"I'm just happy we're safe. It was dumb of us to even be here." Her comment was met with a tense silence from both males. Maria had opened up a whole new discussion. Doug recovered first.

"We've lots of time to talk about that later. Let's get you up this embankment and home for some dry clothes. I'm sure your mothers are worried." He turned toward the slope and, after exchanging a secret anxious glance, the miscreants meekly followed through the inky darkness.

At the top of the bluff, Maria and Charlie knew their anxiety was justified. Mr. Lupozzi stood by the Chevy, his face revealing confusion, relief and anger—but mostly anger.

"Why you both down there? What happen there? You are wet from in the river?" He moved toward Maria who shook in fear. But his big work-roughened hands gently touched her face, carefully pushing strands of long wet hair from off her muddy cheeks. He took her in his strong arms and silently began to weep with thankfulness for her safety. Nor could Maria hold back her own tears.

"We bring you home to *Mamma*." Forgetting or ignoring the Thompsons, Donato took his daughter's hand and led her, still crying, toward their car and home. She did not risk a backward glance.

"Well, young man, we can't get any wetter. So let's start walking." Doug put a fatherly arm around his chastened son, and the two soaked Thompson men began their five-block walk home. They noticed the rain had suddenly stopped.

cells 1. ... ... clot foi.n....un.

SPECIAL WEATHER BULLETIN

The hurricane is expected to continue on its Northerly course, reaching the Eastern end of Lake Ontario about midnight tonight. In crossing the Allegheny Mountains the hurricane will decrease markedly in intensity with winds not expected to exceed 50 miles per hour on the open water of Lake Ontario.

Dominion Weather Service, Friday, October 15, noon

CHAPTER THIRTY TWO

When it finally reached Toronto early that evening, Hazel was technically no longer a hurricane, downgraded to an extratropical storm. As predicted, its power had dissipated over the Alleghenies. But no one could have guessed that it would be reborn to resume its destructive rampage northwest. After colliding over Lake Ontario with a massive cold front moving south, Hazel renewed her energy. With regained strength and intensity, she invaded Canadian waters and set sights on Ontario's capital city. But Hazel was not the only villain.

It was the cold front, preceded by heavy rain, moving across southwestern Ontario during the day, which brought the first drenching. By 7 p.m., the leading edge of Hazel had crossed Lake Ontario and blocked the cold front's progress just west of Toronto. As a result, the weather over the city temporarily cleared.

* * *

Katie had kept supper heated for the missing family members. From time to time she would open the oven door to check on the sliced roast beef, mashed potatoes and peas, arranged on two plates, sitting on the upper warming rack. Each was covered by a second plate to keep the food from drying out. She had listened as usual to the 6:30 evening news on CFRB, albeit with greater attentiveness than usual. Jack Dennett referred to the ongoing heavy rain and high winds but gave the impression it would end overnight. There was also mention of flooded underpasses leading to road closures and detours and further entangling Friday rush hour traffic.

Mary had long since finished and was quietly doing paper doll cutouts on the living room rug. She lived in the moment, not worrying that her father and brother had yet to show up. She knew they would. However, she was curious to find out the reason for their lateness. Maybe Charlie was with his new girlfriend—her bashful big brother with a girl!—and somehow in trouble with their father. She suppressed a giggle at the thought.

Katie was less sanguine. Doug's phone call had been two hours ago. By now, he should have located Charlie and fetched him home.

Where in the world could my son have been all this time? If a friend had asked him over after the game to wait out the storm, that would make sense. But most families had phones. He would have called—if he had a friend. Maria's a friend. Maybe he's with her!

Katie remembered the angry porch scene with Mr. Lupozzi and shuddered. No one wanted a repeat of that encounter. She returned to her dishes in the sink. Any chore was a welcome distraction from her growing concern. At least the rain had let up.

Then she heard the screen door slam. She had been trying to teach her children to close the door quietly behind them when they came in through the porch. At that moment, however, it was the most reassuring and welcoming of sounds. And there they were, drenched and bedraggled, especially Charlie whose clothes were covered in mud, his shirt badly torn. Katie was stunned.

"Were you in a fight?"

Doug quickly interceded: "Katie, let Charlie have a bath and get cleaned up. Lots of time for explanations." His abruptness surprised her, but she accepted his direction, once assured that the dishevelled young man standing sheepishly before her was indeed alright.

"Let me look at you, son." She drew closer, touched Charlie's dirty face and found a large ugly purple bruise beginning to form on his right cheek. She involuntarily gasped but said nothing. Like Doug said, her son was safely home. Explanations—and dinner—could wait.

* * *

While Charlie was wearily scrubbing off the Humber mud—though unable to wipe away the memories—Doug told Katie the whole story, which Charlie had confessed on their walk home.

"I don't know what Mr. Lupozzi will do next. He stormed off really angrily."

"Doug, I can already guess one thing for sure: Charlie won't be seeing Maria anymore." She felt sad for her son. Then the much heavier weight of the day's events overwhelmed her.

"Doug, he could have been killed today, and to think that Maria saved him. No matter what happens now between them, we need to somehow let her know how very grateful we are. It was an answer to prayer." These last words slipped out before she could censor them and, as usual, Doug stiffened; they both knew God doesn't always answer prayer. But he said nothing and instead picked up his remaining daughter in a hug so tight Mary had to laughingly beg him to loosen his grip.

Rosa Lupozzi was also keeping a meal warmed for her missing family. Since Donato's phone call almost three hours ago, she had heard nothing. She puttered around her tiny kitchen, trying to find something to distract herself from worrying. Rosa was not used to being idle, yet all her routine chores had been completed long ago; and unwelcome empty minutes stretched before her like a book without words. As always, when feeling anxious, she turned to her saints. Holding on to a sturdy chair for support and ignoring painful arthritic joints, Rosa managed to kneel reverently.

Santo Cristoforo was the patron saint for many needs, including travel, storms and children. Rosa remained kneeling for a long time, fervently requesting his divine intercession for all three.

Once she finally struggled back on her feet, Rosa returned to her window vigil, in the hopes of seeing their old car rumble up the gravelled driveway. The sight greeting her was so disorienting that she felt dizzy. Somehow, the Lupozzi's half-built little house had been moved to the water's edge. A second look provided a different and more frightening theory: the Humber had overflowed its banks and was now swiftly encroaching on her property. Rosa hurried to the wall phone. In place of a familiar hum, the line was dead.

* * *

Donato Lupozzi's prolonged silence was proving to be far more frightening to Maria than any lecture. As they approached their car, her father stormed ahead, leaving her to follow behind in exhausted misery.

They drove along Westdale toward home, each lost in their own isolated world. For Maria, her mind was a whirlwind of thoughts:

What's going to happen once we get home? Mamma is going to be so upset. I want to apologize to Babbo but I'm afraid to say anything right now. He looks so angry, like he could kill me. I know he has good reason. Charlie and I really messed up. I sure won't be able to see Charlie again— at least until I'm older and on my own. But I'm only in grade nine, that will be forever. I can't believe I could keep his head above water. No, I won't think about that. I need to figure out what's going to happen once we get home. I know they'll be really disappointed with me. I lied to them. I'm in big trouble.

Then more angrily but again only to herself:

All I wanted to do was see Charlie without having to sneak around. If they hadn't been so old-fashioned Italian strict, none of this would have happened. It's not all my fault. And now I won't be able to see him at all, ever. None of this needed to happen. Shit!

Donato was gripping the steering wheel with both hands to keep them from shaking, his mind racing on a parallel path to his daughter's:

I almost lost her. My only bambina. That boy, it was his fault. Why did she lie to her Mamma and me? That's not my girl. It's that boy. He's no good for her. Why would she want to be with him? What would my life be without Maria? What should I do when we get home? I can't spank her like she's a child. She's fifteen. I can't believe Maria's fifteen. Back home I could have her already promised to a good man. But this is Canada. The rules are so different here. So difficult for immigrants. I'm not sorry we're here. And his father's a good man—except he can't control his own son.

The tired old Chevy moved steadily along Westdale through light traffic. Approaching Danton Road, Donato increased his speed, anxious to finally get home. The road dipped beneath a CPR train bridge, where he saw water pooling in the underpass. Unwilling to consider a longer detour, Donato headed straight through, his tires sending cascades high into the air on both sides of the vehicle.

Then the engine died. He repeatedly pressed the starter button but was answered only with an ominous silence. Glancing into his rear mirror, Donato was momentarily relieved to see there was no other car about to rear-end him. The road was empty. Now what?

He thought quickly. They needed to find a tow truck. Or walk home for help; his neighbour António had a John Deere tractor and could easily pull their car out of its watery prison. Or they could stay in the car until the water went down and the sparkplugs dried out.

In the darkness, they could see the flashing red lights of an emergency vehicle. A shiny black police cruiser stopped behind them and a tall, heavy-set officer emerged, quickly pulling on his long black raincoat.

Donato exited his own car and stepped into swirling water which reached his knees. A powerful flashlight shone in his face and then illuminated the stranded car.

"Are you alright?" The voice was concerned, not threatening like in the old country. "My car won't start. My engine she's wet."

"I'm putting barriers up to close this underpass. You'll have to leave your car here and walk out. Do you need a hand?"

Donato stood silent for a moment, reluctant to abandon his vehicle but realizing there was no other option.

"We go." He called for Maria to join him and father and daughter sloshed through the water to higher ground beside the policeman.

"Where were you headed?"

Maria was used to answering for her family when dealing with English-speakers "We're trying to get home, on the other side of the Humber. We live on Sanderson."

The constable looked shocked, but only for an instant before quickly regaining his professional calmness.

"You might have trouble getting over there. The river's really high with all this rain." He kept to himself other vital information. Why provoke unnecessary fears? After all, these early reports could be false.

Donato and Maria locked the car, not that anyone was likely to steal it under these conditions and began to trudge along Westdale toward home. By now, the wind had picked up enough speed to almost knock them off their feet. The rain, which had abated earlier, returned even heavier, as if to make up for lost time. The winds had shifted to the east and, for some strange reason, the temperature was climbing above 60 degrees, not falling as one would expect in mid-October.

Left behind at the roadblock, the lone constable received a crackling message over his car radio. The calm of the past hour was in fact the eye of what, a few hours earlier, had been a hurricane. Far worse weather lay ahead. He resigned himself to a later than usual night shift.

Given this wild night, his wife would understand.

Donato and Maria walked steadily, despite the driving rain which sandpapered their faces. They finally reached the familiar bridge over the Humber. They stared down in shocked silence at the torrents of water roaring beneath their feet, then quickly pressed on toward Sanderson. Another cruiser blocked their path. Again, they were engaged by an officer.

"You can't go past here. Sanderson is under water."

"My mother is down there. She's alone and we need to get to her."

"You'll have to wait until the water levels go down—unless you want to go in by boat."

Donato had caught enough of the English conversation to be alarmed "My wife, she there." He pointed toward their darkened street, realizing at the same moment that the hydro was off. He also realized their path home was truly blocked.

"I'm sorry, sir, but you can't go further. You can wait here in my car and get out of the rain," he offered.

Reluctantly, the two Hazel-soaked travellers acquiesced to the policeman's direction. It was now almost 10 p.m. The Lupozzi family had experienced spring flooding last year when the Humber spilled over its western bank, throwing huge jagged chunks of ice onto nearby fields.

Within a day or two, the river had retreated, to be confined once again, like a recaptured zoo lion.

Donato rested wearily in the back seat of the police car and found comfort in assuming this year's flood too would turn out to be of no real concern.

...The intensity of the storm has decreased to the point where it should no longer be classified as a hurricane. The weaker storm will continue northward, passing east of Toronto before midnight. The main rainfall associated with it should end shortly thereafter, with occasional light rain occurring throughout the night.

Dominion Weather Service Bulletin, Friday, October 15, 9:30 pm

CHAPTER THIRTY THREE

They might as well have lived in two separate worlds. For Katie, the night was stormy with driving rain and wild winds which rattled their windows and blew her remaining potted fall zinnias off the verandah.

Yet Doug and Charlie were safely home. The family turned out their houselights around 10 p.m. and eagerly sought sleep, everyone except for little Mary who, upon seeing Doug and Charlie, finally understood the danger and was emotionally and physically worn out. Katie knew that bad weather always passed and would soon be forgotten. Indian Summer was almost there, with sunny skies, tree garlands of leafy golds, reds and yellows, and a final burst of warmth before winter clamped its icy hold on the land. Before turning off the radio, she had listened to the latest weather synopsis from the CBC. It was reassuring:

Only a few blocks away, but on lower more vulnerable terrain, the night brought with it a far different tale.

Rosa Lupozzi huddled in the family's basement as the rain pounded on her roof like a home invader demanding entry. She had lit a candle, partly for light and partly for prayer to her saints. Donato had built his house foundation expertly, tightly sealing every joint in the concrete block walls. No water from the flood would penetrate and seep into their home. Next spring, he planned to finish their long-awaited first floor, when they would at last vacate the basement which had housed them under crowded but cozy conditions. Under the onslaught of water, however, their tarpaper temporary roof was taking a bad beating from the wind. Rosa feared it might be torn off, giving an entry point for the rain.

Still, she was more worried about her husband and daughter. Without phone service or electricity, she was cut off from the outside world of information. For an instant, she thought of trying to leave her home, before realizing it was too stormy even to join her Italian neighbours. Besides, the water had begun to swirl around the perimeter of the house. She could only wait, alone with her anxious thoughts:

Maybe they've gone to the Thompsons and aren't able to phone to say they're safe. I wonder where he found Maria. I hope he wasn't too harsh with her for missing curfew. After all, the game may have gone on longer than expected, or she might have met friends afterward and gone for sodas at Macleod's. She wasn't with that boy at his house when Donato called. Though they might have found each other at the river. The thought of our daughter with him scares me more than the pounding on my roof.

Several miles north, the Humber was nearing its crest, an unprecedented and horrifying twenty-five feet above normal. Two hundred million tons of water would drop from the sky before the night gave way to daylight. Long ago four dams had been built to help keep the river in check, with two of them open to offer free passage for the deluge. The bridge at Woodbridge, choked with debris, acted as a temporary dam, holding back the river tide. Once it was breached by the relentless water pressure, the last protective barrier and hope for protecting thousands of unsuspecting homes further south was gone.

* * *

No hurricane had ever threatened Toronto. There was no emergency plan in place, ready to be actualized in this kind of natural catastrophe. Toronto was far better prepared for blizzards. In addition, weather forecasts on October 15 failed to register the severity of what was about to unfold on the sleeping metropolis.

When the Woodbridge dam gave way, a torrent of water immediately rampaged south, uprooting massive trees and obliterating riverbanks. Every home in its path was endangered. Some were flooded, drowning inhabitants as they slept; others left families marooned helplessly on roof tops awaiting rescue which, in many cases, never came. The Lupozzi home was targeted by a massive tree trunk which bore down on it like a medieval battering ram.

The fallen tree, its force fueled by a powerful current, crashed against the northern wall of the house, knocking it off its cinder block foundation. The wounded structure was quickly swept downstream, bobbing in the river like some giant's toy playhouse. After only a few horrific moments, it broke apart. Jagged chunks of metal siding and torn sheets of plywood wall panelling scattered in the flood among furniture, clothes and other remnants of what had stood as a proud immigrant's first home. But by then, Rosa was already dead.

* * *

Around midnight, a tired-looking police officer returned to his cruiser and drove the two passengers a few blocks to a high point on the eastern bluff from where they could look down on the far side of the river.

"Can you spot your street from here?" he inquired anxiously.

Donato and Maria desperately scanned the scene below. All they could see was devastation. There was no longer a street and certainly no longer their house. In its place was a small swirling lake where the Humber had aggressively advanced far beyond its confines.

Rosa, devoted wife and mother, a proud New Canadian who loved her garden and her little home, was eventually counted among the eighty-one who perished during that long day and night when Hazel struck Toronto. Another four thousand families were left homeless. Damage was estimated at 25 million dollars. Two hundred million tons of Hazel-borne water, dumped on an unprepared city, had left this unforeseen legacy of death and destruction.

Her body was found late Saturday afternoon by a gangly pimply-faced boy scout whose troop had volunteered to assist soldiers, police and firemen in a frantic search along the riverbank for survivors. She had been swept downstream about two miles. When the teenager came across her, he thought it was just another log pushed against the shore by the powerful currents of last night. But as he drew closer, he saw a head and upper torso protruding from the sand and mud.

Instead of a survivor, the poor fellow had stumbled across a corpse with a rosary in her lifeless left hand.

CHAPTER THIRTY FOUR

In nomine Patris, et Filii, et Spiritus Sancti, Amen Gloria tibi, Domine
Donato Lupozzi knelt rigidly beside Maria on the kneeling bench in the front pew of Saint Mary's.

It was not weariness that held him fast in its grip. Rather, it was the words of the funeral service that tore at his soul. *How can I offer glory to God after He took Rosa and left a child without her mother? How am I supposed to raise her on my own?*

Maria sensed her *Babbo*'s anguish and gently placed her hand on his. Donato had been to many funerals in Italy, a sad reality of the war years. For a few moments his mind escaped the church service and found itself back home. He remembered neighbours—Anna and Tomaso, Giuseppe and his infant bambina, Angelica—all killed in the air raids. Even after the bombs had stopped, sickness and starvation claimed many more. Yet, somehow, these losses were easier to bear because he was not alone. In Calabria, Father Luigi would drone on in Latin, the words familiar enough in their comforting rhythm though mostly a mystery in their liturgical meaning. Rosa sat beside him then, her tears offered on his behalf to the saints because his own were safely locked away. They carried their grief together.

Now she was no longer there to help him say goodbye. He would have to lift the load of mourning on to his own shoulders. Maria's hand, warm against his, offered comfort; but Donato knew she too was gradually slipping away from his grasp. Only with her, it wasn't the flood snatching her from his arms, but this new country with its different ways.

Finally, Rosa's funeral service was over and he was once again outside in the fresh air of a warm mid-October afternoon. Outside, where there was no sign of the disaster which had claimed so many lives only a mile away. Maples still displayed their beginning display of fall wardrobe, with which the oaks and chestnut trees, with their dull yellows and browns, couldn't hope to compete. Zinnias and climbing roses resisted the fate of their flowerbed companions, those tulips and daffodils which had long ago lost their youthful brilliance and remained only as a leafy green promise for next spring.

Donato observed the orderly rows of brick houses around the church. Neighbours were raking leaves and tending to their backyard gardens where the last of the beefsteak tomatoes and the root vegetables—carrots, beets and potatoes—waited to be discovered. Green squashes and cucumbers shared tangled vines with brightly-coloured pumpkins. Once the ground was dryer, men or their sons would be pushing their clacking lawnmowers, eager to complete the final pre-winter lawn trim before a first blanket of snow made it impossible.

The new widower felt an unexpected rush of anger rising from his belly. Why is the world carrying on like before? Don't they know or care? Their inconveniences were trivial: A few broken branches and tipped-over patio furniture. Why should their lives remain untouched when his own was shattered?

Maria sensed her father's helpless rage and silently took his work-calloused hand as they walked slowly toward their car. She recognized with surprise that it was her father who needed strength and comfort. Just as Charlie had.

During the funeral service, Maria's attention had been drawn toward the confessional booth. She was familiar with the sacrament. It had brought relief from guilt over the past few months when her adolescent yearning for independence collided with her parent's European ways. Usually a quarrel would follow, with her doing most of the shouting—in both languages. Afterward, she always felt regret that she had caused them pain. She remembered the troubled expressions on their faces—surprise and anger softened with uncertainty—when she would angrily challenge a curfew or some other limit arbitrarily imposed on her freedom.

She vowed to return to confession as soon as it could be arranged. She was desperate to be unburdened of the guilt she now carried, a pain far heavier than she could hope to carry alone. She had caused her mother's death and taken away her beloved father's wife.

* * *

Charlie was secretly relieved when his father advised against attending the funeral. The Thompsons hadn't learned of Rosa's death until three days after the flood, when the Telegram printed a long list of its victims. Charlie was distraught, feeling a sudden and overwhelming outpouring of empathy for Maria. What must it be like to lose a parent when she was so young: no mother to talk with, to be there after school? He wondered with an involuntary shudder how he and Mary would manage if either their mother or father died.

His parents had always been there for them, and it seemed they always would be. Mom in the kitchen when they returned from school, Dad home by supper time. He could hardly contemplate the loss of his grandparents. Death had been something that happened to other people and other families. This past week, it had moved much closer.

I've never even been inside a Catholic church. I wouldn't know what to do. But that's not the real problem. What would I say to Maria and her father? He might come after me right in church. I wouldn't blame him. Maria and I were wrong. I'm not telling Dad, but I'm glad he advised against me going.

Yeah, that could turn out really bad—as if things could get worse.

As the day of the funeral arrived Charlie trekked to school as usual but, once there, remained distracted by the heavy thought of his Maria crying in a church pew, sitting beside her *Babbo*. He envisioned her furtively glancing around, hoping through teary eyes, to see him walk respectfully down the aisle and quietly slide next to her in the pew. But then his thoughts would turn to Mr. Lupozzi and his murderous scowl. No, his father was right; to attend the funeral would only create tension and accusations, with Maria once again caught in the middle.

By French period, Charlie had determined that he would give Maria a few more days before meeting her on her return from St. Francis. Once that decision was made, he found conjugating the verb "*etre*" to be a welcome distraction from deeper concerns.

* * *

Monday October 25. Charlie had circled it in red on his bedroom calendar, from Farmer's Co-Op, which his grandfather had given to him. He was up early that morning, fretting over what he should wear to school—or, to be more exact, to meet Maria.

Charlie figured she would return to classes today, the start of a new week, after remaining home for a couple of days to be with her father. Mr. Lupozzi would understandably need her comforting presence by his side during those empty first days after the service.

Then it dawned on Charlie: "Home for a couple of days?" There was no longer a home for her to return to for those couple of days. The Telegram reported that temporary shelters were available for homeless flood victims. So where was she living: a church basement, or the home of some relative? Would she really be back at school? There was only one way he would know.

By 4 p.m. Charlie was walking quickly toward St. Francis. By the time he reached Layton Avenue his pace had slowed while his eyes scanned the sidewalk ahead. For a moment he allowed his mind to reminisce, to return to the last time he travelled this route. Was that really only nine days ago? It seemed like months had flown by between the promising beginning of a romance and where matters were now.

What should I say to her? Of course I need to tell her how sorry I am that her mother died. But that sounds so stupid, and inadequate. I need to ask about their home and where she and her father are now.

Charlie felt an irrational impulse to invite them to stay until their house could be rebuilt. Imagine having her around every evening and all weekend! They could do homework together, watch Ed Sullivan and Red Skeleton and laugh together. Side by side on the chesterfield, she might even snuggle up closer to him, as long as her father was not looking.

The image of Mr. Lupozzi scowling in Katie's kitchen snapped Charlie out of his fantasy.

What a stupid idea, never mind they didn't have a family room. Besides, his parents would never go for it.

Maria was almost in front of Charlie before he recognized her. She was walking with three other girls, all in identical brown flared skirts, white blouses and red blazers. What was different was her face. A frightening sadness and weariness had pushed aside the warm smile and that glow which once radiated both happiness and sensuality.

Caught off guard, Charlie fumbled for an opening comment, but Maria never gave him the chance. She paused, while her friends looked on with a mix of curiosity and an open hostility.

"What are you doing here?" There was an ominous coldness to that familiar voice.

"I wanted to walk you home. Like before" He looked awkwardly at the semi-circle of protection around Maria. He was now at a loss for words or direction.

"You don't need to do that. I'm okay."

Charlie started to blurt out that he knew she didn't need him to walk her home. It was him who needed to walk her home. As Maria moved away, he felt her slipping inexorably out of his life and dreams like water through a cupped hand.

"Can't we talk for a minute?" He knew the answer before his sentence was finished.

"No, I can't see you." A pause. "Not ever again." She flung the words over her shoulder as she continued to move down the street, her phalanx of protective friends on either side. Then abruptly spun around to face him:

"And, by the way, you can't walk me home because I don't have a home. Or a mother."

Charlie watched in misery as Maria strode hurriedly and resolutely away from him. But after a few steps, she paused, looked back and half-smiled a sad goodbye before finally walking out of his life.

He could not see the tears stinging her eyes nor the pain in her heart. He could not hear the concerned voice of a priest gently admonishing her within that tiny confession booth three days ago, his words now echoing in Maria's thoughts:

"My child, you have suffered a terrible loss with the death of your mother. She is safe in the arms of Jesus now. And our Lord said: 'Blessed are those who mourn for they shall be comforted.' I pray that our Heavenly Father's comfort will help you and your father through this difficult time. But Maria, this boy has led you to lie to your parents. He is not even Catholic. God loves you and has forgiven you but you know that you must not see him again. Now go and reflect on these words. In the name of the Father, Son and Holy Spirit. Confession is over."

As Charlie slowly found his way home, still in a daze, he clung to a faint hope like a drowning person clings to a tossed, lifesaving ring. In his mind he replayed Maria's words over and over until their familiarity blunted his pain. He grasped at one final straw of hope:

What she said was that she can't see me again. I know she was told that by her father. I can understand his anger. We were in the wrong. But she didn't say that she didn't want to see me again. Maybe there is a difference between "can't" and "want." Maybe, one day, when we are older and she's on her own, away from him, we can try again— if she still wants to.

He could wait. After all, she had smiled at him in the end. He pictured himself turning down other girls next year in grade ten. The incoming grade nine girls would want to be with him, would cluster together and giggle around the cafeteria table and wonder: Why was he playing so hard to get? Is it true he has a beautiful girlfriend waiting somewhere for him. Lucky girl!

He tried to return to his comic books, to Wonder Woman and the jungle girls who had been the focus for his adolescent desire. Now they lacked allure. Instead, he would turn the pages of his time with Maria, illustrated not on paper but in his memory. Yes, for now, that would be enough. Who knows about the future? After all, Maria never said she didn't want to see him again.

EPILOGUE

Of course, Maria never returned to Charlie. The pull of her faith, especially the guilt which stuck to her like river mud, held her back as did a daughter's duty to care for her *Babbo*. To his credit, Mr. Lupozzi insisted Maria finish the school year. By summer, despite his loneliness for Rosa, he surprised himself by regaining much of his former strength and resilience. He gave her his blessing to complete high school. Then in 1959, he returned to Italy and to his home village in Calabria for a summer vacation.

That said, Donato Lupozzi had an ulterior motive for this trip: he had reconnected by airmail over the past two years with Angela Combardo, a neighbour whose husband had been killed fighting the British in North Africa. Both widowed and lonely, they were married in their old parish church. In 1961, Angela was admitted to Canada to begin life with her new husband.

Maria went on to study civil engineering at the University of Toronto, one of the few women in her class. Drawn to that difficult program by a deep desire to design bridges and dams better able to withstand flash floods, Maria graduated with honours in 1963. She was married three years later to a young man who shared both her Italian heritage and Catholicism. In fact, Tony had been a neighbour to her family before Hazel struck and starred as a running back for St. Francis's football team. As Charlie had supposed, Mr Lupozzi even liked him!

The family home was never rebuilt. Their land, like all adjoining properties, was deemed to be on a flood plain and expropriated by the city at fair market value. Eventually, a system of attractive riverside parks was linked together under the newly formed Toronto and Region Conservation Authority. The Humber was finally controlled, flowing where directed, safely contained and tamed for the safety of future generations.

Maria never completely forgot about Charlie. While life had brought her a deep new relationship, the experience of first love continued to occupy a special place in her heart. For Maria, it would always be reawakened by a certain kind of river. Of course, she couldn't bring herself to return to the Humber; it had stolen her mother. As an engaged couple, Maria and Tony would talk animatedly of their future during frequent hikes through the Don Valley; even then, she would find herself glancing toward the riverbank. Later, when canoeing down the Saugeen with other young married couples, there were times she could almost hear Charlie's voice amid the churning of the rapids.

While those unexpected fleeting images could not be denied, Maria refused to give them a place of prominence. She made sure the past stayed where it belonged.

Charlie's family continued life much as before. Doug was promoted to supervisor, easing the years of accumulated wear and tear on his back. His crew spoke fondly of the boss's fair-minded leadership. Katie enjoyed the youngest Thompson child's journey through her teen years, as Mary somehow remained immune to the lurking temptations of drugs and sex which characterized the sixties. Church continued to be the central theme of Katie's Sunday mornings even after Pastor Hanson was called to a new much bigger new suburban congregation. Doug continued to resist. As a couple they agreed to disagree about Jesus.

As directed by scripture and her female church friends, she dutifully prayed for Doug to not remain lost but to be saved and come to faith. No one knew that, inwardly, she struggled with the thought that he was never would. She could only hope God saw him as she did: good enough just as he was. Katie was never comfortable with her new pastor's rigid preaching about sexuality, and his dogmatic teaching on abstinence from alcohol, make-up, movie-going and card playing. But she still found abiding love and acceptance within her church family and ongoing comfort and security in the old hymns and now-familiar Psalms.

Mary's child-like unquestioning acceptance of evangelical Christianity was mostly swept aside once a wave of the more permissive '60s rolled in during her late teen years. Yet her rooted faith ultimately held fast as an anchor against this decade's tide of changing values. Adulthood brought a return to church, albeit in a more mainstream progressive denomination.

Despite his mother's reassuring promise, Charlie never "filled out" even once his growth spurt ended. He retained the thin frame which had always been his genetic destiny. But to his surprise, it was also to become an asset.

It was the day after Maria's painful rebuff that Brock's cross-country coach received a visitor at his office door. Mr. Tavener remembered the ease with which a young ninth grader had led his classmates, seemingly without effort, around the red cinder track during gym period and then briefly practised with the Junior team. He quickly conscripted a still-doubtful Charlie to rejoin his runners for the balance of the fall interschool meets, then on to track meets in the following spring. Over the next four and a half years this unlikely athlete dominated the competition and ended up winning an athletic track scholarship to Iowa University.

Despite the disappointing way their relationship had ended, Charlie eventually recognized he had good reason to be grateful for his short-lived romance with Maria. After all, it was a fact she had been attracted to him and, once entering that relationship, obviously liked the young man she found there. Charlie concluded that he must have something to offer the opposite sex. It was as if Maria had waved her magic wand and transformed a reclusive shy boy into a more confident young teenager.

Admittedly, this wand-waving would take several months to work its full magic. But only a few weeks after Charlie had discovered his athletic gift, he once again ventured with renewed energy and optimism into the uncertain world of female relationships. By this time, he had finally shifted his brown bag lunch from self-imposed outdoor exile to the cafeteria. Invitations to sit with teammates made the adjustment far easier than expected. Between bites of peanut butter sandwiches, Charlie cautiously entered into conversation with the girls who sometimes shared his table.

Over the remaining months of that grade nine school year, a more secure and relaxed young man would walk home with one or two of those female tablemates, spend time on the phone continuing these pleasurable conversations and eventually share a few movie dates. By the time Charlie was in his senior grades, he had enjoyed several deeper relationships, though none came close to capturing his heart the way Maria had.

It was late August, two months after Charlie had graduated from grade thirteen, when he stopped by the river one last time before leaving for college.

In the oppressive humidity of late summer, it seemed that the water was moving sluggishly, too lethargic to quicken its journey. As ever, Lake Ontario waited patiently for the Humber's eventual arrival. Finally free of the paralyzing fear that plagued him as a boy, Charlie could now sense his life flowing like the river soon to disappear around that fateful bend a quarter mile south from where he sat. In a few days he would leave the comforting familiarity of home and family to embark on a new unknown chapter in his life journey. Iowa seemed very far away to a boy who, except for a special weekend trip to Buffalo with his grandparents when he was ten, had never been out of Ontario. Though he had never before even been on a train, safe in a bedroom drawer lay the CPR ticket sent by the University.

In those moments, Charlie finally made his peace with the Humber. For several months after the hurricane and flood, he had cursed the river, though it continued to roll past, oblivious to his anger. He had blamed the water for what it had stolen from him. Over time, however, he grew to understand how much more Maria had lost that terrible night. Fueled by heavy jolts of guilt, he determinedly nudged his adolescent self-pitying toward a more mature compassion. Her mother had been cruelly and suddenly snatched away by the powerful grasp of that same river, now moving placidly below his familiar vantage point.

In the months after Hazel, Charlie also began to realize the same river had brought her into his life. That first memory of Maria stepping gracefully from rock to rock along the water's edge like a tightrope walker would be forever etched in his brain. The image, as vivid as if it were yesterday, continued to arouse in him a mix of sexual yearning and untainted love every time he indulged the memory.

He allowed himself one lingering stare at the spot where they once sheltered under the canvas tarpaulin. Smiling to himself, he relived that awkward but still unforgettable romantic afternoon when they huddled together before the water rose. He raised his eyes to follow the Humber as it found the bend and disappeared out of sight to discover what lay ahead. Glancing at his new Bulova watch, a graduation present from his proud parents, Charlie stood up, spanked the dirt from his jeans and turned toward home. He had a suitcase to pack.